MW00647709

FALLOUT

William Hunter

ALSO BY WILLIAM HUNTER

Sanction

ISBN 13: 9781732949904
Library of Congress Control Number: 2018913422

For Callee, Charlotte, and Catherine

Cherish those who seek the truth, but beware of those who find it.

Voltaire

PROLOGUE

East Berlin
November 1984

*T**he lone figure stood in the shadow of the Oberbaum Bridge. The weather was miserable, even for November, and a thin layer of ice covered the shallows of the Spree River. The man, code-named Castor, clenched the collar of his overcoat, but the wind racing along the water like a rusted East German Reichsbahn checked any effort to stay warm.*

The agent should have exfilled a day earlier and a hundred miles to the south. His part of the operation should have been over, but Castor had discovered a critical security breach involving the Stasi directorate in East Berlin, and stayed behind in a desperate bid to bring the intelligence across the border. He should have already been debriefed and sitting over a pint in a West End pub.

Should have.

The epitaphs of dead and missing operatives scattered across Soviet-occupied Europe could be summed up in two words.

Castor knew he could wait no longer, and stepped from the darkness of the underpass. Behind him loomed the watchtowers that manned the approach to West Berlin. On the opposite bank, he could see the backside of the "You Are Now Leaving the American Sector" sign.

Never mind the death strip with its Czech hedgehogs and tripwire mines, or the overlapping patrols armed with Kalashnikovs, attack K9s, and shoot-to-kill orders—the Spree measured four hundred feet across. The full length of a football pitch.

I might as well queue up to escape the pull of a black hole, Castor thought to himself.

His ID card showed him to be a twenty-eight-year-old resident of Kreuzberg, a painter who crossed several times a month to teach courses in the East. As he was routinely checked through with two other artists, Czech agents working with British Intelligence, any attempt at a lone reentry might raise suspicion. Enough, at least, to be singled out and handed over to a more seasoned official, and Castor wasn't confident that his German, or backstory, would weather prolonged questioning.

Castor hesitated before stamping out the cigarette he had pretended to smoke. He rescaled a stairway to the bridge and joined the somber line that stretched back from the boom gate, the dismal hallmarks of a city split by concrete and barbed wire. An older man near the front was abruptly pulled aside, and Castor wondered if any of the buildings housed two captured spies, surrounded by guards and a crack Stasi colonel patiently awaiting the last of their team to make his attempt. The line moved, but Castor did not, wondering whether he should retreat back to the momentary safety of Friedrichshain. Beyond the barricade he could see the section of Schlesisches Tor Station not obstructed by the partition that bordered the free bank of *the river, and Castor suddenly feared his fellow agents were already sitting safely in a westbound train.*

Castor considered the intelligence he had concealed in his sketchbook, information vital to British interests in West Germany.

In a singular moment of clarity, standing alone at that sector boundary, it became clear to Castor what was in play. An expendable agent. A cocksure handler emboldened by past Huzzahs. An operation cooked up after one too many, by someone with too comfortable a view of the Thames.

Something this critical should not be resting on the shoulders of an operative so soon out of university, never mind the IONEC's good-luck-staying-the-fuck-alive-on-that-side-of-the-Wall six-month short crash course. Hopes pinned on an Oxbridgian who was recruited as much because he was the heir of a long-dead life Peer of Parliament, than that one grandfather's side of the family hailed from the Rhenish Palatinate.

Bloody hell.

Despite the cold, Castor could feel a column of sweat pooling at the small of his back, while his heart raced to the point he was certain it could be heard bounding off the bridge. He stepped out of line, almost involuntarily, and began a casual stroll back toward Warschauer Strasse.

The command from the checkpoint, bracketed by the menacing growl of German Shepherds, was immediate.

"Halt!"

Bloody fucking hell.

It was then that the panic, which had slowly siphoned off any remaining self-control, forced its way to the surface in a manner that betrayed who the agent was and why he was on that bridge. He bolted back down the concrete steps to the quay wall, near the underside of the bridge. Castor could hear the commotion above, and the marshalling of boots. Mass confusion and more shouts, and a well-armed phalanx now pouring from doorways on either side of the overpass. He moved to the water's edge and marked a spot on the far bank. Louder and more animated shouts of "Wo ist er?!" and "Halt!" as GDR soldiers, many of them barely out of school themselves, began to zero in on the lone silhouette.

The MI6 operative knew he was absolutely bollocksed.

The champion swimmer, who had bested all-comers on Hampstead Heath when life was about bread pudding in a Batman-themed bowl and Clangers on the telly, lunged into the Spree. The frigid water overwhelmed his senses and dampened the thunderous roll of automatic rifles from above. Castor pulled himself deeper and farther out with powerful strokes, but already his lungs demanded oxygen. Gunfire raked the top water, and he could see the bubbled trace of bullets flash by, before they disappeared into the blackness below. The agent fought off the dizzying ache and was forty yards across when his options, reduced to breathe or drown, forced him up and into the concentration of muzzles at high ready. There was another deafening volley from the riverbank, and a searing pain sliced through his left leg as Castor dove back down. Water mixed with an involuntary wince, and he resurfaced too quickly to throw off snipers still locked onto his last position.

A single shot echoed from the tower, and the young man

from Highgate, and Hertford College, with the right past and a bright future, foundered, and drifted into darkness.

PART I

CHAPTER ONE

Washington D.C.
September 2018

Banastre Montjoy cycled between sipping a black coffee and skimming the case summary of a South American operation that had gone belly-up almost as soon as two of his more trusted agents had arrived in Rio De Janeiro two weeks earlier.

Near the end of that spring, long after Montjoy's beloved Everton side were knocked from title contention but not before they had guaranteed their annual mid-table Premiership survival, MI6 had been made aware of a potential mole in the office of the Chinese Consulate-General in São Paulo. The intelligence had come in the dubious form of a dead-dropped anonymous note written in Portuguese and left at the British Embassy in Mexico City. It claimed that a high-ranking attaché from Beijing, with familial connections to the Ministry of National Defense, was privy to information about a state-sanctioned team of black hat hackers who had allegedly gained brief access to the mainframe at GCHQ, Britain's security branch in charge of signals intelligence, ten months prior.

The missive stipulated that a proxy of the officer would

be willing to meet to discuss a quid pro quo, which meant the man wanted money rather than asylum or, God forbid, simply to make the world a better place. Greed over ideology was usually the motivating factor with the majority of turncoats, Montjoy knew, though it also meant that the potential prized catch could cut and run at any moment, in search of a higher bidder.

An agency asset already in country, fronting a sinecure at an HSBC banking branch in the same borough of Mexico City that housed the embassy, made contact with the surrogate and reported back even odds that the man and the meet were on the level. A formal sit-down was agreed upon to take place a fortnight later, in Rio, when the young captain in the People's Liberation Army Navy believed he could better ensure its secrecy and his safety.

A month passed, and with it, no further contact from the stand-in who had reached out in the Mexican capital in March. Three weeks later and out of the blue, MI6's man in Cuauhtémoc received a cryptic message at a prearranged mail drop that the officer was ready to rendezvous, immediately, and demanded one hundred-thousand-pound sterling for information related to the cyber break-in. The British agent relayed the details of the proposed meet to Montjoy, who by that point had decided to personally manage the risky tête-à-tête from London.

Montjoy quickly gave the go-ahead to two agents waiting in Argentina, who made the two-day trek via train under the guise of heirloom collectors anticipating a browse and buy with a rare antiquities dealer from Southeast Asia. Once they arrived at *Central do Brasil*, the two men made their way to Campo de Santana Park, across from the main station.

It was then that everything turned into an absolute shite storm.

Local authorities, teamed with a squad of *Polícia Federal*, had been tipped off by a junky squatter from a local *favela*, shantytowns that littered Rio's outskirts, concerning a pair of British drug dealers who were in possession of a large shipment of heroin bound for the criminal organization *Amigos dos Amigos*. The SIS team were singled out and surrounded by nearly forty armed officers, whose feverish shouts and brandishing of automatic weapons sent families scattering in a terrified frenzy. In the ensuing panic, someone collided with a policeman, who inadvertently fired his weapon, hitting several people and setting in motion a scene of complete bedlam. In the chaos, the MI6 agents were able to escape the Keystone Coplike encirclement and make their way back to Buenos Aires, before exfilling to London.

Montjoy rubbed his temple as he reread the file and considered slipping a shot of Bailey's into his carafe.

Fortunately for MI6, the repercussions from the Brazilian operation had so far been limited to internal only. Authorities in Rio were seemingly clueless as to the identities and intentions of the foreign operatives in the park, and ignorant of their intended objective, who had failed to show. Montjoy acknowledged the agency's good fortune that the response team had not included CORE, the elite tactical unit of the city's police force, or he would be dealing with a diplomatic headache much larger than the actual one which had plagued him since the evening prior.

Montjoy had suffered his fair share of them since his ascension to deputy chief of MI6 three years earlier. He had been with the Service for nearly three decades, and for much of that period had languished as a high-functioning semi-alcoholic counterintelligence agent, and then head of section. Montjoy's salvation had come in the form of an operation that involved the assassination of a Cambridge professor and the bombing of the London Underground. Though the damage had hit close to home, Montjoy had ultimately tied the terrorist act to a larger conspiracy which involved the highest echelon of SIS and the British government. The resounding success had gained him considerable notoriety in the intelligence community and propelled Montjoy to his current position, for better or worse.

While he conceded that the view was far better from the peak, Montjoy now better understood why his predecessor, William Lindsay, seemed to manage the Service with an almost semi-detached air. Though the political fallout from operational failures tended to trickle downward, more than once Montjoy found himself sitting atop a malodourous pile that he alone seemed responsible with sorting out.

At the moment, he needed to determine whether the fiasco in Brazil had been a cock-up or a set-up. If what happened was a misstep on their part, someone's head needed to be on the block for sodding up a promising source inside the Chinese government. If MI6 were being played, however, Montjoy needed to determine who was behind it and whether there had actually been a breach at GCHQ, or if SIS were being fed misinformation solely intended to send them on some bootless errand.

Montjoy stared through the small port hole of the private jet that had been chartered to take him to South Carolina from Washington D.C. He had arrived in the epicenter of the US intelligence universe two days earlier to meet with Robert Riley, head of Europe Division for the Directorate of Operations at Langley. The two men had known one another for nearly two decades, and three years earlier the CIA officer had played an instrumental, albeit unknowing, role in the capture of the mastermind behind the King's Cross bombing. The sit-down had been routine but brief, as the meet was cut short by an unforeseen issue on Riley's end.

With an extra day suddenly at his disposal, Montjoy decided to tour some of the more popular tourist venues. He had always enjoyed his visits to the American Mid-Atlantic in fall, though Montjoy was chagrined to discover he had arrived in the city too early to fully appreciate the auburn hues that would soon blanket the National Mall. He had nonetheless walked much of the downtown, and even took a water taxi to Arlington and Old Town Alexandria.

A horn sounded outside the plane, and for a brief moment Montjoy caught a glimpse of his own reflection as the lights from a passing luggage dolly illuminated the window. Growing flecks of gray reminded the deputy chief that his own seasons were beginning to pile up and pass with more urgency than a younger man could ever envision, or worry about. Though he was a year shy of sixty, the former lieutenant commander in the Royal Navy had long been convinced that any emerging deficiencies, physical or otherwise, were limited only to preconceived notions of age. Until one knee began to routinely ache, and his doctor further suggested it was time to schedule semi-invasive procedures reserved for people Montjoy once considered ghastly old. The stark realization that he faced less years ahead then were behind him had inspired Montjoy to reinstitute a rigorous physical daily regime of weight lifting and boxing at his former gym.

Montjoy had also been forced to acknowledge that he hadn't taken a personal vacation in nearly three years, and decided to use his trip to the States as an excuse to rendezvous with his half-brother, Sean, an expat who now lived in the mountains of North Carolina. Their grandmother, Madeleine Halliwell, also planned to join them, traveling from Ballachulish in the Scottish Highlands to spend several days on the southern coast.

The high-pitched turn of the jet's twin engines and sudden jump forward from its hitherto wheel-chocked position induced Montjoy to snap from his rumination and fasten his seatbelt. The first rays of light had yet to irradiate the capital skyline, and a slight rain began to pelt the glass of the porthole.

Montjoy poured another coffee and committed himself to fully enjoying a few days in the American South before heading into whatever the next storm back home might be.

CHAPTER TWO

Johns Island, South Carolina

The skiff turned into the Stono Inlet. The man who steered the flat-bottom jon watched a squadron of Black Skimmers encircle Bird Key and set down near the dunes on its leeward side. Their distinctive bills and white underbellies made the birds recognizable even in the half-light. The pilot remembered that local fishermen would know boats were forbidden above the tide line during nesting season, so he throttled up and pushed past the island sanctuary and its endangered rookeries.

The man at the bow, the more experienced of the two Chechens, cast his partner a disapproving look. The reprimand was less for the sudden shift that threw him off balance than because they were moving too close to the shallows, whose sandbars would be difficult to spot in the chop. Though the men were in front of the storm that would soon engulf the entire South Carolina coast, heavier winds had begun to rake the top water where the Kiawah and Stono Rivers met, making it difficult to steer the twelve-footer smoothly.

The operatives barely knew one another, but the promise

of a lucrative payday offset any potential risk to the point that the two men would trust each other's provisional loyalty and skillset just long enough to ensure the success of the mission.

"*Ärroo áaghor verza*?" the man who had flown into Charlotte a week earlier as Kevin Greene asked, as the boat began to pitch in the strong current.

"English," John Riker replied, not for the first time, but affirmed with a nod at the query concerning their bearing.

Greene accelerated to right their direction, and maneuvered into the mouth of the Stono River.

"How deep?"

Riker surveyed a map sealed in a waterproof case. "Enough."

Greene switched off the motor and loosened two clamps screwed into mounting brackets on the transom. The boat began to drift as he struggled to hoist up the outboard and drop it into the channel. It disappeared with a splash as Greene flipped down and turned on the trolling motor. The absence of an engine capable of transporting the men down the seacoast from the Outer Banks would reinforce their appearance as local angers, at least from a distance and in the dark. Should they be stopped and randomly checked by patrolling DNR officers, the two killers were prepared with a well-rehearsed backstory, their cover as German tourists who had decided on a whim to rent a boat and head out in search of speckled trout and redfish.

Riker had gone one step further and studied the Lowcountry, which boasted a history as rich as its wildlife. The largest and most violent slave uprising in early America had been ignited not far from where he would rendezvous with Greene later that morning. Riker's approaching insertion point was only a stone's throw from British General Henry Clinton's own in the winter of 1779, en route to his capture of Charleston and George Washington's entire Southern army. Finally, the high-value target the assassin had been contracted to eliminate would die at almost the exact location where a heavily outnumbered Confederate cavalry turned back Union forces in the summer of 1864. The encounter at Bloody Bridge had been lost in the historical shadow of an iconic fort in the Charleston Harbor whose shelling had set in motion a civil war that sealed the fate of 750,000 men.

They kept to the middle of the channel, wary of their underside cargo and in order to avoid contact with others. Other than two crabbers hauling up early-morning traps, they had encountered no one else on the waterway. Greene again consulted the tide chart from Limehouse Bridge, his destination upriver, which listed the high-water mark at just after 2 a.m. He glanced at his watch and gauged that Riker had plenty of time to alight and set up before sunrise.

Riker glanced in several directions before he rechecked two lines lashed to the oar sockets, which secured a neoprene case beneath the boat. In the waterproof container were outfits and equipment, North Carolina driver's licenses, American passports, five thousand dollars in cash, two hundred rounds of ammunition, and a Russian Dragunov SVD-1 rifle. Both men also carried Heckler & Koch VP9 pistols.

"We're close." Riker again checked their wake as the boat rounded a bend in the channel.

"*Há*," Greene replied, then corrected himself. "Yes."

"There." Riker pointed to a cove near a small tributary, sufficient to allow the jon boat access. "Pull up the troller and use the oar."

Greene hesitated long enough for Riker to realize his partner hadn't fully understood, so he repeated the instruction in Chechen.

"*Há*," Greene answered, this time not bothering to revert to English.

Riker acknowledged the man's skill was top notch, but he planned to inform their handler that Greene's English would need to improve before he could work outside of Europe again. Riker cut one end of the rope and snapped the case free. He hauled it over the portside gunwale as the boat came to rest at the water's edge. The jon bobbed in the swell, and its hull tapping against rows of jagged oyster beds created a rhythmic, almost soothing sound. While the assassin cut the heat-sealed seam and organized his gear, Greene watched fiddler crabs scurry through cord grass and disappear down holes dug into the bank.

"It stinks," Greene remarked, referring to the smell of pluff mud.

"I like it," Riker replied, as he separated his equipment. The pungent odor reminded him of childhood summers spent on the Caspian Sea, where Riker and his grandfather would pass the days in an old dory on the tidal flats of the Volga Delta. It was on the largest enclosed body of water on Earth, fed by the longest river in Europe, that the boy and his *neena* would angle for the world's biggest freshwater fish. Over a small fire on shore, the pair would clean and cook the beluga sturgeon they caught, hoping each time for the opportunity to harvest its highly valued roe.

It was along the same riverbanks that Riker learned to shoot. At age ten, the young Cossack could hit any wild boar that wandered within two hundred yards of the Fedorov Avtomat rifle his grandfather had used during the Soviet-Finnish "Winter War" of 1939, and the devastating conflict that followed. As an eighteen-year-old private in the Russian Army, Riker's effective range had increased to seven hundred yards. By the time the First Chechen War broke out, the highly trained Spetsnaz sniper had recorded seventy-four confirmed kills, three of them from more than one mile out.

The storm was pushing in faster than Riker had antici-pated. Now dressed in black and wearing rubber hip waders, he stuffed the new credentials, cash, and the remainder of his kit into a watertight pack. He conducted a quick check of the Dragunov, and zipped the rifle into a modified fishing rod tube. The soft sleeve looked like any other drop-safe case used to transport gear, though the reel compartment had been elongated to accommodate the stock and receiver of a long gun, including two thirty-round magazines. Riker donned the rucksack and slung the case over his shoulder.

"*Udachi*," Greene said, this time in Russian.

His partner had routinely switched between English, Chechen, and Russian, which led Riker to wonder where the man's loyalties ultimately lay. Greene was Chechen, but his father was a Muscovite and had served in the Russian Army. The former captain's refusal to fire on citizens during the First

Chechen War led to his arrest and brief imprisonment. At his court-martial, the disgraced officer argued that he had ordered his troops to stand down because of poor strategic planning rather than any allegiance to those fighting for the breakaway republic.

Like Greene, Riker was born in Grozny, but unlike the man's father, the sniper held no reservations as to who the enemy had been during his time in the conflict. Every rebel he centered in the reticle of his Swarovski scope only hardened Riker's conviction, and added to his total.

"I won't need luck," Riker responded. He pulled himself out of the boat and immediately sank down into the mud. "The plane is scheduled to arrive at 7:45 a.m. Stay on the river as long as you can, but make sure you're at the extraction point no later than eight o'clock."

"*Há*," Greene replied as he pushed off the bank and turned upriver. He was not far from the put-in at Limehouse Bridge, where a black Denali and tow-trailer had been parked two days earlier. After the contract was carried out, the two men were to abandon the boat at a campground near Santee, South Carolina, en route to Charlotte Douglas International Airport. There, they would split up, Greene on a Scandinavian Airlines flight heading to Oslo, and Riker on a nonstop Lufthansa bound for Barcelona.

The assassin watched the boat fight the current for a moment, before he turned and disappeared into the marsh.

CHAPTER THREE

Limehouse Bridge Boat Landing

Kevin Greene steered to the water's edge beneath Limehouse Bridge. He throttled down the trolling motor as he approached the groundout dock, and the underside of the boat scraping up the concrete ramp echoed across the landing like sandpaper pulled over coarse wood. As he secured the craft, Greene eyed the black SUV he had earlier parked near one of the massive pylons of the overpass.

It was colder than seasonal averages predicted, and the growing cloud cover signaled that conditions would only worsen over the next twelve hours. Sunrise was an hour away, but Greene knew that first light would bring out early-morning fishermen looking to troll for red drum and flounder. He had just circled the trailer when he sensed someone nearby, and heard a voice.

"Morning."

The Chechen turned and watched a man in uniform exit a nearby truck. Greene quietly cursed himself for not surveilling the vehicles well enough to pick up the shadowed silhouette in the driver's seat of the F-250. The officer was not wearing the outfit of a policeman, but was law enforcement of some kind, evidenced by the badge on his shoulder and large-caliber weapon holstered on his hip. Greene strained to make out the agency, but it was too dark and his English too poor to read the inscription.

Greene had yet to respond when the DNR agent spoke again. "In from a late night out?"

Greene was not certain he understood what the man had said, so he only nodded.

"What are you after?"

Damn these Americans, Greene thought to himself. The basics of their language were easy enough to master, but their tendency to speak fast and in choppy vernacular made it nearly impossible to pick up rapidly spoken everyday jargon. "I've been fishing," Greene responded flatly, hoping that if he sounded tired and disinterested, the man would leave him alone.

"So I gathered. Anything biting?"

"Mosquitos," Greene replied, but pronounced the word with a strong '*qu*.'"

"Which are about the size of F/A-18s," the agent joked. "Listen, I won't keep you long. I just need to see your license."

Greene smiled, having understood the request, and produced a North Carolina driver's license along with a South Carolina non-resident fishing permit.

The agent glanced at the documentation. "What were you fishing for?"

"Red drum."

"Out deep?" The man held up the license. "This is for freshwater only."

Greene gathered himself enough to point further east. "I've been inland."

"Not on the Stono. It doesn't die out in freshwater."

Greene remained silent, unsure of what to say. He assumed the officer would have recognized that the size of his boat and small trolling motor effectively restricted his territory to inland waterways, and that the visiting angler had simply misspoken, but his limited fishing knowledge and a lack of language acumen combined with the welling panic to prevent Greene from saying anything.

"Whereabouts are you from in North Carolina?"

"Raleigh." Greene gave his prepared response, ready with street names and landmarks, if pressed.

"You a State fan?"

Greene heard the word "*estate*" and considered his response. "Sure."

"Me too. Love the Pack. Born up in Henderson myself, though I haven't been to a game since I moved to South Carolina. Do most of your fishing along the Banks?"

Greene again failed to understand the query, and began to consider his dwindling options.

"Listen, I've got to write you a citation."

Greene thought he heard "*gotta*" and "*righteous*," and watched the man pull a small pad from his pocket. The agent turned toward the Denali, and the Chechen saw metal cuffs cased on the back of his belt.

"Is this your SUV?"

"*Há*," Greene answered without thinking, but then quickly followed with, "it is."

The agent didn't register that he found anything unusual in the answer as he continued to jot down Green's information. "Normally, I could let you off with a warning, but they're making us crack down on out-of-state infractions."

He said something else, but the Chechen ignored it, having decided on a course of action. "I have another license in the car."

The agent stopped writing. "You should have it on you."

"Let me get it." Greene pulled the keys for the vehicle from his pocket and pressed the remote. The locks snapped up in unison and the back hatch rose slowly as compressed air hissed out. Greene straddled the hitch trailer and pretended to shuffle through a small storage bin that had nothing in it, as he kept the DNR agent in his periphery. He noticed the man casually glance back toward his own truck. At that moment, the operative spun and snapped his wrist in one quick motion, causing a telescopic blackjack to whip from its casing. The agent registered something was wrong just as the metal baton smashed across his neck, just below the ear. The electrical knockout was immediate, and reduced the man's response to little more than dropping like a marionette with its strings cut.

Greene quickly recanvassed the parking area, which remained still and quiet. He policed the area, shoving the logbook and pen in the unconscious man's pocket, before pulling him inside the car and binding his hands and legs with flexicuffs. Greene struggled to push the rear door closed quicker than the auto-shut feature wanted to allow, as he surveilled the surrounding area for any security cameras he might have missed. The Chechen backed the Denali to the ramp, hitched and locked down the boat, and drove to where the entrance of the lot intersected the main road. The plan had been to stay at the river access until it was time to head to the pickup location, where Riker would be waiting. Since Greene was now transporting a bloodied and unconscious law enforcement officer, he decided to drive to the extraction point early and wait there for his partner.

Greene rolled to a stop at the main road just as the DNR agent began to groan and regain consciousness.

CHAPTER FOUR

Charleston Executive Airport

John Riker moved along the edge of a creek that forked inland from the Stono River. His map showed the waterway would soon turn east and peter out on the edge of the Charleston Executive Airport. The entire region, he knew, brimmed with tentacle-like tributaries that branched off its main river systems and created a massive, five-hundred-square-mile swath of wildlife-enriched swamps, woodlands and marshes. It also contained the type of wet mud that made walking, at best, a chore, and at worst, nearly impossible. Each plodding step that Riker took produced a sucking sound, like an airtight container opened for the first time.

The inconvenience was necessary, for the route gave the sniper access to a wooded area with a direct line of sight to where passengers deplaned at the small airport. The distance of the shot was manageable, one Riker could have taken when he was eighteen. His target that morning, however, would be considerably larger and far slower than the jackals he had hunted as a young boy near Bryansk, and the hefty price this particular hide would bring made the kill far more valuable than what the Kazakh villagers used to haggle for back home.

A 7.62x54 round fired from the Dragunov rifle traveled at roughly three thousand feet per second. Five hundred thousand Euros for one-half of one second's work was not a bad payday, the sniper acknowledged.

As Riker trudged through the muck, he envisioned himself an officer under Henry Clinton's command, navigating the same patch of ground and in the same conditions more than two centuries earlier. The prize then had been George Washington's Southern force and the strategic port city in which they were entrenched. For a brief moment, Riker wondered if he should pay homage to the ragtag band of American revolutionaries who had bested the world's most powerful army. In the end, however, he viewed those rebels no differently than their modern-day counterparts in Chechnya. Both were insurrectionists who needed to be dealt with accordingly.

Riker did admire one patriot, a New Jersey marksman named Timothy Murphy, whose long-range effort from elevated cover at the Battle of Bemis Heights knocked British General Simon Fraser from his horse, and into history. That single, nearly impossible shot, taken from three hundred yards out with a Swiss-made double-barreled Golcher rifle, helped turn the tide of the Revolutionary War improbably in the favor of the poorly equipped people's army of farmers and shopkeepers.

Murphy's superior feat had been born from experience and skill, and while Riker was certain he could make his own shot cold bore, the guaranteed payday for a successful kill left no room for error. As a result, the sniper would rely on a digital scope with an integrated laser rangefinder, wind gauge, internal environmental sensor suite, and a ballistics calculator that could plot a solution to the center mass of his target.

Riker reached the end of the rivulet and stepped onto firmer ground. The knee-high wading boots that had facilitated his trek along the pluff banks now hindered his progress, but the fishing attire was necessary in case he encountered anyone curious as to what he was doing. Fortunately, it was a short walk to the perimeter of the airfield. Riker could make out the end of the runway through the fog, which had already begun to burn off in the morning heat. It was humid even for late September, and the sniper marveled at how British soldiers, always dressed in canvas cloth and heavy wool, would have been able to withstand the stifling climate of the American colonies. No wonder more of them died from heat exhaustion than enemy fire in several battles.

The Chechen reached the tree line and searched for a suitable place to set up. Though crosswinds from the incoming storm had increased, he was not concerned, for Riker had made kills from far longer distances and in worse conditions. At least he would not be firing through exposed rebar from a concrete hole amidst the deafening percussion of heavy artillery.

Riker located two trees whose lowest boughs had become intertwined parallel to the ground, nearly eight feet high. The sniper grappled up the twisted limbs and unloaded his backpack on a neighboring offshoot. He found a spot that afforded him a relatively comfortable position, and rested his rifle on the stem of a branch that formed a natural Y-notch.

The Cessna, a private charter out of Washington, D.C., would take several minutes to taxi to the only lot the airport offered its incoming flights to deplane. Riker gauged he would have approximately one additional minute to adjust for changing conditions. He pinged several distances with the rangefinder and plotted three successive shots, rotating between the runway and the building closest to its terminus. Riker verified the computer's formula using his own mental calculations, and then closed his eyes.

It was now a waiting game, something a sniper learned to do better than pulling a trigger.

Within thirty minutes, Riker heard the reverberating engines of an approaching aircraft. He checked his watch. His target was early. The assassin watched the plane drop through the clouds and struggle against the coastal wind shear, until it finally steadied its descent. The small plane hit hard, bounced twice, and touched down. The private plane, with red trim along the tail section, slowed to taxi speed and turned onto a perpendicular run that accessed the main parking lot. He confirmed the plane's *N* number as it rolled to a stop.

Intelligence from his handler listed the target at just over six feet tall, with light brown hair, slightly graying. Other than a minimal flight crew, the manifest from the private charter numbered the passengers at three, with two of them women.

A turn of luck put the plane's exit door broadside to Riker's position. At this range and considering his target's height, the man would sit at just under two mils on the scope. Riker reverified the distance, seven hundred and forty-four yards, and took one last wind reading.

A door opened and several people exited. The assassin could not discern facial features at this range, but he was able to dismiss both passengers, one a woman and the other a younger girl. A third person appeared, a man wearing a dark sport coat, who matched the height, general weight, and hair color of the target. He descended halfway down the airstair, then stopped for a moment and turned to face the wooded area, offering Riker a clean shot.

The sniper was now forced to make a snap decision. If he couldn't be certain, Riker had been instructed to follow and finish the man at close range. This course of action involved added risk, particularly to Riker's own health and well-being.

Thirty seconds.

He recanvassed the runway. No other passengers had exited the aircraft, and the women had already begun to make their way toward the hanger. The target loitered a moment longer and then slowly walked down the remaining steps to the tarmac. Riker slowed his breathing, sharpened his focus, and flipped off the safety. He paused, and for a split second reconsidered the potential danger of delaying the kill. Of having to rely on Greene and his broken English for a prolonged period.

Take the shot or the alternative.

Riker reminded himself that his success, his very life, had often rested on his own battlefield judgment, a certain wisdom that could come only from wartime experience. He readied the shot, and drew in one long breath, holding it as he relaxed his right pointer. *Squeeze, don't pull*, he still reminded himself, though the movement was reflexive.

The sniper was seldom fully cognizant of the chain reaction that followed the recoil of the rifle and the spit of a 150-grain armor-piercing round from a suppressed muzzle. Even though the feeling was second nature, that singular moment, between compression and the sending of a bullet downrange, always created the illusion that time momentarily stood still. It passed instantly, and Riker gazed through his scope to watch the scene unfold much as it always did in a setting where people did not expect to witness someone's chest split open from the high-speed impact of a boat-tailed ball of lead jacketed with a copper alloy.

The target was down, and nobody moved.

The bullet had entered below the neckline, near the heart. Upon impact, the man's arms and head had reflexively pitched forward, as if he had been shoved, while the lower half of his body gave out. He then collapsed, before the awkward angle at which his legs folded caused his body to recoil backward onto the pavement.

There would be no ambulance with flashing lights speeding through stopped traffic in the hopes of making it to Bon Secours St. Francis in time, nor any trauma team working feverishly to repair life-threatening injuries.

Terms such as laceration, cavitation, and soft tissue damage were irrelevant.

The man was dead on arrival.

CHAPTER FIVE

Ascoli Piceno, Italy

Geoffrey Charlton stepped onto Via Giudea and returned a familiar late-morning salutation to a man standing in the doorway of a corner barbershop. He entered the *Piazza del Popolo* just as a waiter at Caffè Meletti popped open the first of three massive umbrellas that covered its patio. One of Ernest Hemingway's early haunts, the storied restaurant had opened a century earlier in what was considered one of the country's most beautiful *"squares of the people."* It had also become Charlton's preferred place to sit and watch the unworried Italian world go by.

The Englishman slowed as he approached the Palazzo dei Capitani, a majestic structure that once housed a powerful medieval order known as the *Captains*. The former head of MI6 ensured that his daily promenades often passed within sight of the eight-hundred-year-old building, not only because of its aesthetic beauty, but for what it represented.

It reminded Charlton of a time when he ruled the most powerful order of spies in the known world.

"*Buongiorno, Luca.*" Charlton smiled at the waiter laying out espresso cups and serviettes. "*Sono i primi?*"

"But of course not, *Signore* Charlton," the young man replied, eager to practice his English. "You are right on time, as always."

"*Bene.* At your pleasure, I'll have my usual, at my usual." Charlton referred to a Caffè Americano and the first table inside the restaurant, in the corner and back from the doorway. He would have preferred to sit outside on such a pleasant day, but old habits died hard for those who long minded their backs for a living.

"Luca!" An older woman at the doorway snapped her fingers and jerked her head in Charlton's direction.

Charlton smiled at the easygoing university student, who flashed his ubiquitous grin. "Take your time, my good fellow."

"Only if I want my mother to harass me all day," Luca muttered under his breath.

"Luca Giovanni!"

"She hates it when I speak English. She thinks I'm talking about her."

Charlton smiled. He liked the Italians, their conviviality and embrace of *la dolce vita*. The first time he set foot in Rome, en route to London after an assignment in West Berlin, the Cold War operative knew he would make some part of the country his home once he retired from the Secret Intelligence Service. That happened to be thirty-five years later in the wake of several setbacks and the very public shakeup that followed. Charlton had landed on his feet, and in Marche, on the central Italian coast. Since then, one of MI6's most pivotal and polarizing chiefs had done little other than sip espressos and peruse *The Times*.

Charlton dropped his newspaper on a nearby table for some other expat, and rued the waning peace and quiet of the piazza, which would soon be overwhelmed by noisy tourists and traffic. His spirits lifted when he spied an old acquaintance making his way across the square. The man entered the cafe and when he saw Charlton, he flashed a wry smile, the consequence of some inside joke between the two men.

"Geoffrey." Gianfranco Rossi clasped his hands together in mock surprise. "Imagine my shock to find you here, *amico mio.*"

"*Ciao*, my old friend. I hope life is treating you well."

"If I am here tomorrow, then it is." Rossi sat down across from Charlton, and the Englishman watched his retired counterpart scan the piazza through an open window. He had first worked with Rossi while on assignment in southern Europe, when the cocky young officer from Rome was still with the *Servizio per le Informazioni e la Sicurezza Militare*. Early operational successes had fast-tracked Rossi through the ranks of military intelligence, until a string of scandals that had been considered brazen even by Italian standards of corruption derailed his espionage career. Thanks to family connections, Rossi embarked on a highly lucrative venture in finance, ultimately capped by a windfall payout with the merger that formed Banca Intesa twenty years earlier.

"I hope you are well, despite shortcomings beyond your control," Rossi said, teasing the Londoner about England's national football team.

"The measure of a man is to be found in a stiff upper lip."

"Something your ancestors were forced to invent out of necessity, I think."

"We are all haunted by our ghosts," Charlton replied. "This is why you should be wary of Greeks bearing gifts, or guns."

"*Tsk, tsk.* This is low, even for you, my friend." Charlton had alluded to heavy losses suffered by the Italians during their failure to defeat an underwhelming Greek Army in 1941. The debacle forced Adolph Hitler to intervene, delaying his invasion of the Soviet Union long enough to ensure that a stalwart Red Army and harsh Russian winter finished off the German advance on the Eastern Front, along with any hopes of the *Wehrmacht* winning the war.

"It could be worse," Charlton added, deciding to up the ante. "You are from the South, no? Some distant relative was likely Spanish, and part of the Armada."

Rossi jumped on the opening. "And if your national side could defend as well as its navy in 1588, you would have more than one World Cup trophy to crow about."

Charlton attempted to suppress a smile, but could not, and both men laughed aloud.

"It's all in good fun, Geoffrey, and you're a good sport." Rossi raised his demitasse. "To the Three Lions."

Charlton tipped his own. "To the *Azzurri*."

Luca returned with *cantuccini* and two espressos, but Charlton shook his head and tossed a ten-Euro note on the table. "Unfortunately, I must go."

"What's this?" Rossi replied in surprise. "I've just arrived. Certainly, you have time for one more café?"

"I'm afraid not." Charlton handed Luca twenty Euros.

"*Grazie*," Luca said.

"No, Luca, thank you for your hospitality and exuberance. I shall miss it."

"*Grazie*," Luca replied again, confused. "You are going somewhere, *Signore* Charlton?"

"*Sì*, and I don't know when I shall return."

"Would you excuse us, Luca?" Rossi handed the waiter a wad of Euros from his own pocket as he pushed Charlton's money back across the table. "I don't like it when you speak in this manner, Geoffrey. What in the name of St. Catherine is going on?"

"No need to concern yourself. Just a journey, nothing more."

"It is always something more with men like us," Rossi replied. "Are you in trouble?"

"Not anything I can't manage, and nothing that would hold a candle to what we went through in the old days."

"Is it something in Italy? I have favors I can call in."

"I wouldn't be doing you any, getting someone else involved. Thank you, but no, I will handle it."

"And when will you return?"

"Sooner than you'll miss my jokes."

The two men strolled several blocks without speaking, when Charlton suddenly stopped and extended his hand. "This is where I leave you."

Rossi nodded, an unspoken acknowledgment that he indeed might not see Charlton again. "Until next time. And don't forget, you owe me an espresso."

"I owe you a great deal more than that, Gianfranco."

"Watch your back, Geoffrey."

"And yours, my friend."

CHAPTER SIX

Charlton quickened his pace. He was a few blocks from his flat, a five-room loft that occupied the entire third floor of what had once been a palace dating to the Renaissance. It had been fully renovated and was quite posh by Italian standards, though he was certain the plumbing still operated by nineteenth-century norms, judging from the sound of the pipes and the erratic water pressure.

Charlton slowed as he approached the corner adjacent to his building. He had already packed two small suitcases and had intended to leave directly from his afternoon coffee, but decided to wait until after lunch to request the taxi that would take him to the *stazione* for his train to Munich.

His mobile rang, but Charlton ignored it as he entered the foyer and climbed two floors to a small stoop outside the door of his flat. Winded, he listened for a perfunctory moment before inserting his key and twisting the lock until it snapped open. Charlton stepped inside, and froze. The bags he had packed were gone from the couch, and in their place sat a well-worn woman. Though she was young, the heavy eye shadow and caked rouge produced the opposite of its intended effect, and Charlton guessed that the girl was the same kind of low-grade prostitute who populated the back streets of most moderately sized Italian cities.

Charlton's ability to call on the reflexive skills required to respond in such situations had been dulled by age and distance from the field. Before he could step back into the hallway, to momentary safety and the pistol he carried, he saw a man leaning against the kitchen entryway. His right hand was pulled far enough behind his leg to hide the gun from the woman, but not Charlton.

"*Buongiorno*, Geoffrey. It's been a long time. Please join us."

Charlton entered his flat and walked slowly to a chair near the window, certain that he had never seen the man before. The hooker, clearly strung out on something, sat unmoving and with no visible anxiety. As Charlton sat down and faced the pair, the man directed the woman to the bathroom in rapid Italian, instructing her to remove her clothes and remain there until she was summoned. She complied, glancing once back at Charlton before she closed the door to the lavatory.

Both men eyed one another for a moment, until the intruder finally spoke. "Have you worked it out? Why, you must be wondering, have I been sent here?"

Charlton took note of the innuendo. Any queries concerning the *who* or *what* of the man's presence were ultimately immaterial, for he was clearly not there to administer a slap on the wrist. Charlton sensed he would be unable to chat his way out of the situation, so he remained silent.

"No?" the man asked. "Shall I enlighten you? Men such as you send others to do their dangerous work, a coward who wrings his hands of any responsibility from a safe perch in some privileged hall. One of those operations is in fact the reason you find me standing here today, in a place you clearly believed would provide safe harbor."

Charlton finally broke his silence. "You would need to be more specific, mate."

"No doubt, the filth so long removed from your finger-nails." The man paused, and then said, "*Turnkey.*"

Charlton did not respond, though from his muted reaction the revelation had clearly produced the intended effect.

"I see I needn't remind you of its particulars."

"And what could you know of it, other than a name?"

"You are all the same, prancing about like the viceroy of some colony that still flies the Union Jack. *The sun never sets*, isn't that what everyone used to sing?"

Charlton took note that the broadside had begun to take on the tinge of something personal, a sentiment that went beyond the directive of whomever was behind the man. Charlton saw an opening, a way to initiate a longer conversation and perhaps a way out. "You seem familiar with our top-secret operations."

"Enough of this pointless chit-chat," the man suddenly replied. "Would you like to know how this ends? The girl is a cheap hooker, this much you have worked out for yourself. She thinks she is here to pleasure both of us. She is, of course, as good as someone your age could expect to get, so you should thank me."

Charlton watched the man begin a slow arc around the room, all the while threading a suppressor onto his gun. He reached into a backpack on the floor and pulled from it a handful of bondage and S & M magazines, which the man scattered on the table. He also produced a whip, which he threw on the couch. "I've been shadowing you for the last few weeks. What a boring life you've led in retirement. Since the death of your wife."

Charlton could well recall the day, one year to the week that the woman to whom he had been married for fifty-three years had finally succumbed to a slow, painful cancer.

"Not to worry. I've refashioned a far more exciting last act. *You*—" the man accentuated by gesturing with his gun, "the retired spy with a long-hidden sick side, have spent the better part of your golden years in a scenic corner of the Italian coast on strung-out whores and sadomasochistic pursuits. When the *polizia* arrive, they will deduce that she shot you, and then, still wearing the strap-on she was paid to use on you, killed herself, beside cooked-out heroin spoons and little blue pills." The man laughed. "Can you imagine the conversation around Vauxhall Cross when that story breaks? *Che peccato!*"

Charlton suddenly felt sick to his stomach. "I was only head of section at the time. I had superiors."

"You ran the operation from West Berlin," the man snapped. "But, do not worry, the 'others' to whom you refer will be dealt with in due time."

Charlton's mind raced at the implication, and he shifted his position, hoping to push the gun in his waistband higher for quicker access.

The man watched him intently. "Yes, go for your weapon. I think you will find it is identical to this one, the gun that will kill both of you," he replied, bringing attention to his own pistol. It was a Walther PPK/E, a .32-caliber ACP, the same model Charlton carried.

Charlton slumped. He recognized that a lifetime of achievement would soon be trumped by shock and gossip. All he had done, every operation that had built his career and put him in the Chair at MI6, would forever be replaced by hushed talk of dominatrixes and dildos. "Who are you?" he asked.

"I haven't gone by my given name for many years, but if you want something to remember me by—in fact, it will be the last memory you have—I am the agent you betrayed at that checkpoint thirty-four years ago. Since I have been sent here to deliver you from this life, let me also deliver a message. *Spindle* says hello."

Charlton's eyes grew wide with disbelief, and it was then the ex-chief realized that it would be the only reaction he could muster this late in the game.

"Mia Cara!" the man then called loudly toward the bathroom, before turning back toward Charlton. "I'll leave the five-hundred Euros I paid her so that everyone will know what a generous pervert you were."

With that, the assassin raised his pistol and shot Charlton between the eyes.

CHAPTER SEVEN

Munich, Germany

T he two operatives had rotated their surveillance every fifteen minutes over the last three hours. Neither man was native to the crowd who populated the popular park, but in one of Europe's largest urban green spaces, located in one of its biggest cities, the killers blended in easily enough.

The more experienced of the pair, Mykhail Vann, hailed on his mother's side from the Tyrolean region of Austria only one generation back and looked less traditionally Slavic than his partner, Artem Ivanenko. Vann's features were softer and his German perfect. Anyone who had spoken with the man since he had flown in from Copenhagen, and that number had been limited to as few as possible, would have presumed his Bavarian to be fairly local. Ivanenko's bearing and familiarity of regional customs complemented his own near-fluency, which was sufficient to pass for someone who had immigrated to Germany and worked hard to assimilate. Together, the team of ex-Spetsnaz soldiers formerly attached to the Alpha Group of Ukraine's Security Service confidently shadowed their target as he walked carefree along the Oberstjägermeisterbach River.

William Lindsay made a second pass by the *Englischer Garten*. It was appropriately named, he acknowledged, for strolling through it reminded him of a youth spent romping around the gardens of Milton Abbey, in the southwest of England. How quickly nine decades had passed, the former deputy chief of MI6 thought as he stopped at the base of the Chinese Tower, an impressive five-story pagoda at the southern end of the park.

While he admired the structure, Lindsay continued to discreetly monitor the garden from his periphery. He had marked one of his pursuers shortly after finishing lunch at the restaurant *Hirschau* an hour earlier. Lindsay had caught his trailer using a large window to observe his movements, and since leaving the beer garden, the retired spy had singled out the man's partner and the rotating system of surveillance they employed.

Their timing was too coordinated and not random enough to work on someone who had spent a lifetime obsessed with his surroundings. Lindsay's issue, however, was not that he hadn't spotted the pair, for his mind was no less sharp than the first day he had entered the Security Intelligence Service sixty-five years earlier. Indeed, he had survived as one of the few operatives left in the Special Operations Executive, whose ranks of saboteurs had been all but decimated by the Nazis. Like the scattered SOE agents who remained, and their number was few, Lindsay had been absorbed into MI6. By the time he had finished his meritocratic march up the intelligence hierarchy, the extremely popular deputy chief had carved for himself no small fiefdom of loyal protégées.

Lindsay's problem was that he had foolishly left his sub-compact 9mm at his flat, allowing the prospect of a leisurely stroll on such a nice day as the grounds to momentarily forget the maxim that it was better to have a gun and not need it, than the contrary. The aging spy was painfully aware that no matter how keen his wits remained, it would be difficult to physically shake the men loose, especially if they turned out to be more professional than their ability to follow a seasoned target suggested.

Experience demanded that Lindsay assume the two men were familiar not only with his daily routine, but also the location of his flat. A long and healthy career in the field also suggested that the pair might be part of a larger team, which meant he would not so easily make an MI6 safe house located on the opposite side of the city.

Lindsay kept his pace even and assumed that neither man would move on him in a public venue. He exited the park and passed by the U-Bahn station at *Universität*. Lindsay considered hopping the next train in an attempt to make it back to his flat, and his waiting pistol, but he feared there was likely someone already there in anticipation of his eventual return.

He considered seeking assistance at the closest *polizeistation*, or simply walking into the nearest hospital and feigning chest pains. Neither option would help Lindsay in the long run, he knew, and worse, it would give away that he was aware of his surveillance.

For one of the only times in his career, the man who had beaten the Germans and bested the Soviets, and weathered countless failed operations, hesitated, before making his way back to Prinzregentenstraße.

The British Consulate was just across the Isar River, less than a mile away.

CHAPTER EIGHT

Johns Island, South Carolina

John Riker zipped the Dragunov into its case. He carefully policed the area beneath his perch and located the spent shell casing. As he pulled the backpack over his shoulders, the assassin kept an eye on the scene at the tarmac, which had quickly become one of panic and confusion. The two women who had flown in with the target had been joined by the pilot and several airport staff, including one who was on the phone and gesticulating wildly.

Riker gauged that he had seven minutes to get to the pickup location and get moving before paramedics arrived, assuming first responders adhered to the average response times for Charleston County. Twenty minutes after that, police would cordon off the immediate area and search for witnesses, until detectives arrived and took over the investigation.

And when they discovered the identity of the dead man, an alphabet soup of federal agencies would swarm the small airport like mosquitos in March. Men in black suits and overpriced sunglasses would stand around oversized SUVs, scribbling on notepads and pointing officiously in various directions. A few would see what others had missed, assume things local authorities would not, and someone might even retrace the path of the bullet back to the tree line. But a handful of bent branches and a few footprints muddled by the coming downpour would be as close as anyone would come to solving the brazen murder of the sitting deputy chief of Britain's Secret Intelligence Service. By the time the news began to reverberate throughout the known world, Riker would be at a safe house in Spain.

The extraction point was less than a mile away, but walking was still difficult. Riker cut his way as quickly as possible through heavy brush and across patches of semi-wet marshland, which combined to slow his pace and restrict mobility. The sniper acknowledged that if the plane had been late or the rain had come early, he likely would have been unable to make the meet location in time to clear the first wave of law enforcement and any perimeters they put up.

Riker pushed through the last bit of undergrowth and stopped short of the rendezvous spot, situated off a dead-man's curve on a single-lane unpaved road. He spied the Denali idling on the soft shoulder with its running lights on. Greene had been instructed to move to the passenger seat so that he would not be the one dealing with any situation that might arise on the drive to North Carolina. Riker could see his partner was still behind the wheel.

The assassin stepped from his concealed position and moved cautiously toward the vehicle, scanning the area as he approached. As Riker neared the SUV, Greene exited without speaking and walked to the rear door. The sniper sensed something was wrong, and as Greene raised the hatch, the bottom of two boots attached to a man lying alert but bound in the tailgate confirmed the suspicion.

Govno, Riker said to himself. *Shit.* "What happened?" He eyed Greene as he pushed the door shut.

"My fishing license was no good."

"Of course it is, you idiot," Riker snapped. "We were sent separate permits for fresh and saltwater. Did you show him the correct one?"

"I don't remember," Greene replied, angry with himself for the slip and irritated at Riker for taking issue with what amounted to an unlucky turn of events.

"And why didn't you just allow the man to write you a ticket?" *Tupoy*, Riker said again, this time in Russian, and began to rapidly cycle through a handful of scenarios and how each could potentially play out depending on what course of action he chose to take. Riker almost laughed aloud as he marveled at how quickly things were guaranteed to go wrong at the worst possible moment.

"What do we do?" Greene asked.

"Help me with the boat." Riker climbed into the jon and opened a small storage bin secured to the center bench.

Greene pulled himself over the gunwale by the oarlock as Riker removed a tarp from the compartment and handed it to him.

"What are we doing?" Greene asked again, confused, and if he had been more attuned to human microexpressions, he might have recognized the giveaway that flashed across Riker's face. It took the gun coming level for the less experienced operative to register what was happening.

"*Ty chyo blya!?*" Greene shouted as he dropped the tarp and reached in vain for his own weapon.

Riker had determined he could not risk the assignment being compromised further, and that his best chance to get cleanly away was alone. Greene's reaction betrayed his surprise as two rounds snapped from Riker's suppressed HK and slammed into his chest, twisting the man off balance and knocking him backward. Greene slumped awkwardly on the center bench of the boat.

Riker watched as his partner struggled to maintain some semblance of control. The man clutched at two entry wounds spurting blood in rhythmic bursts, while a perforated lung labored to pull in enough air to function. Any thought of retaliation was gone as his system began to shut down noncritical functions in a desperate bid to keep oxygen and vital fluids circulating. Greene's body, now in as much a state of panic as his brain, had begun to transition into the decompensatory stage of cardiogenic failure. With his pressure plummeting and respiration nearing full stop, the Chechen slipped into an unconscious state as his shock became irreversible.

Riker pulled the tarp over Greene and secured it to metal rings on either side of the boat. Approaching sirens indicated that the scene at the airport had progressed beyond the first responder stage. The operation was heading into dangerous territory, and Riker knew he needed to get moving. He jumped off the trailer and into the driver's seat. He could hear the bound man in the back of the SUV struggling against his restraints, and what sounded like curses muffled by the towel that had been stuffed into his mouth and duct-taped around his head.

Riker consulted his map and decided to take back roads to his destination in order to avoid major highways.

The sooner he was in Santee, with the bodies at the bottom of Lake Marion, the better.

CHAPTER NINE

North Ballachulish, Scotland

The kitchen and sitting area had been cleaned twice, and the furniture in the main room covered with bed linen. The house had been locked down and readied to sit dormant for several weeks, the longest that Madeleine Halliwell had been away since the death of her husband. A suitcase and small overnight bag sat beside the front entryway, and Halliwell decided to recheck the small lochside home, which doubled as a bed and breakfast, to ensure that everything was in order.

She planned to take the early evening train south to visit her granddaughter, also named Madeleine, who had been in a coma since the bombing of King's Cross Station four years earlier. While their conversations during the monthly drop-ins had been decidedly one-sided, Halliwell was certain that Maddie would soon wake and answer back, as if nothing had happened.

The journey to England that week, however, would be different. After the stopover in London, the long-retired MI6 officer was off to the States to see her grandsons. Sean Garrett had relocated to the U.S. years earlier and was now a climbing guide in the mountains of North Carolina. His half-brother, Banastre Montjoy, deputy chief of MI6, was in Washington, D.C. on official business. The family had arranged to meet in the Carolinas and head to the coast for holiday, their first together in a while.

Halliwell had retired from SIS nearly twenty years earlier after a long and lionized career. During World War II she served as a saboteur for the SOE, and had endured numerous missions in Nazi-occupied Europe, several times returning as the only surviving operative. The promising agent joined MI6 after the war, working her way through the ranks until she was made senior case controller, one of the first females in the Service to be promoted to that position. After her career, Halliwell had retired to the Scottish Highlands with her husband, Sir Nigel Aldrich, who had served as deputy chief of SIS through the end of the Cold War. Together, the couple had opened and run a small bed and breakfast, until Aldrich had been killed by the same terrorist bomb that put their granddaughter in a coma.

The retaliation against those responsible, scattered over two continents and several countries, had been swift and unforgiving. Though retired, Halliwell had orchestrated and overseen the unsanctioned operation to determine who was behind the terrorist act. Both Sean Garrett and Banastre Montjoy had been instrumental in its success, which, thanks to then deputy chief William Lindsay, remained off the books and ultimately out of the political and public purview.

How fast it had all gone, Halliwell thought as she turned down the last lamp.

What happened next amounted to nothing more than bad luck and worse timing. Halliwell had long been accustomed to dealing with both, and had always been able to turn each in her favor. But, in the midst of opening the door to leave at the exact moment the man on her stoop was attempting to quietly let himself in, Halliwell, one of the first women to work her way through the highest echelon of British Intelligence, found herself in no-man's-land.

The killer's direct flight from Ascoli Piceno to Glasgow had taken three hours, and he had then made the drive to Ballachulish in just under two. The gain of an hour with the change of time zones allowed him to intercept Halliwell before she left for London. He had cut it close, and though the information on her travel itinerary had been precise, the man would later acknowledge that he had gotten lucky, for any delays in his trip from Geoffrey Charlton's flat to Madeleine Halliwell's doorstep would have cost him his second target of the day.

Halliwell was able to process who it was only after shaking off the disbelief that followed her delayed recognition.

Before she could say or do anything, the visitor spoke. "Hello Maddie. It's been a long time."

Unlike Charlton, Halliwell recognized the agent on her doorstep, despite the distance and time of their last meeting in East Berlin, thirty-four years earlier. "They said you were dead."

"And yet, here I am," he replied. "Like Lazarus."

Halliwell did not immediately respond as her mind raced, cycling though what skills she had honed over a long career that might see her free of the situation. "Then I should put a kettle on, to celebrate your return," she suggested, thinking of the .45-caliber pistol in her sugar drawer.

"No thank you, Maddie, I don't take hollow points with my tea."

Halliwell sensed that she was out of options for the first time in her life. She began to tear up at the realization that there would be no more visits with her granddaughter, nor any days with Sean and Banastre. Halliwell stared at the man a moment longer before she responded calmly, "I made my peace a long time ago."

"And I found mine in a KGB dungeon," he hissed.

"Langley bollocksed up *Turnkey* and you bloody well know it."

"The Americans, I remember, were quite good at interfering in East German operations," the main replied, having returned to a calmer state. He reached into his pocket and produced a cigarette, which he lit. "In the end, it was you and Charlton who sabotaged the operation. And, thanks to *Spindle*, I know why."

"*Spindle*?" Halliwell replied, both shocked and confused. "What did that bastard tell you? What's happened to Geoffrey?"

"Allow me to show you," the man replied as he pushed through the door.

CHAPTER TEN

Santee, South Carolina

John Riker exited the highway and turned into Santee State Park. The journey from Charleston had taken longer than expected, owing not only that the drive had been slower along a secondary route, but because the abducted DNR agent had attempted to kick through the back window at the only semi-busy intersection they encountered. The assassin had been forced to pull off on a deserted road several miles outside a small town and climb through the inside of the SUV to choke out the witness to keep him quiet. He had hoped the man would face death with dignity, like a Russian, but that was not the case.

In fact, the officer had thrashed mightily when Riker snapped his neck an hour later on a dead-end lane near a dairy farm in the middle of nowhere. The man was now rolled into a second tarp and lashed to the rear bench of the boat next to Greene, who was already rigid from rigor and turning dark purple from the gravitational post-mortem pooling of blood.

The Chechen circled the campground in search of a suitable put-in for the jon. He would have preferred to access the lake from somewhere other than a public launch, but knew he could not risk the attention of DNR looking to clamp down on early-morning poachers, or drunk boaters still reeling from their weekend revelry.

Although it was eight hundred times smaller than the Caspian Sea, the assassin had heard that Lake Marion offered fishing that rivaled some of his most prized spots back home. Riker had also read that it boasted the world record for channel catfish, and was named for the famous Revolutionary War General Francis Marion, who had terrorized the British with hit-and-run raids throughout the South Carolina Lowcountry.

That evening it would bury two bodies and a boat.

Riker backed into a site near the lakefront. The summer was gone, and with it, the crowds that would have normally flooded the loop with mammoth RVs and loud generators. His spot, a walk-up campsite that could be reserved through a drop box at the park office, was the only one occupied. Though Riker did not expect the campground to attract much attention that time of the week, or season, he nonetheless ignored the pangs of hunger that had peaked in the late afternoon and instead chose to remain in the SUV through dinnertime.

It was near sundown when Riker finally exited the Denali. Only two other cars had entered the loop over the last few hours, but both had continued without stopping. He had paid cash for a week, and beyond that, it would depend on a number of factors as to how long it took for the trailer to be impounded and its owner sought. Riker changed back into his fishing attire and loaded the remainder of his gear into the boat. He rechecked the ropes that bound both men, which would eventually be weakened by water and wildlife gnawing on it and the decomposing bodies.

By that time, the assassin would be one ocean and two continents away.

Riker had already charted several possible sink locations from a nautical map of Lake Marion, and gauged it required only twenty feet of depth for the boat to remain hidden longer than he would need to worry about it.

Riker backed the trailer down the launch, unlocked the pulley mechanism, and fed the boat into the lake. After loading several large rocks collected from the shore, he pushed off from the water's edge and turned on the troller. The assassin motored the boat into deeper water, and initially had difficulty consulting the map as radiation fog enveloped the surface water and mixed with the haze of twilight.

Within ten minutes Riker found what he was looking for, a depression in the lake bed that dropped a full thirty feet lower than the surrounding shelf. He monitored an electronic depth finder and reached the location where he wanted the boat to sink. Riker brought it to a stop and consolidated the small boulders and anchor in the middle of the vessel between the two bodies. He fired a succession of suppressed shots in the shape of a crude circle, and slammed his heel through the metal, causing water to surge around the mass of weight centered between the benches. Riker shoved the 9mm into his backpack and pushed off from the gunwale as the craft began to list. He treaded water for several minutes and watched as the jon bobbed upright on its stern for a moment, before bubbling beneath the waterline.

He quickly swam the distance to shore, stopping only once to monitor the faint outline of running lights moving away in the opposite direction. As Riker pulled himself out of the water, he considered the story he would concoct. His handler would not be happy that he had willingly killed Greene and dumped his body alongside another witness, whose discovery could unravel a complicated chain of events that the assassination in Charleston would soon set in motion. Riker could not hide his partner's death, but he could convincingly bend the narrative into one where Greene had panicked and been shot by a law enforcement officer, who had been wounded in return and then finished off by Riker.

Dangerous loose ends, but ones that had been tied up, literally, at the bottom of a lake.

Riker climbed out of the water near the launch point and drove back to his rented site. He unhooked the trailer and pitched a makeshift camp, which would give the appearance that someone was using the spot. He loaded the remainder of his gear, while ensuring that the surrounding area remained empty of any visitors.

It had begun to drizzle as Riker slowed to a stop at the campground exit. He idled near the front gate and briefly enjoyed the stillness of the moment, before checking his iPhone. The mobile had struggled with spotty signal strength since leaving the city, and he had been unable to contact his handler with an affirmation that the contract had been successfully carried out.

Riker attempted to cycle through web pages, but could find nothing on Reuters or the BBC in regard to the shooting. A throwaway statement from local police had been posted on the website of *The Post and Courier*, but it provided scant details of the murder. It had only been half a day, Riker acknowledged.

Tomorrow morning, there wouldn't be a major news source anywhere in the world that wasn't leading with the story.

CHAPTER ELEVEN

Montreal, Canada

The man strolled along Rue Saint-Pierre, but remained a safe distance behind the twosome he had marked since their exit from the Notre-Dame Basilica. They gave the impression of a normal couple, even if she looked a decade older than her companion. Their route, though it had strayed from the Promenade du Vieux-Port, appeared spontaneous, and while she was committed to popping into whatever shop suited her fancy, which was most of them, he seemed happy enough to oblige her whims.

Emile Chénard, the alias he had gone by long enough to no longer instinctively react when someone else with his given name was randomly hailed, fingered the trigger of the Ruger 9mm in his front pocket.

Some habits were more difficult to break, he acknowledged.

The pair lingered in front of a small eatery, debating. The man glanced at his watch, his patience finally wearing thin, while the woman spoke on her phone. Chénard decided it was time. He stepped from a corner doorway and advanced along an adjacent sidewalk, past a sign painted with a bright red "*Arrêt.*"

Perhaps he should stop, Chénard thought to himself, this habit of hunting sightseers around the streets of Montreal.

He neared his targets. Both were wholly unaware of their surroundings, which was typical of the majority of people, but especially those on holiday. Chénard tightened the grip of his pistol as he approached the couple from behind. The man turned just as Chénard reached him, before Chénard paused and issued a polite, "*Pardon.*" The woman smiled and stepped aside, though her partner did not move, clearly wondering why the stranger had simply not gone around them.

Chénard smiled to himself as he continued up the avenue, toward the café. He had not shadowed someone in earnest, at least with the intent of killing them, in almost twenty years. He had continued the practice in his "retirement," not so much because it kept the skill somewhat sharp, but because the ex-operative had become addicted to the simple reality that such people remained alive only because he afforded them the liberty.

As expected, Olive & Gourmando was standing room only. The scene at the immensely popular and trendy restaurant in Old Montreal was always the same. Locals had arrived early enough after the lunch crowd to be comfortably bunkered into the limited seating space, while a motley collection of tourists waited impatiently in a line that stretched to the street corner. Chénard threaded his way to the entrance, past one particularly disgruntled lot, and through a door that seemed to remain perpetually propped open.

The hostess, an attractive second-year student at McGill University, smiled when she saw Chénard. "*Monsieur* Chénard, I think you will soon become part of the décor," she joked, a reference to his nearly habitual early-evening visits.

"Only if I'm certain to see you," Chénard replied. Though he looked considerably younger than his sixty-three years, Chénard played the part of the harmless grandfather to perfection and was well-liked by the staff. If only the young girl could truly know the man whose given name was Alexei Kirill Arkipov, birthed on a floor in northwest Moscow in a filthy, single-room prefab housing unit that provided even less space than the state-allotted nine meters per person.

Arkipov's father, who had survived World War II, Stalin, and the Great Purge, only to be forced out during the upheaval that followed the sudden demise of "Uncle Joe" from a burst brain vessel, disappeared and was presumed dead before his family relocated to East Germany. While his mother and three older brothers discovered that housing in East Berlin rivaled its Muscovite counterpart in sheer squalor, their flat was considerably larger, and thus to young Alexei, a paradise.

Four years later, two months after his mother and two brothers had perished in a kitchen grease fire, Arkipov was sent to a state-run children's home. Lost among the remnants of the Wolf Children—war-orphaned Germans from East Prussia who were expelled from Russia into the GDR   Arkipov kept to himself as best he could and was by all accounts, and against all odds, a remarkably well-adjusted child. He was finally given to the Heinrichs, a couple fiercely loyal to the Party, and in his new environment, "Markus" excelled in school and at sport.

The teenager showed a particular aptitude for languages and science, and following his one-year compulsory conscription into the military at age eighteen, Heinrich was recruited into the Stasi, the East German Ministry for State Security.

He rose quickly through the ranks of Main Department II, impressing both ally and skeptic alike. Eventually, the young counterintelligence agent was singled out by his case officer to be sent across the Wall as one of the agency's Romeos, operatives consigned to court vulnerable, but well-placed, West German women. The handsome and consummately dashing Markus Heinrich, identified by the deep-cover alias *Spindle*, so named after the poisonous fruit, became one of the Stasi's most effective operatives in Berlin. There to initially seduce and exploit a twenty-eight-year-old interpreter at the American embassy, Heinrich found the sexspionage assignments rather dull, his carnal interludes with a wide range of unsuspecting lovers notwithstanding.

Everything changed in the fall of 1984, in the South Berlin borough of Dreilinden.

Chénard's fleeting reminiscence of the events of that period, and the fallout that ensued, was interrupted by the muted din of the café, and a voice. On occasion, the muddle of his identities, from Arkipov to Heinrich to *Spindle* to Chénard, caught up with the master spy, who was forced to concentrate on what façade he was fronting at any given moment.

"I have saved you a nice spot in the corner," the hostess said as she handed Chénard a cappuccino that had been prepared as soon as he arrived.

"You treat me too well, my dear." Though his nuanced

French was such that neighbors assumed Chénard was a Parisian expat, he routinely spoke only English around strangers and casual acquaintances. Misdirection, he knew, was the best guarantor of anonymity.

Chénard had just taken his seat, near the front window and in view of the same group who had grumbled as he jumped the line, when his mobile pinged. The text sent from Scotland displayed a single number, the signal that the third contract had been carried out. *Three confirmed kills.* Charlton, Lindsay, and Halliwell were dead. Only one sanction remained, though Chénard expected that the Chechen assassin in South Carolina would contact him within the next few hours.

He had settled on a chickpea and pickled beet sandwich for an early dinner when his phone newsfeed buzzed its hourly update. Among the headlines was the breaking story that a man had been gunned down at a small airport in Charleston. Chénard smiled, but only for a moment. Though the details were limited and no identity had been officially released, a local newspaper had leaked that the victim was a forty-four-year-old financier from New York. Authorities, as far as they were willing to admit, were still uncertain whether the man had been intentionally targeted.

Chénard reread the story and swore under his breath in Russian, one of the few times he slipped and spoke in his native tongue. He stood, downed his drink, and left hurriedly without bidding *adieu* to anyone.

The information, if accurate, signified that the wrong man was dead. It meant that the fourth objective of the operation,

Banastre Montjoy, the man who was the reason Chénard had been forced into exile two decades earlier, was still alive.

PART II

CHAPTER TWELVE

Riga, Latvia
December 1984

*T*he building, a grand structure that was originally designed to be a collection of shops and luxury flats located in the heart of Riga, dated to the decline of the Art Nouveau frenzy and the assassination of Archduke Ferdinand. By the onset of yet another great war to end all others, the year of terror had arrived with the Soviet occupation of Latvia. Gone were the trappings of commerce and wealth, and taking their place in "The Corner House" was the Komitet Gosudarstvennoy Bezopasnosti.

While much of the complex housed local government agencies acting as little more than puppets for Moscow's bidding, its basement contained the headquarters of the local KGB. The Kremlin's sinister agency for state security lorded over dank and perpetually dark corridors lined with filthy cells that were kept at a constant eighty-five degrees. Enemies of the State, deprived of medicine, food, and water, were crammed twenty deep in a space with four wooden beds and unlidded shit pots that were rarely emptied. Those who weren't fortunate enough to be summarily executed in a concrete killing room reinforced with sound-suppressed walls and blood drains were subjected to endless hours of torture.

One of its prisoners had been captured two weeks earlier at a well-guarded East German checkpoint. The young agent, caught carrying highly classified documents, had been whisked off in secret to a small corner of the empire to prevent his handlers from discovering his fate. The man was tough, and had so far survived the sadistic abuse a rotating phalanx of interrogators had inflicted on him for ten hours a day. The beatings, burnings, and sleep deprivation, however, had begun to take their toll, and his chief tormentor, flown in specially from Lubyanka, believed he would soon be able to extract a prized piece of information that Moscow was certain the spy was privy to.

A name.

The mole in East Berlin.

CHAPTER THIRTEEN

Cruso, North Carolina

Sean Garrett scaled the last pitch of his run up Devil's Cellar, on the eastern ridge of Linville Gorge. He anchored on a small perch near the plateau and enjoyed the solitude of the moment. The morning had been cloudy but crisp, and the organic leach of conifers mixed with the atmospheric layer to cast the entire Appalachian range in its famous hues of white and cerulean blue. Garrett had made the two-hour drive early in order to beat the inevitable midafternoon bottleneck of *sprayers, kodaks,* and *desk-monkey dirtbags.* At least the last batch, hard-core mountaineers with day jobs, was tolerable, he acknowledged.

A small team had already summited, and Garrett watched as several of the climbers took turns traversing the gorge over a slackline. Because of the growing crowd on the pinnacle, he decided to bypass his routine exploration of a nearby cavern and instead performed a rapid abseil down the mountain face. Garrett packed up and passed an inbound collection of deadbeats who were clearly there to smoke up rather than rope up. A carload of coeds in a baby-blue convertible Prius with a bumper sticker that read *"I'd just as soon be in Boone,"* pulled up as he finished loading his truck. The tiny car seemed to empty out all at once, and one of the girls, carrying a soft Yeti cooler and wearing less than a Revolutionary War soldier would have used to wad a musket, smiled at the ruggedly handsome Garrett. "Coming or going?"

Garrett flashed her a sideways look. "The safer of the two options."

She laughed, having gotten the joke.

One of her friends gave him a pouty look. "If you change your mind—"

Garrett smiled as he backed out, grateful that he was long-gone from his early twenties. The former Special Forces operator in the Royal Navy's Special Boat Service had recently hit his forties, and though he looked a decade younger and still moved with the agility of an extreme athlete, age was beginning to catch up with Garrett. To combat the creep of nagging, short-term injuries, he had ramped up his daily regimen of trail running and climbing, working as hard as he had during his days in the SBS. Though he had maintained his training in Muay Thai and Krav Maga, Garrett had recently been awarded a black belt in Brazilian Jiu-Jitsu from an RGDA Gracie dojo nearby, something that took him seven intense years.

The drive home was uneventful, primarily because Garrett was able to clear Asheville before its inevitable backlog of afternoon fender-benders gridlocked the main thoroughfares of the city.

Garrett had also found himself free and clear of any consequences from the unsanctioned SIS operation to gather intelligence from Mohammad Ahmad, an esteemed, and now dead, professor at Cambridge who had been connected to the London Underground bombing of 2014. Garrett had furthermore managed to outlive two encounters with the professional assassin sent to kill Ahmad. David Laurent had since dropped off everyone's radar, and as a result, Garrett's Glock 20 10mm remained on his person at all times, with the exception of weekly climbs in the Western North Carolina mountain range. If he was unlucky enough that Laurent could corner him halfway up Laurel Knob, then so be it.

Garrett's cabin, tucked into a mountainside north of Brevard and not far from the East Fork Pigeon River, was typically accessible by four-wheel drive, even when the road wasn't coated in a layer of snow and ice. The way in was gated and its ten acres patrolled by a German Shepherd named Bandit. Garrett veered off Route 276, and after several switchbacks, came to a stop near a secondary lane that bordered his property. Though the red swing barrier was closed, he could make out the faint outline of fresh ruts, where tires smaller than his own had fishtailed as they struggled to gain traction on the steep grade.

Garrett parked his Chevy near the gate and grabbed his backpack. It was a half-mile hike via an access trail that he had cut up the backside of the ridge, which allowed an unseen approach to his property from the rear tree line. He slid the Glock into a belt holster and fast-tracked the winding ascent in just under five minutes.

Garrett knelt behind a young yellow birch that had grown sideways from a sloped earthen rockface and scanned the property. On the parking pad was a rented black BMW with South Carolina license plates, caked with mud. The porch door had been left open to allow a fall breeze to blow through the screened back entrance, and a light was on in the kitchen.

Sitting on his back deck and petting Garrett's dog was Banastre Montjoy.

Garrett wasn't expecting to see his brother for another two days, when he was scheduled to pick up their grandmother in Charlotte and drive her down to see Banastre on the South Carolina coast. Nor did he expect to see the deputy chief of MI6 by himself.

Garrett emerged from the woods and Montjoy smiled as he tipped his flat cap. As he climbed the stairs, Garrett gave his brother a nod and his dog a look of disapproval. "Aren't you supposed to be accompanied by a phalanx of bodyguards and a personal masseuse at all times?"

"I gave them the slip, old boy," Montjoy joked as he shook Garrett's hand. "How are you, Sean?"

"Good, but I should be asking you the same. I'm surprised you haven't broken out in hives now that you're Stateside."

"I can assure you that if I don't find a good tea soon, I will."

The two men entered the kitchen and Garrett pointed to a cabinet near the sink. "Third shelf."

"Taylors Yorkshire?"

"None other."

Montjoy smiled. "I'll put on a kettle."

Garrett shrugged off his backpack and set his pistol on the counter. He had picked up the habit of conducting a quick sweep of the house each time he came home, even if from a short walk, but decided to forego it that day. "You've shed some pounds," he observed, as Montjoy poured the black tea.

"A full stone to be precise, nearly down to my Royal Navy weight. I'll be fifty-something this year." Montjoy drew out the number as if he couldn't remember his exact age. "I've taken up boxing again, though someone seems to have made the workout bag heavier and not as reactive to a right hook." Montjoy handed Garrett a cup.

"Ta." Garrett raised it in toast. "Good to see you sooner than not, though I'm a bit surprised. I assumed your schedule was fairly tight, what with your lot saving the world on a daily basis. What brings you down so early? Grandmom flies in tomorrow and I didn't expect to see you until the weekend, in Charleston."

"My sit-down with the CIA was cut short and I was afraid I'd miss the holiday altogether if I didn't jet in for the first part of the week. I changed my charter, and instead of Charleston, I flew in through Greenville, South Carolina. Lovely little downtown, by the way."

"How long can you stay?"

"Saturday." Montjoy's phone began to buzz. "If it's not one bloody thing—" he muttered, and moved to the opposite corner of the deck to take the call.

Garrett watched as his brother listened intently without speaking. His face betrayed nothing, but something was clearly wrong. Montjoy finally said something Garrett couldn't pick up, and then hung up.

"I'm surprised you got a signal up here."

"Which explains why the office has been trying to ring me all day. I'm sorry, brov, but I've got to head back to London, as soon as. How far is Charlotte?"

"Two hours and a bit. Since I've got to collect Grandmom from the same airport, I'll drive you in your rental and return it once I get back."

"There's no need, Sean, and there's no easy way to say it," Montjoy replied. "Grandmother passed away yesterday."

Garrett did not respond, but only turned toward the mountains, resting his elbows on the railing as he glanced out over the range. "She was ninety-two, good enough for anyone, I suppose. How?"

"Heart attack, they say."

"Whiskey?"

Montjoy nodded. "That will do nicely."

CHAPTER FOURTEEN

Foreign Intelligence Service
Moscow, Russia

Vasily Markov sighed as he stared down a row of boxes that lined one entire wall of the makeshift workspace to which he had been reassigned ten months earlier. His former office, near the top floor and with a picturesque view of a large forest, was located in the section of SVR headquarters that had caught fire and burned a year earlier. It had been comfortable and spacious and at the end of a hall near the vending machines and a coffee maker. More importantly, the reams of past intelligence he had long put off organizing had been hidden in a closet and not staring back at him from a converted, windowless breakroom opposite a noisy elevator bank.

Born of scant means in the Caucasus, Markov had found his way out of a life destined for peasantry or factory labor and had attended university before being recruited into the KGB. Though he had risen steadily through the ranks of Russian Intelligence over the last four decades, Markov secretly acknowledged, particularly on the back end of several vodkas, that it was only during the early period of his career when things actually got done. Prior to 1990 and the fall of communism, he had been with the First Chief Directorate of the Committee for State Security, the KGB, who answered to almost no one and got answers from nearly everyone. Now, Markov was attached to the office of the deputy director of Directorate K, tasked with counterintelligence abroad for the Foreign Intelligence Service.

What's in a name? Markov liked to joke, quoting Shakespeare. While he and his colleagues used to command an all-powerful organization known and feared the world over, they were currently employed by a service, which had its own website.

What the former field agent really longed for, what he and most of the remnants of the old guard referred to as the *staryye dobryye vremena*, was the Cold War. That glorious period during the *good old days* when he was an operative in Berlin, ground zero for espionage, betrayal, murder, and women from nearly every corner of the world who were willing to do almost anything that a man of power desired.

When anyone now mustered up the energy to grouse about the slow downslide that had occurred in the aftermath of the dissolution of the USSR, Markov would assure them not to worry, that only the acronym on the company letterhead had changed. They remained as overextended and burned out as ever, but at least the crappy pay remained the same.

Markov poured himself another black tea and made up his mind to work even harder to ignore the looming task of organizing the files. Not for the first time, he closed his eyes and reminisced back over his career.

First, a counterintelligence agent in East Germany.

Then, a line officer in a unified Germany, in charge of infiltrating local intelligence services.

To Paris and Madrid, tasked with monitoring GRU officers in France and Spain.

Back to Moscow, to oversee new programs aimed at recruiting the best and brightest from the country's top universities.

And now, having been promoted as far as he would go up the intelligence hierarchy, Markov seemed to do little more than oversee an endless parade of orders, requests, appeals, and anything else that could be printed on A4 paper and pushed across his desk. Over the last forty-four years, he had moved from the KGB to the FSK, and then temporarily to the FSB, before being assigned permanently to the SVR. If the Russians couldn't always outwit their Western adversaries, he would silently muse, they could at least confuse them by shifting acronyms.

Markov readily conceded that he should have retired a decade earlier when he was still young enough to enjoy what modest benefits working for the new Russian government would allow. He had hesitated in buying a dacha on the Baltic Sea when it was far more affordable, following the financial crisis of 1998 and the redenomination of the first Russian Ruble. At present, his salary, combined with what he had saved, wouldn't accommodate one month in a vacation home in any place worth visiting.

Markov especially missed the days when money could be made in myriad other ways. One memory in particular was stirred as he read something that had come across his desk that very morning, a summary that had piqued his curiosity more than had anything else in the last few years. Several communiques, originating from agents operating under diplomatic cover out of embassies in Italy, Germany, and the U.K., had all reported the same bit of remarkable news. Three retired MI6 officers, each under intermittent SVR surveillance in their respective countries, had turned up dead or missing in the last forty-eight hours.

The agents, William Lindsay, Geoffrey Charlton, and Madeleine Halliwell, were of particular interest because Markov had crossed paths with each of them while stationed in East Germany in the 1980s.

One officer he knew especially well. It had been a particularly cold winter in East Berlin in 1984, a February to forget. But Markov could well remember one bleak afternoon when Geoffrey Charlton asked to buy him a drink. Over a warm beer, in a freezing shithole of a bar in Friedrichshain, SIS's head of section in West Berlin made the Russian an offer.

To become a double-agent for MI6.

CHAPTER FIFTEEN

Saint-Armand, Canada

The plan to kill Geoffrey Charlton, William Lindsay, Madeleine Halliwell, and Banastre Montjoy had been a painstaking operation to piece together. It had taken Emile Chénard thirty months and hundreds of hours to analyze and organize how, and if, it could be done.

The need for revenge, on the other hand, had been simmering for two decades.

Chénard had relied on a team of former Alpha Group operatives whom he had commanded during the First Chechen War to locate the three retired British agents. Lindsay had proven particularly difficult, but after Charlton and Halliwell were tracked down, a separate team was dispatched to monitor their movements and mobile communications in Italy and Scotland. Within two weeks, they had been able to locate Lindsay in southern Germany, based on intercepted phone conversations with Charlton.

It took far longer to determine a way to get to Montjoy. The deputy chief of MI6 was well protected, and it would have been nearly impossible to kill him in England. Chénard had neared the point of abandoning his fourth and final target when one of his men, by sheer happenstance though a monitored communication with Madeleine Halliwell, discovered that Montjoy would be meeting his family in Charleston, South Carolina for vacation near the end of September.

Chénard had acknowledged that it was better to be lucky than good any day of the week.

Montjoy's brief sojourn in America would present the perfect, and perhaps only, opportunity to carry out the brazen plot to kill all four former Cold War operatives at the same moment. The deaths would garner scattered attention in the outside world, but the timing would set off alarm bells within MI6.

Someone was hunting its agents, past and present.

Chénard sat patiently in a line of cars queued at the U.S.-Canadian border. He had opted to cross over near Saint-Armand in order to skirt Lake Champlain before cutting directly across Vermont to New Hampshire and down through Massachusetts. It was the first time he had ventured out of the country in almost three years, and though Chénard wasn't concerned about his counterfeit credentials, there was always that moment of nervous tension when a customs officer took extra time to double-check his passport and biometric data against the system.

When news first reached him that Banastre Montjoy had escaped his fate in South Carolina, Chénard wondered if his intel on the deputy chief's itinerary had been wrong, or whether the man had been tipped off. The latter was unlikely, as the ease with which each of his other assassins had located and liquidated their targets indicated that none of them had been warned. Though all three deaths had been confirmed by the killers, only Lindsay's was yet to make the news, which likely meant that the team tasked with his murder in Munich had done their job perhaps too well, and that the man would remain permanently missing.

As he drove though the countryside, and there was no better time or place than New England in the fall as far as Chénard was concerned, he considered his next move. If Montjoy suspected that the three deaths were linked, and that an attempt on his life had also been sanctioned, the game was over. MI6 would double his security and ensure that no one came anywhere near him anytime soon. If that was the case, Chénard could return to his life in Montreal and chalk up the overall operation as a success.

If not for the fact that Montjoy remaining alive and well would eat away at Chénard like acid slow-dripped onto soft metal.

Sitting in his comfortable living room a day earlier and mulling everything over a string of whiskeys while staring out across the St. Lawrence River, Chénard decided he would come out of hiding and take one final crack at the prize that got away.

CHAPTER SIXTEEN

Glasgow International Airport

The flight from Charlotte Douglas had been packed, the proverbial standing-room only, and Banastre Montjoy would have happily accepted a stand-by deferment in order to avoid the cramped eight-hour ordeal, if not for the death of his grandmother. He was originally booked to fly directly, and comfortably, to Heathrow via a first-class ticket on British Airways, but had instead decided at the last minute to divert his return trip through Scotland on an American Airways overnight that connected through Philadelphia.

As he waited to pass through customs in Glasgow, Montjoy considered what he knew.

The information he had received while in North Carolina was that Geoffrey Charlton had been found dead in an apparent murder-suicide in Italy. Montjoy had served under Charlton during several postings, first in West Germany and then again in London after Charlton was promoted to head of section once the Berlin Wall came down. He liked the man, and much of what Montjoy learned in his earliest days was the result of Charlton's acumen and keen intuition as to who could best be manipulated to do what, on both sides of the Bloc. He had neither seen nor spoken to Geoffrey since his rather ignominious ouster from MI6 years earlier, and it saddened Montjoy that his former chief's legacy was now sullied by the sordid rumors which had already begun to circulate around Vauxhall Cross concerning the nature of his death.

Moreover, while on layover in Philadelphia, Montjoy received word that William Lindsay was missing. Once the body in Italy was discovered by local police and the British Embassy in Rome notified, a member of staff discovered that Charlton had booked a one-way train to Munich, ostensibly to rendezvous with his Cold War colleague. SIS reached out to Lindsay, who had retired to the Bavarian city, and, unable to contact him through any channel, dispatched a team to Germany only to discover a deserted flat and no sign of its ex-deputy chief.

Lindsay had been Montjoy's last chief, and it was he who had recommended Montjoy to assume the post in the wake of the Mohammad Ahmad assassination and the fallout from the professor's connection to the British government and bombing of King's Cross. Unlike Charlton, however, Montjoy had remained in relatively close contact with his former boss, and indeed planned to see him that Christmas during a planned party for past and present MI6 officers.

That was the extent of what Montjoy was certain of. What he privately suspected, particularly where his grandmother's death was concerned, held far more sinister implications. Considering that three of MI6's best and brightest had died or gone missing in the same twenty-four-hour window, Montjoy harbored a growing fear that the timing of Halliwell's heart attack went beyond mere happenstance.

A visit to the cottage in North Ballachulish where he had spent much of his boyhood would determine Montjoy's next move.

CHAPTER SEVENTEEN

Boston, Massachusetts

J ohn Riker turned off Atlantic Avenue and found an empty parking spot on a finger wharf near the Boston Waterboat Marina. He had made the nearly thousand-mile drive from South Carolina to Massachusetts in just under sixteen hours, stopping only once to disassemble and discard the Dragunov.

The call he had received a day earlier came through just as Riker reacquired signal, on a Lowcountry interstate that should have taken him to Charlotte Douglas International Airport and out of the country. It was roughly the same moment he became aware of the breaking news from Charleston, that a New York businessman had been gunned down at a small airport near the city.

The wrong man.

Riker barely had time to slam the steering wheel and curse aloud before his mobile rang. He did not need to check the number to verify who it was, nor answer to find out that his handler was less than happy. The conversation was short and to the point.

Boston, Christopher Columbus Park, as soon as.

Riker dropped the Denali keys into a trash bin as he exited the lot. The assassin had already wiped down the limited areas of the SUV he had touched. Any other fingerprints would lead authorities to an end that matched the man who left them. Whether the dead Chechen at the bottom of Lake Marion had a file at Interpol, or military dossier in Grozny, was not Riker's problem, for neither would come back to him.

As he passed the Marriott Long Wharf and approached the park, Riker tapped in a quick text that he had arrived. He was instructed to proceed along Harborwalk until he came to a bench where Emile Chénard, wearing a Burberry cap and reading a newspaper, would be waiting.

As he passed a playground teeming with families enjoying a pleasant September afternoon, Riker, who was born Kostya Petrikov, briefly made eye contact with the man he had met as "Alex" twenty-five years earlier in Chechnya. It had been two years since the small federal state on the fringe of the former Soviet Empire declared its independence in 1992, and Chénard, known then as Alexei Arkipov, was an ex-Stasi colonel and KGB officer in command of an elite squad whose purpose was to wage a covert war in the breakaway province.

Each of its twenty-two operatives was highly special-ized, and all of them killers, let loose in a conflict rife with targets and ripe with opportunity for anyone willing to oper-ate with ruthless efficiency and outside the bounds of any moral authority.

The units were divided into separate cells, their sole objective was to mete out as much death and destruction as possible.

Company "A," recruited from Ukraine's Special Group Alpha, hunted down, kidnapped, interrogated, and disposed of high-ranking defectors to the newly formed government.

Company "B" was charged with intercepting and monitoring mobile conversations, seeking to match voice signatures to those on file. Once recognition was confirmed, or at least narrowed down to an acceptable probability, coordinates were relayed to Russian attack aircraft, who would level target locations with tactical missiles.

Riker, one of only two Special Forces snipers assigned to Company "C," was tasked with neutralizing immediate threats on the ground. He was instructed not to concern himself with *jus ad bellum*, authorized use of force, or justified kills. There was no ambiguity to his directive.

Aim and squeeze.

Riker distinguished himself quickly, questioning only whether he had gauged the correct windage and distance to the scores of dissidents he eliminated from behind camo paint and cover. Chénard had taken a special liking to the Spetsnaz sniper, and schooled Riker in espionage tradecraft during mission downtimes. After the first war ended, poorly for Russia, Chénard disappeared and Riker was recalled to his army unit. Three years later, during his country's follow-up effort against the same separatists, the sniper redeployed with his official unit. He continued his impressive tally, and the result this time for the aggressors was decidedly different from the first campaign.

Riker remained enlisted until the wide-ranging reforms of the Russian Armed Forces were enacted in 2008. He left disillusioned, and drifted as an itinerant mercenary selling his services to paramilitary actions in South America, Africa, and Asia. It wasn't long before the skilled shooter found a far more profitable calling, as a contract killer. Getting a taste for adventure and easy paydays, the newly minted assassin recognized that he needed anonymity. Not long after, Kostya Petrikov relocated to Canada and ceased to exist, becoming a second-generation Torontonian, by way of Ukrainian immigrants, who went by the name John Riker.

While his reputation as a professional killer quietly grew amongst a select global clientele, Riker fronted the façade of a comfortably retired businessman who traveled the world. By his tenth contract, an American pharmaceutical rep in Uruguay who had been skimming from the heroin he moved for the Serbian mafia, Riker had earned enough money to call it quits.

If not for his own addiction to the life of an assassin.

It was near the moment he truly considered slowing his pace that Riker was contacted by a man who everyone presumed had drowned while on vacation twenty years earlier. Alexei Arkipov, who had also chosen Canada, and the name Emile Chénard, to escape a possible war crime tribunal for his actions in Chechnya, had tracked the sniper down through an intermediary from their unit whom Riker had remained in loose contact with, against protocol. After Chénard good-naturedly chided him for disobeying a direct order concerning their mutual war acquaintance, he made Riker a lucrative offer: to come on board a team much like the one from the old days. The rules would be the same; there were none. Riker was to be partnered with another Chechen professional, and be paid handsomely to hunt and kill one man, the sitting deputy chief of Britain's Secret Intelligence Service.

A job he had failed to do.

Riker leaned against a railing and watched water traffic crisscross Boston Harbor. A crowded amphibious car slowly toured the wharf, readying to come ashore. The assassin looked on in amusement until, in his periphery, he caught Chénard stand, tuck a newspaper under his arm, and begin to make his way along the walk.

Riker waited several seconds and then followed. Chénard circled back through the park to the MBTA Blue Line stop near the Aquarium. He entered the station and pulled two tickets from his pocket, running one through the electronic turnstile and leaving the other on top of it. Riker collected the all-day pass and fed it into the machine, then descended a second set of stairs onto the subway platform. The pair moved to the tunnel entrance at the far end, where cold, dank air mixed with the distant squeal of brakes.

The two men eyed one another, before Chénard smiled at the same moment Riker broke the silence. "I was forced to make a split-second decision. It was a case of extremely bad luck."

"Should I take that as an apology, Kostya?" Chénard asked.

"Colonel—"

"Your bad luck, as you put it, has upset the balance of a carefully planned operation, and brought me out from behind a very comfortable rock."

The platform began to fill with travelers while an automated announcement preceded the approach of an inbound train.

Riker was about to respond, when Chénard raised his hand. "Time is of the essence, so you can enlighten me at some other point as to what exactly went wrong."

"What do you want me to do?" Riker asked.

"The job you were paid to finish." Chénard produced an envelope and mobile. "Logan to Heathrow, tomorrow morning. Wait in London for my instructions."

"*Da*," Riker responded, and boarded the waiting train just before its doors closed.

Chénard watched the line of railway cars disappear into the darkness of the tunnel at the far end of the platform. He lingered another moment as the last of the commuters emptied through the underground exit. Riker had failed him, and while he would allow the former soldier under his command a second chance in Europe, Chénard decided that he could not afford another letdown.

As he began to slowly ascend the escalator to ground level, Chénard pulled a phone from his pocket and punched in the number of a mobile in Sweden.

CHAPTER EIGHTEEN

Ballachulish, Scotland

The hired BMW idled on the graveled pad as Banastre Montjoy surveyed the cottage, barely visible through a film of Highland mist that coated the windshield. His focus was fixed on a section of wall where the whitewash had been worn off by a thatch rake his grandmother habitually leaned against a leafmould cage. Though the bin was empty, he was certain he could still pick up the redolence of its organic rot. The peaty scent, and more than a few memories, hung around the entryway as pleasant remnants of another time and place.

The abrasive squeak of a faulty wiper arcing over the windshield jolted Montjoy. He glanced back at the bare patch of brick and remembered his promise to repaint it by summer, that year marking the third he had made such a pledge to his grandmother.

Montjoy sighed and shut off the engine.

He bypassed the house and walked along the rear boundary of the property, which shadowed a craggy beach below. It was near the end of the fishing season and a small trawler tugged through the tidal current of Loch Leven. Montjoy could recall how eagerly he would count down the end of term, to the beginning of his month-long furlough in the Highlands. He would barely arrive and discard his uniform before Montjoy was out the door, his grandmother chasing behind with a jumper, and sweet biscuits rolled in wax paper. The daring schoolboy would drift the South Deep for brownies, who always seemed more interested in the fry hiding amongst the brown algae of its banks than Montjoy's homemade jig.

He knew the curve of every inlet, which shallows to avoid, and how long it took his dinghy with its twelve-volt troller to putter home once the dinner bell echoed across the channel. Somewhere in the fog a horn sounded, and startled an Osprey that had been fishing the shallows. For a moment Montjoy considered navigating the rocky slope to the water's edge, but knew his schedule prevented it. He closed his eyes and breathed in the salt air. It was then that Montjoy decided he would keep the small estate, no matter the cost or inconvenience of upkeep. He lingered another minute and watched the bird settle into the shoals further down the shoreline, before Montjoy began a slow trudge back to the cottage.

His grandmother had died of heart failure, the report concluded, though no inquest was ordered because of her age. She had enjoyed a long and fulfilling life, the coroner had perfunctorily assured Montjoy over the phone, without having the slightest clue as to whether that was actually the case. Moreover, her loved ones could take comfort in that she had passed without pain, the man added, and was prepared to reiterate his condolences when Montjoy politely cut him off by thanking the medical officer for his time and kind words.

Madeleine Halliwell had suffered scores of SOE colleagues executed by the Nazis. At MI6, she ran operations throughout Soviet-occupied Europe that sent agents to their deaths, some who were first interrogated by torture for weeks by the KGB. Considering that she had recently endured the murder of her husband and seen her only granddaughter comatized by a terrorist bomb, Montjoy knew his grandmother had experienced significant pain over a long life and career.

He unlocked and entered the front sitting room, and smiled. His grandmother habitually covered the furniture with white linen each time she traveled, even if only for a short period. Everything was in its customary order, though the interior of the bed and breakfast was colder than it should have been. Montjoy walked to the kitchen and discovered that a window over the sink had been uncharacteristically left open.

It was at that moment he sensed something was not right. Montjoy returned to the entryway and scanned the room. His grandmother had been found facedown near the fireplace by a family friend from Glencoe, a retired dairy farmer who still delivered milk to her doorstep twice a week. The man had come to pick up empty bottles and became alarmed when he saw her car sitting on the pad. *Wasn't Madeleine off to the States on vacation?* He then saw what he thought was a body through a side window and alerted local authorities.

Montjoy glanced down at two suitcases left by the entryway. He stepped back and closed the door, revealing a pile of letters that had been dropped through the slot and pushed into the corner the last time it was opened. A small bundle of

mail secured by an elastic band sat on a foyer table, ready to
post. The curtains of two front windows had been pulled back
to let in light, presumably by the police. A book of poems by
Rupert Brooke sat in a chair by the window.

Nothing out of the ordinary.

And then he saw it. On the mantel above the fireplace, in
the rear row of photos that ran the length of the hearth. An
empty frame, barely noticeable among the forty or so filled
with family and friends scattered over sixty years and countless places.

*Montjoy as a boy, shooting pheasants with his mother in
Ross-shire.*

*His grandfather, writing at a desk and smoking a
Castleford.*

Maddie, his sister, after graduation.

*Sean, standing with his mates from the Special Boat Service,
each of them tanned and shirtless and holding rifles in some
foreign desert.*

The frame was unusually heavy, carved from oak, and
slightly larger than the others. With its photo missing, the glass
façade reflected Montjoy's concentrated effort to remember. He
turned it over and noticed that the brace to keep the picture
upright had been snapped off.

*It had been late summer some years back and he and Sean
were wrestling when the frame toppled over and broke.*

And suddenly it came back to him. His brother joking
that he had intentionally knocked over the photo because
their sister Maddie had commented that Banastre was now
the more handsome brother, standing outside Number 10 in

his new Savile Row suit. He could recollect that exact day, in May, exactly one week after his favorite side, Everton, had bested Manchester United for the F.A. Cup title.

1995 was also a good year for his career. Montjoy had just turned thirty-five and had been with MI6 for over a decade. The Service had moved to the Embankment eleven months earlier, while Montjoy had steadily moved up its ranks, having been assigned to Europe Division that spring under its newly appointed head of section, William Lindsay.

Montjoy's early success with British Intelligence was the byproduct of many factors, not least among them that he had been born into a family of spies. His grandmother, grandfather, two uncles and a score of extended relatives had served in some capacity in MI6. Montjoy's own tenure had begun after university and a four-year stint in the Royal Marines, where he served in the Balkans, and then the Falkland Islands in 1982, where he received commendation for his actions during *Operation Paraquet.*

After the war, and his recruitment into the Service, Montjoy was posted to West Berlin, where he served under Geoffrey Charlton. Montjoy moved between assignments throughout Europe and the Middle East before returning to London in 1994. He served under Lindsay for a decade, and when his head of section was made deputy chief in 2005, Montjoy was promoted to his position.

It was during this period that Montjoy first began to feel the weight of the world bearing down, often turning to drink to assuage the pressure of keeping pace during a period of massive budget cuts and constant queries by clueless politicians as to what exactly their spy apparatus was accomplishing, particularly in the wake of the 7/7 bombings. It wasn't until the King's Cross Tube bombing in 2014, which killed his grandfather and put his sister in a coma, that Montjoy snapped from his mid-life stupor.

He reconsidered the empty frame. The missing photo meant nothing at first glance, until Montjoy recalled standing in the backyard only minutes earlier and glancing down. At his feet lay discarded cigarettes that he assumed were from a lodger enjoying one last view of a too-short vacation. But it was the marking on one of the burned fags that stirred a memory, and Montjoy's suspicion.

He traced his path back to the overlook and found them. A hollow cardboard tube, unfiltered, and with its end flattened. Montjoy recalled asking a colleague about it years earlier, having witnessed an informant from Minsk squash one side of a cigarette nearly flat before lighting up. *It makes that particular brand easier to hold,* he had been told. Montjoy bent down and examined the remains. On one edge, barely visible, were three letters. "б Е Л." Cyrillic script. *B-E-L.*

Belomorkanal.

Russian-made cigarettes.

CHAPTER NINETEEN

Hammarstrand, Sweden

T he cottage, sparsely outfitted and in transition to a
state of disrepair, was trimmed in white and bedecked
with a red tinge common to dwellings throughout Sweden.
The color was reminiscent of the *falu* dye excavated from the
copper mines centuries earlier and stained into wood slats to
resemble the brick exterior of the homes owned by the wealthy
tradesmen of Europe. The pigment's use as a decorative and
durable outer layer dated back over a millennium and was
rumored to last a hundred years.

The weathered façade of the man's summer house, chipped
and cracked from the constant wind and wet climate of the
region, was in desperate need of a new coat of paint.

He sat on his front porch and sipped a straight rye whiskey,
his third of the early afternoon. A pack of cigarettes lay on
the table nearby, opened not long before but already reduced
to only a few sticks.

The man rarely spoke, never mind that there were few
people nearby with whom to converse even if he had something
to say. The former operative was good at keeping quiet, and

to himself. He had learned this early in life, when his father ensured the maxim that children should be seen and not heard was one taken to the extreme. In a rare moment when he might offer up some meager opinion to family guests around a finely laid dinner table, the patriarch would assert that whatever the boy had said was a *mute point*, purposely amending an old English expression. As one branch of their family hailed from Kent, outside London, part of the gathering would get the play on words and laugh, at the boy's expense. The other side of his grandfather's family, from southwestern Germany, would merely stare and wonder what was so funny.

The boy had learned quickly the benefit of keeping quiet.

And, as a man, he had not said a word in that hellhole of a KGB dungeon. At least, very little that was intelligible, between the screams.

The man had taken pains to ensure that few people were privy to the places where he had permanently disappeared, having refused to return home after being betrayed and discarded in the aftermath of the failed operation at that damned checkpoint. He had settled on the name Tomas Karlson, his real one abandoned in the wake of those many weeks in the company of the Committee for State Security. Through much of the early years after, he had bounced between the free countries of Europe, until the Wall came down and he could more safely widen his travels. When it was time to find a place to live permanently, Karlson first favored Denmark, before settling in Sweden.

Karlson glanced out over the Indalsälven River, at a man and his sons fishing from the opposite bank. He stood and leaned on the railing, flicking the last of the ash from the burned-out cigarette, before searching for its replacement. Downriver, Karlson could see the dam lock and accompanying bridge, the one he would cross if he decided to accept the new contract offered by his handler.

Karlson peeled back the plastic on a second pack of Belomorkanals. The carton was missing the stamped tax sticker that was typically affixed over the front flap, sealing the box and indicating they were legally produced in some factory in Latvia or St. Petersburgh. He had acquired a taste for the cheap cigarette while in Berlin, and now Karlson wondered if an affinity had grown because of the KGB. His chief interrogator and tormentor had expertly swung between sympathy and sadism over the course of a week. The man had allowed Karlson to smoke as much as he wished, during those brief interludes in which he was not being tortured, in order to induce his cooperation in a less painful way. In the end, "Dimitry" seemed to prefer a pair of pliers to beguiling persuasion, and Karlson was convinced that he now favored the foul-tasting and filterless brand because of some lingering symptoms of Stockholm Syndrome.

It was rare that he ventured from either of his modest residences in Copenhagen or Hammarstrand. That had changed a year earlier, when Karlson was offered the opportunity for revenge against those responsible for his suffering. It was his chance at rebirth, at redemption, and he had taken up the mission with the same passion and determination that put him in the predicament which had permanently scarred him thirty-four years earlier.

Geoffrey Charlton had been an easy kill. Karlson had stalked the ex-chief of MI6 for two weeks in Marche, gleaning his habits and itinerary, all the while devising the perfect way to exact retribution while forever sullying the man's legacy.

Halliwell had been different. She was Karlson's point of contact during the East German operation, and he had grown fond of her in the weeks leading up to his exposure and arrest by the Stasi. That she was the one ultimately behind his betrayal had been hard to stomach, though when the time came to finish the job, standing on her stoop in that picturesque corner of Scotland, he had not hesitated.

Karlson chain-lit a cigarette and considered another man, one who had existed before him. An earlier iteration of himself, a newly-minted spy who believed he would change the world. Certainly not someone who would have sacrificed an innocent woman, hooker or not, to slake a nearly unquenchable thirst for revenge. But that man had died long ago, broken in the bowels of a Soviet cell.

The line of Prussian-blued storm clouds that had moved steadily across the horizon for much of the afternoon now turned in Karlson's direction. A frigid rain would soon follow, the kind that drove most people indoors, to the refuge of a roaring fire. For Karlson, the visceral chill served as a welcomed respite from the memories of needles and electrical nodes, of truncheons and heated iron, all seared into his psyche.

Now, it was neither warmth nor cold which brought him comfort. It was the chance to settle a score with those who had sold him out. Though the deaths of Charlton and Halliwell had only served to agitate the need, Karlson knew there had been others attached to *Operation Turnkey*, higher-ups for whom the call to cut away loose ends would have been far easier than SIS foot soldiers directing operatives like Karlson from ground level.

It had been only twenty-four hours since he had been contacted by the very man who had offered him the chance to eliminate Charlton and Halliwell. Karlson's handler had kept the details to a minimum, other than to relay that a second operation had been run parallel to his own, targeting two others connected to *Turnkey*.

One had escaped assassination, the sitting deputy chief of MI6.

Karlson had spent the better part of the day trying to decide whether coming out of the shadows once more, this time to kill Banastre Montjoy, was worth the risk. His contact in Montreal had assured Karlson he would soon be given the target's location, and that the job would be clean and quick. If he accepted, Karlson would also be given the chance to remove one more piece off of the board, from a game that had been intentionally stacked against him, the ultimate sacrificial pawn.

Karlson crushed out his Belomorkanal and decided it was time, his turn, to move.

To play one final gambit.

He would travel to London, and await instructions.

CHAPTER TWENTY

Cruso, North Carolina

The storm crested the rim of the gap and converged on the leeward side of the range as it often did, with little warning. Sean Garrett's property rested in the shadow of the two largest peaks, *way up the holler*, as any local would declare, and comfortably removed from the main arteries that linked the chain of tourist towns throughout the valley.

Garrett sat on his deck in the growing darkness, his back against a half-finished wall of stonework. He watched the clouds roll over the mountain and hug the ridgeline, like an unroped climber desperately clinging to a slick overhang. The weather effect was not unlike the rush of water pooling into turbulent eddies on the downfall of a spillway.

Or of a man pushed to his limit.

Soon, the pressure of the conflicting systems would come to a violent head, and erupt.

She had been murdered.

Banastre had not minced words during the short call two hours earlier. The rushed autopsy results had been returned that morning, while a second classified pathology test had also verified that trace amounts of potassium chloride, microscopic but unmistakable, had been found in the bloodstream of Madeleine Halliwell.

Injected to induce, and mimic, congestive heart failure.

His brother had been less than forthcoming with any further details over the phone. At this point, there was little the deputy chief could do than speculate that the assassination was the likely consequence of some long-shelved operation. Indeed, there would have been nothing to suspect the cause was anything but natural, if not for the coincidental murder of Geoffrey Charlton and the disappearance and assumed death of William Lindsay.

Officially, Montjoy had taken a leave of absence to deal with the passing of his late grandmother and to settle the affairs of her estate. Off the record, he and a hand-picked group at SIS were operating under the assumption that a connection did indeed exist between the deaths of the operatives.

Garrett got to his feet awkwardly, a double whiskey in one hand and a Glock in the other complicating the movement, and leaned against the railing. The concrete dust caked to his flannel shirt began to flake off as the wind picked up. He scanned the blackness and acknowledged how easily a skilled assassin like the man he faced three years earlier, or the one now after Banastre, could enjoy an uncomplicated kill from somewhere in the dark.

Twenty years earlier, it was Garrett who had been the one feared from some hidden place. As the saying went, *from somewhere you cannot see comes a sound you will not hear.* After growing up and attending university in England, he had followed in his brother's footsteps and joined the Royal Navy. A gifted athlete at six feet tall and a solid two hundred pounds, Garrett had been invited to join the Royal Boat Service, and after passing the rigorous selection process and advanced training, he deployed to the Middle East. After three combat tours, two in which he received commendation for exceptional bravery under fire, Garrett was sent to North Africa to conduct joint training exercises with American Navy Seals. It was there that he injured his back when his parachute failed to properly deploy during a high-altitude jump.

It had taken Garrett six months to fully heal, and after a stint in the SBS Reserves, he moved back to the country of his, and his father's, birth, and had been living in the mountains of North Carolina ever since.

In the distance his Shepherd barked, not unusual for that time of night and season, as maturing coyotes began to disperse the pack and nomadically patrol newly formed territories. The click and chatter of a Barred Owl echoed from the tree line and competed with the rasp of bullfrogs in a nearby creek. Garrett relished the sights and sounds, and acknowledged that while his childhood, bracketed by the deaths of both parents, had been far from ideal, his life since moving to the Smoky Mountains was as close to perfect as possible.

A world that had been thrown back into disarray.

Garrett was scheduled to co-lead a trek of five *bumblies*, new and inept climbers, in Chattanooga in two days, which was certain to drag out for another slow and painful five. Banastre, however, had requested his help in managing their grandmother's final affairs in Scotland. With her death, their sister, in a coma in London, was the last of their family, and Garrett was due to depart Hartsfield-Jackson early the next morning.

The anger wouldn't subside anytime soon, certainly not with the closure of seeing his grandmother one final time, nor walking the loch property in North Ballachulish that he had so often visited in his youth.

His only hope, something that could at least provide temporary respite from the rage he felt, would come from standing in front of the party responsible for the murder of his grandmother.

And snatching the life from them with his bare hands.

CHAPTER TWENTY-ONE

Johns Island, South Carolina

The area around which the dead body had lain, itself encircled in a fading outline of fluorescent paint, was still cordoned off with yellow and black police barricade tape. The off-limit section proved a considerable inconvenience for the airport, not because it prevented planes from accessing the terminal, but that it stood as a stark reminder that someone had been gunned down in broad daylight on one of its tarmacs.

That *someone* happened to be a wealthy hedge fund manager from Manhattan, who had flown in via Washington, D.C. with his family for several days of golf at Osprey Point, on Kiawah Island. The killing was all over the local news, but had not yet piqued any noticeable volume of national interest, as local authorities were unsure whether the man had been intentionally targeted, or was the unlucky victim of an unintended bullet. The banking executive was, by all accounts, well-liked by colleagues and well-respected by competitors, all of whom vouchsafed that Robert Harris was that rare man without enemies.

John Perry, a police detective in the Central Investigations Division of the City of Charleston, had learned over a twenty-five-year career to approach every case with the exact opposite presumption. It wasn't that he believed an individual should be considered guilty until proven otherwise; it was just that those who had done something wrong typically stood out like a sore thumb when pressed. Innocent people tended to come across as exactly that from the outset.

Standing aside one of the runways and recanvassing the scene, Perry knew he needed to assume *everything* in order to narrow down to the *one thing* that might break open a case with few leads.

The police had already determined, from eyewitness reports and the position of the body, that the shot originated from a tree line seven hundred yards to the north of the outer runway. The Lowcountry was overrun with deer, and its season had recently opened, so it was plausible that someone hunting near the airport, illegally, had fired the errant round and then fled once they realized what had happened.

Ballistics had not yet returned a report on the type of ammo, though Perry didn't expect it would tell him anything he already didn't know.

The detective was waffling on whether to re-walk the bullet's trajectory to its origin, and had convinced himself that it was probably pointless to get muddy all over again, when two uniformed officers pulled up. The tandem, each in their late twenties and both with only eight years of experience between them, had been on patrol on Johns Island the day of the shooting. They were the proverbial first black-and-white on scene and the first to canvass nearby neighborhoods.

Perry had already taken their statements, but he requested they investigate a wider area in order to determine if anything had been missed or overlooked on the first pass. The tree line itself had produced little in the way of leads. There were no spent shells, footprints, or anything else to suggest that anyone had been in the area when the banker was gunned down. It was unlikely, but could not be dismissed, that a panicked hunter would have had the wherewithal to clean up a casing and erase any signs of their presence.

There was also the matter of the faint trace of tire tracks found on a gravel road in a neighborhood near the airport. The driver had seemingly backed over the same spot several times, perhaps in an effort to muddle the tread imprints on the soft shoulder. All forensics could tell Perry was that it was some sort of SUV or large truck, towing a trailer. He had subsequently asked the officers to widen their area of inquiry and investigate all boat landings within a reasonable distance of the airport.

The officers exited the squad car in unison, and their creased uniforms, spit-shined shoes, and steel-rimmed mirrored Ray-Bans made the pair almost carbon copies of one another. Both had served in the military and each had already compiled exemplary service records considering their brief time on the force.

Perry extended his hand. "Gentlemen, I appreciate you coming out on your lunch break."

"It's not a problem, sir," the first officer replied, shaking his hand.

Perry handed each of them a twenty-dollar bill. "Beers on me, after your shift."

"Thank you, sir," the other replied.

"Your message led me to believe that you've found something?"

"That's correct, sir. On a wider search, we found the vehicle of a DNR officer who has been reported missing."

"Where?"

"Limehouse Bridge. The agent, Jeffrey Cox, last spoke to his wife three days ago, at 6:30 in the morning. According to her, he was heading to the boat put-in to conduct random license checks. She called around lunch, but Cox didn't answer, and hasn't since."

"Any outgoing calls from his mobile during that period?"

"None, though the carrier was able to track his phone as far as Eutawville before it either died, or went out of tower range."

"Up near the lake," Perry said aloud, but to himself.

"We spoke to his supervisor and she said that a section of Lake Marion falls within their jurisdiction, and it was feasible, though unlikely, that he traveled there during his shift. Cell reception can be iffy out that way, so it's possible he's still in the vicinity."

"Anything is possible at this point," Perry replied, donning his sunglasses. "Though, it's been seventy-two hours, awfully long even if Cox decided to head off on some post-shift bender with a buddy." He glanced back toward the tree line. "Thanks, fellas, and well done."

"Thank you, sir."

The officers exited the airport, and Perry remained a moment longer to watch a plane descend below the clouds and begin its final approach.

The missing DNR agent, combined with the circumstances of the airport shooting, unconnected or not, demanded that the detective reevaluate the case and pass the information up the chain.

CHAPTER TWENTY-TWO

Ballachulish, Scotland

The drive from Glasgow Airport had taken Sean Garrett longer than expected, owing to a drove of Highland cattle that had broken free of a paddock on the outskirts of Glencoe. The rogue herd had refused to budge from a single-lane detour off the A82, and by the time their owner arrived, one had been backed into by a tour bus attempting a three-point turn.

Banastre Montjoy was leaning against his hired car outside their grandmother's cottage and sipping a tea when Garrett pulled up.

"Alright then?" Montjoy asked, handing Garrett a cup.

"Trouble with some locals," Garrett replied. "Ta, brov."

As they entered through the kitchen door, Garrett was immediately aware of how cold and empty everything suddenly felt. He had spent his formative years in that place, surrounded by generations of love and laughter, and now it was as if none of it had ever existed. He remembered his last visit, of hugging his grandmother and fearing that the next time he returned it would be to shutter the cottage for good.

Garrett spied the book of poetry on a table near the door. *"If I should die, think only this of me: that there's some corner of a foreign field that is forever England—,"* he recited aloud, though lost in some other time and place.

"In hearts at peace, under an English heaven." Montjoy added the finishing lines of the famous poem by Rupert Brooke, penned a year before his death during World War I. "He died from an infected mosquito bite, if memory serves."

"Worse than the Kaiser's bullet," Garrett replied. "Did you know Churchill wrote his obituary?"

"I didn't think it was possible to not know that."

Garrett smiled. "Was anything out of place?"

"A photo missing from the mantel."

"Which one?"

"Of me, on the doorstep of 10 Downing."

"The one we broke?"

"Aye."

Garrett walked to the fireplace and picked up the empty frame. "Significance?"

"Perhaps nothing."

"Cue the caveat."

Montjoy gestured toward the rear door, and Garrett followed him through the patio and into the backyard. They walked the property line until Montjoy stopped at a bluff that jutted from a steep crag.

Garrett could recall standing on the small overlook as a boy and hopelessly attempting to heave stones into the surf below. "Do you remember the hidden shoal in the channel off the island?"

"The one I warned you about only to have you blunder into it anyway?"

"Most people would agree that shouting 'look out!' at the last moment constitutes excellent seamanship," Garrett replied. "The swim back was cold."

"Yes, it bloody well was."

Neither man spoke for several moments, each reminiscing in his own way as the wind began to whip and wail in advance of the coming storm.

Montjoy finally broke the silence. "The short of it is, I'm sure the photo was here when I visited Grandmother a week before her death." He then pointed to his feet. "And I found several spent fags in this spot two days ago which I'm quite certain were not." He pulled several cigarettes wrapped in plastic from his pocket and handed them to Garrett.

"I recognize the label," Garrett said, turning the bag over. "Russian, cheap and strong, and smoked by nearly everyone east of Warsaw."

"The same brand that was also found in the flat where Geoffrey Charlton was killed."

"Not by a strung-out hooker, I'm now guessing."

"Which, at the moment, is as good as mine," Montjoy replied. "There is something else. Did you read about the New York businessman gunned down in Charleston?"

"The same day you arrived, yes."

"The man flew in on a private jet out of Washington, D.C. It was the same charter and time, in fact, that I was booked on but was forced to cancel at the last minute due to a scheduling conflict at Langley. If it's not an extraordinary coincidence, there's only one conclusion that can be drawn from the deaths here and in Italy, of Lindsay's disappearance and presumed murder in Munich, and the cocked-up assassination attempt on me in Charleston."

"Someone's hunting," Garrett replied, seeing his grandmother and again struggling to suppress the rage.

"Indeed."

"Why the four of you?"

"The million-pound question. We'll comb back through our files to see if something, or someone, turns up."

"That someone will know that Charleston was a failure, and still come after you."

"It's the other way around now, old son."

"Even so, you're not safe in the open," Garrett said, turning back toward the cottage and surveilling the surrounding area. "You'll need to stay off the radar until this is sorted."

"And you'll be in want of an alternate identity."

Garrett glanced at Montjoy. "I had a hunch you needed help with more than just settling Grandmom's affairs."

"I need help settling a score," Montjoy replied. "I'll remain on leave from MI6 until the job is done, and the debt to Lindsay, Charlton, and Grandmother is paid."

"An eye for an eye, is it?"

"We're well beyond that now."

Garrett picked up a stone and launched it toward the beach below. After a moment, he asked, "Where?"

"Amsterdam, the Bijlmer District. Seek out a Czech named Havel Sokolov, a harmless old libertine who runs a small restaurant of the same name near the arena. He would be in his early sixties and likely still dodders about with a limp. Look for a perpetual scowl and a scar across the back of his left hand."

"Who is he?"

"A black market forger, tip top, back in the day. His job was counterintelligence with the StB, the Czech secret police. Sokolov spent most of his money and waking hours on vodka and hookers, and finally got caught in a honey trap, with another bloke, in London."

"He's a puff?"

"No. The CIA drugged him and set the whole thing up, photographing an unconscious Sokolov in compromising positions with a male prostitute in Soho. MI6 was close to recruiting him at the time, and, for reasons unknown, did not want to share the asset with Langley. William Lindsay put together an operation that lifted the negatives of the feigned liaison off the Yanks, all the while fooling them into thinking it was the Russians who had foiled their blackmail scheme."

"What do I tell Sokolov?"

"That *Zephyr* is calling in a favor. Other than that, only what is necessary, and you'll be lucky to get five words in return."

"Do you trust him?"

"Of course not, so keep your head about you."

"It's yours I'm concerned about."

"Better to be seen than viewed, mate. Besides, Everton's already safely removed from any sight and sound of Premiership glory. The dry spell sits at a sodding quarter-century, and God won't take me until just before the Toffees are certain to hoist the trophy again."

"Then you'll live to be a hundred," Garrett, a dyed-in-the-wool Tottenham supporter, joked. Both men laughed for a moment, standing at the loch edge and thinking of better times.

Blackening clouds covered the horizon, and Garrett could see a wall of rain moving in their direction. His dark mood suddenly returned, as quickly as their brief bout of levity had broken up the somber reality of their grandmother's murder. "Alright, brov. I'll go to Amsterdam. We'll see this through together, to their end, or ours."

"After you find Sokolov, I need you in Zurich, Credit Suisse on *Paradeplatz*, box 4917, if you please." Montjoy handed Garrett a key. "I'm off for a quick stop in London, and then I'll be on the mainland, in Strasbourg, and in touch as soon as."

CHAPTER TWENTY-THREE

Munich, Germany

D r. Martin Becker finished his fourth coffee of the afternoon and fished for another paracetamol. He had been battling a dull headache for the last five hours, and while the caffeine exacerbated the discomfort, he knew he would also need it to counter what would likely turn into a typically long night. Becker couldn't decide if the evening prior was the problem, though the nurse he had stayed up all hours entertaining had definitely been worth the lack of sleep, or whether it was the thought of another seemingly endless shift that induced the intermittent pounding on his temple.

Becker wanted to pretend it was going to be a slow and steady rotation until he could stumble home and crash for two straight days, before he was next on call. However, he also knew *Murphys Gesetz* guaranteed that whatever could go wrong, would. Besides, he hadn't experienced a quiet Friday in the ER since his first week of residency eight years earlier. He and several other doctors had already pooled their money as to whether it would be drunks who had fallen down and injured themselves, or drunks who had gotten into fights with other drunks, that would take the top spot on the triage docket.

At the moment, Becker was hard-pressed to decide what was to be done with the first case he had tended to that evening. The unidentified gentleman was older, likely in his eighties, and though his German was fluent, he was not native. The patient had been brought in several days earlier, half drowned and mostly incoherent. A passing policeman had fished him out of the Isar River and performed CPR, which had saved the man's life. He had barely been conscious when he was admitted, rambling on about someone in imminent danger. In a brief moment of lucidity, and clearly frustrated that he was not being taken seriously, the man had written down a mobile number with an England prefix, accompanied by the word "Spindle." He had pleaded with a nurse to text the message, but she refused, her only goal to calm the patient and keep him relatively sedated. The attending physician recommended administering haloperidol, but Becker had overruled his colleague, as the man was not psychotic, only panicked and exhausted.

Several calls to the number had gone unanswered, and as there was no voicemail, the consensus was that it must not be legitimate. The man had no identification, and no one had inquired at the desk about a missing person or lost grandfather. It was the assumption of the staff that he was likely suffering from Alzheimer's, and had either walked out of a care facility or wandered away from a family member in one of the nearby parks. No one knew what do with the man pulled from the river who had suffered a mild concussion and exhibited early symptoms of walking pneumonia.

Unless *Max Mustermann* awoke and could shed some light on who he was, the hospital would soon transfer the mystery patient to a longer-term care facility on the other side of the city.

There was one other option, and as it was against protocol, Becker had hesitated in taking it. However, the recurring headache, and a steady stream of "*Herr Doktor*, you're needed in—" helped to make up his mind.

Becker summoned a nurse into the break room and instructed her to text the hospital's information, a brief description of the patient, the details of his admittance, and the single-word missive the man had insisted on sending, and see if anything came back.

CHAPTER TWENTY-FOUR

Moscow, Russia

Vasily Markov had ignored the intermittent knock on his office door throughout the afternoon, as well as the LED flash on his mobile that signaled the semi-permanent presence of unread texts and voicemails. The staff meeting earlier had been little more than a perfunctory rehash of the previous week's agenda, the most pressing issue being that the hot drink vending machine had malfunctioned, again. At least when the country was communist, someone quipped, everyone expected the machines to take their money without dispensing anything.

A stack of cartons lay open and discarded, while reams of paper had been sorted into haphazard piles of no particular order. The Russian counterintelligence officer was irritated that much of the Cold War operational case files had been so poorly organized when they were packed up after the Wall came down. Everything was an absolute mess, and Markov was certain that no one had gone through the documents since they had been haphazardly tossed in boxes three decades earlier.

He would have gladly continued to ignore them as well, but

Markov was looking for something specifically related to operations in Berlin between 1984 and 1987, the only period he was sure Geoffrey Carlton and Madeline Halliwell had overlapped assignments with one another in West Germany, and his own posting in East Berlin. Markov recalled that William Lindsay had been a head of section in London during that period, but also remembered that the Englishman's fingerprints had been all over compromised Stasi and KGP operations throughout much of the 1980s. It was irrelevant what the listed manner of death was for Charlton or Halliwell, or Lindsay, if he was more than simply missing, the timing was too coincidental to be anything other than intentional.

While the situation involving the retired British agents was puzzling enough, Markov had learned that very morning that Banastre Montjoy had taken a sudden leave of absence from SIS. The current deputy chief had left London, apparently without any protection detail and with his destination unknown. Markov did not remember ever directly crossing paths with Montjoy while the young agent was stationed in West Germany during the last few years of communist rule, but Markov had a hunch that whatever was playing out with the recent carnage among MI6's retired ranks was possibly connected to the last place each of them had worked together, West Berlin.

Markov took a momentary break from the files and recalled his last exchange, in person, with Charlton. The man had reached out to Markov on more than one occasion during their years on opposite sides of Berlin, and each time the Russian spy had agreed to join his counterpart not just for a free drink, but in the off chance he might be able to glean some bit of useful information from the Englishman to pass on to, and curry favor with, Moscow. Each time Markov informed his superiors of the details of the sit-down, and every time thereafter the KGB would have him followed for a brief period after the most recent meet.

Perhaps it was his own paranoia that prevented Markov from filing his usual report one miserably cold and unproductive February in 1984.

It was mid-month when Charlton suggested he and Markov rendezvous to discuss a matter of utmost importance. Unlike all other previous approaches, however, the MI6 station chief went out of his way to contact Markov surreptitiously, and choose an unknown bar near a less than desirable section of East Berlin as the meet location. Against his better judgement, Markov did not clear the rendezvous with his *Rezidentura*, and it wasn't long after arriving at the poorly heated hole-in-the-wall that he understood why Charlton had taken great pains to conceal this particular encounter.

General Secretary Yuri Andropov is dead, Charlton said, *and the Politburo has replaced him with the terminally-ill Konstantin Chernenko. Certainly, you of all people, Vasily, must realize that it is only a matter of time.*

Markov recalled that before he could object with a polite smile and customary wave of his hand, Charlton suddenly reached out and grabbed Markov's wrist. *We can get your wife and daughter out as well,* was all he said. Markov remembered that he quickly glanced around, but the few people in the place paid scant attention to either man. It was then that Markov realized the "bar" was filled with Western agents, along with an East German bartender who clearly worked for MI6.

The blast of a car horn from somewhere on the street below arrested Markov's attention long enough for him to refocus on his office, and a photo of his family on the desk. He picked up the frame and blew the dust off a picture that had been taken nearly forty years earlier. It was of his wife and their young daughter on vacation near the Baltic Sea. Markov could remember every detail about that day, and of snapping the Polaroid, and of promising Matilda that things would soon get better, and that he was on his way up the KGB hierarchy.

Five years later, sitting across from Charlton in that dingy bar, Markov had realized that whatever dreams he had for his profession and family were not dependent on how hard he worked in East Berlin, nor how productive he was for the KGB. He damn well knew that the credit for his intelligence gathering was being hijacked by those immediately above him on the chain jockeying for their own favor with those further up it. Vasily Mikhail Markov was simply another expendable agent who was competing with an army of other middling officers hoping to grab one of the few chairs left once the music stopped.

While regular citizens might wait fifteen years to buy a *Trabi*, the cheap, crappy, slow, and noisy official vehicle of the GDR, Markov had suddenly envisioned how long his own wait would last for anything that resembled a successful career.

He remembered saying nothing to Charlton at that moment in Freidrichshain, which clearly spoke volumes to his counterpart. Charlton pressed, *you only need stay in East*

Berlin and work for us for six months, and we'll get all of you out. You can start a new life in England and leave this behind.

Markov carefully placed the photo back on his desk, and redoubled his efforts to locate all files between 1984 and 1987 that involved any operation against the British in West Berlin, and specifically involving Charlton, Halliwell, and Montjoy. It was Markov's hunch that the key to whatever was going on, and however his behavior three decades earlier might have played in it, lay somewhere within the bale of A4s that now littered his office floor.

He just needed to find it.

CHAPTER TWENTY-FIVE

London, England

Banastre Montjoy leaned against a railing near the center of the Blue Bridge in St. James's Park. Big Ben sat to his back, and from a distance he watched a cluster of tourists alight a sightseeing bus at Buckingham Palace and swarm the East Front.

Montjoy had grown up just around the corner, in Belgravia, and had spent much of his childhood roaming the neighboring chain of London's more famous Royal Parks. He and his best mate would pretend they were marauding pirates, one Blackbeard and the other Henry Morgan, but not before arguing endlessly over who was which, for neither wanted to be a buccaneer from Llanrumney that no schoolboy had ever heard of, nor a Welshman to boot.

One winter holiday, with both boys refusing to concede, Montjoy was sentenced to walk the plank. This consisted of his leaping, with scant encouragement, from the overwalk and into the lake. He immediately seized up in the freezing water and would have drowned if not for a constable eating lunch nearby. Montjoy had never seen his mother so angry.

As punishment, he was forbidden to go out for one full week, with the added indignity that Montjoy was to play Morgan for a fortnight afterward. No doubt his mum, who had a delightfully mischievous sense of humor, livened up her weekly ladies' luncheon when she capped off the story with that punch line.

Montjoy smiled at the thought, standing near the exact spot from which he'd jumped fifty years earlier. His ruminations were interrupted by a muted salutation.

"Good afternoon, sir."

"Gavin," Montjoy replied, and gave his subordinate a nod in the direction from which Abbot had come. The two men walked without speaking until they cleared a crowd standing around a lone pelican resting on a park bench and waiting to be fed.

"I'm surprised to see you back in the city, what with the sudden leave of absence." Abbot seemed unusually ill at ease and kept his attention on the nearby scene.

"Always the last to know," Montjoy acknowledged, also watching the bird wolf down whatever was tossed its way. "I remember the feeling, mind you, those early years at Six. About the moment you resign yourself to it, they go and up your clearance and bring you in on all the nasty goings-on around HQ, by which time you realize you were better off in the black."

"In the black?"

Montjoy pointed to the pelican. "Not waiting for a handout. Not owing fifty favors across the Embankment because of it." Abbot nodded, and Montjoy smiled to himself, a silent affirmation of the maxim that what needs explanation can't fully be understood.

Abbot then knocked Montjoy for a loop. "Rumor has it there's something unpleasant in play concerning your grandmum."

Montjoy eyed his protégé. "Already in the red, are we?"

"Word is she didn't expire of natural causes."

"If she were a bloody bottle of milk, you'd be spot on."

"I'm sorry, sir—"

Montjoy waved him off. "No need. I appreciate the candor." Abbot had been instrumental in uncovering the mastermind behind the King's Cross Tube bombing three years earlier, and Montjoy had full confidence in, and wholly trusted, the former Oxbridge math prodigy.

Montjoy began to stroll along the lake path, and Abbot followed. Neither spoke until Montjoy gestured over his shoulder in the direction of the Wellington Barracks. "One of my uncles was Queen's Guard, did I ever tell you that?"

"No, sir."

"He was the black sheep." Montjoy then whispered, "Army." He stopped next to a grove of trees and surveilled the area. "Eight generations of Montjoys at sea, *Virginia Capes, Trafalgar, Jutland, Bismarck*, the *Falklands*, and my father's youngest brother becomes a *Percy*," he added, using a derogatory term the Royal Navy attached to soldiers in the British Armed Forces.

"*Pongo*, isn't it? In reference to the rumored stink of the *Tommies*?"

"'*Where the wind blows, the Pongoes*—'" Montjoy quipped,

as he pulled a piece of paper from his pocket. "I need something from records, and because of *its* potential stench, you must tread carefully."

"If that ever weren't the case, I'm not sure what I'd do," Abbot replied lightheartedly, though his deputy chief did not react in kind.

Montjoy produced a churchwarden and began to methodically pack layers of sweet burley. "I need you to collect files on every operation Madeleine Halliwell, Geoffrey Charlton, and William Lindsay collaborated on in the Eastern Bloc. The earliest year they would have all served together was 1972, so begin there and work your way forward. Focus on, but don't limit your search to, Berlin and Moscow."

"That might take some time."

"And I don't have it, if you must know."

"Yes, sir." Abbot reached for the note.

Montjoy instead held it up. After a moment, Abbot nodded. Montjoy struck a match and lit his pipe, before torching the scrap. "Quick's the word."

"Sharp's the action," Abbot replied as he turned to leave, until his habitual curiosity got the better of him. "What am I looking for?"

"I'll know when you find it."

CHAPTER TWENTY-SIX

Amsterdam, Netherlands

S ean Garrett stepped off the metro and into an unusually bright afternoon sun in the Bijlmer District of Amsterdam. Renowned for its sundry mix of culture, and petty crime in the small hours, he knew the southeast section of the Dutch capital would pose no problems, provided he find Sokolov and conclude his business before sundown.

His destination, a small eatery called Sokolov and Son, served American-style burgers and fried chicken and was ironically positioned between a McDonald's and a KFC. Though his route from the station followed an almost straight path into Bijlmer-Centrum, Garrett remained alert for Amsterdamian cyclists, renowned for racing around the city with reckless abandon and who had been dubbed "whispering death" as a result.

Garrett arrived at the marketplace unscathed and weaved his way through lunch patrons that seemed to crowd every shop, save one. The restaurant in question, whose logo was a smiling hamburger with arms and legs waving an American flag that contained only forty stars, was so sparsely outfitted that Garrett wondered if it was still in business. He cupped a hand to his brow and pressed his forehead against the glass façade. The interior was completely dark and he saw no one, customer or otherwise, in the front sitting area, but then noticed a shadeless lamp burning on a small table in a room near the back corner.

Garrett received no response after rapping several times on a sign that indicated the restaurant was indeed open. He had just made up his mind to return later when he saw a face peer around a backroom doorjamb. The young man to whom it belonged stared blankly, and without blinking, for a long moment, clearly hoping the interloper would go away. When Garrett did not, the boy gestured at a clock on the wall, a terse prompt that they were closed and to go away.

Garrett only glared through the glass and pointed to the door. The young man's embellished reaction was typical of someone his age, and he took his time walking through the dining room to the front door, which he barely cracked.

"We're not open," he said, in heavily accented English.

"I'm not hungry."

The boy was clearly accustomed to this type of response, for he sized Garrett up before pushing the door open with his foot just wide enough to step through. Garrett did, and the young man glanced up the street before he shut the door and snapped the lock.

"He's in the back."

Garrett walked down a short hallway to a room with curtains in place of a door, which were drawn. He could make out the sound of a Bohemian polka playing at a low volume and heard someone bid him to enter. Garrett pushed through the mismatched drapes and saw an older man hunched over a table, working intently on a model boat made of wood. He was nearly bald but with long hair growing over his collar, while a hypertrophic scar ran along the back of one hand. The room was cluttered with odds and ends stacked on tables and shoved onto the shelves of old bookcases, while paraphernalia from the Czech Republic, particularly Cold War propaganda, adorned the walls. The man did not speak, and Garrett could smell something fried cooking in another room.

"The boy sent me back," Garrett said. "Your grandson, I presume."

"I don't have any children," the man replied, without looking up.

"Sokolov?"

"Yes siree, Bob."

Garrett brushed off the man's odd use of an outdated Anglicized expression, as well as the contradiction between his admission and the restaurant's name, and stated bluntly, "*Zephyr* is calling in a favor."

"What is it this time?" Sokolov asked sarcastically, but then quickly cooled his tone and smiled. "Would you care for a tea?"

"No," Garrett replied curtly, but then added, "thank you."

Sokolov set down the soldering gun and dusted off his hands, accentuating the gesture. "So, what can I do for my English friends?"

"I need an identity."

"And who is I?" Sokolov asked playfully.

"Someone from the U.K., England specifically and the South preferably, with a passport, driver's license, and credit card."

"Those are biometric now, quite costly."

"I'm certain that whatever arrangement you've made with our mutual acquaintance will be satisfied."

Sokolov furrowed his brow. "That is what I was afraid of." The teapot whistled. "The new format is more complicated and will take some time. How quickly do you need it?"

"Immediately," Garrett responded, and pulled five hundred Euros from his pocket. "Quicker, if you're inclined."

"You'll find I'm easily inclined," Sokolov replied, taking the note and backlighting it against the lamp. "This is from *Zephyr*?"

"Me."

"You'll have it in three days."

Garrett pulled another bank note from his jacket and held it up, along with two photos he had taken of himself.

"Two days," Sokolov said, grabbing the second bill and then glancing at the headshots. "I should be able to pull facial geometry from these. Shall we say Wednesday, here, same time?"

Garrett shook his head. "Overnight it to this address."

Sokolov took the scrap of paper. "Switzerland? Should I subtract the cost of posting it from what you've paid?"

"Two days," Garrett reiterated. "Send it in care of Gareth Walker." He pushed back through the partition and past the boy, who was irritated about something and mumbling to himself as he rolled cutlery into cloth napkins.

Sokolov picked up his phone as he pulled back the curtain and watched Garrett leave. After his host, waiter, and part-time cook locked the door and flipped the front sign to "closed," Sokolov dialed a number he had long ago been forced to memorize. After several rings, a click signaled that someone had answered, though nothing was spoken.

"It's Sokolov," the Czech forger said as he glanced at the photo of Garrett. "*Zephyr* made contact."

CHAPTER TWENTY-SEVEN

Strasbourg, France

Banastre Montjoy downed the last of his pint on the patio of a beer garden in Place Gutenberg, near a statue of the fifteenth-century inventor who had bested Shakespeare, Newton, and Einstein as the most influential person of the previous millennium. Though he had tasted better lagers in the Alsace region, Montjoy acknowledged that the timber-framed medieval city near the Franco-German border provided a cultural setting that was second to none.

Montjoy had opted, at the last minute the evening prior, for an early-morning ferry from Dover to Calais. He had followed the ninety-minute crossing with a four-hour drive through the French countryside en route to Strasbourg. The deputy chief had, for the first time since his early days as a field operative, used an alias to book the crossing and hired car. The burgundy jacket of his alternate passport, which he had long kept hidden in a Covent Garden safe house, was layered in dust, and Montjoy thought he barely recognized the photo of the younger man inside.

He dropped two coins on the table and made his way

through the crowd toward a younger woman, blonde and attractive, who was eating a vanilla soft-serve near a double-decked carousel. The near-empty ride turned methodically, while its ubiquitous melody, one of the most recognized sounds in the world, momentarily filled the square.

"And here I was all set to buy you a *crème glacée.*"

Samantha Anderton gestured to the bronze figure. "Printed books from Asia predate his by six hundred years, but who gets all the credit?"

"Name history's most famous boatmaker," Montjoy asked. "In fact, name any you can, other than Noah."

Anderton pursed her lips, a tacit recognition of Montjoy's point. "I'll Google it and get back to you."

"*Ibid,*" Montjoy replied. "No one has ever suggested, 'Yahoo it.'"

Anderton smiled. "It's good to see you, sir."

"It's good to hear you're doing so well," Montjoy replied as the pair began to walk in the direction of the Ill River, which connected to the *Canal des Faux Remparts* and fully encircled the city center, creating an island of sorts.

It had been three years since the young sergeant with the Metropolitan Police had accepted Montjoy's offer to abandon a promising career in London's territorial force for the Secret Intelligence Service. Anderton had been an up-and-coming officer with the Met, working under renowned chief inspector Roger Holland, when she was assigned to investigate the terrorist bombing of King's Cross. Holland had ordered Anderton to conduct her inquiry off the books, fearing the case would ultimately be commandeered and its findings classified. While her dogged determination eventually led Scotland Yard to the nefarious origins of the bombing, it also meant that Anderton had become privy to highly-classified documents damning to a variety of politicians and government officials.

Holland, a university roommate of Montjoy, recognized that the explosive implications of the findings could also sully the careers and reputations of no small number of intelligence officers, some of them long retired. Holland buried the results of the investigation and Montjoy offered Anderton a place at MI6. While the overture was initially one born of self-preservation, Anderton had quickly developed into an exceptional agent.

Montjoy quickly learned that his new recruit, a star student and former stellar athlete, had disappointed an over-achieving English father with expectations higher than that of a London *Bobby*. Anderton herself had determined that to carry on the familial tradition of law simply did not suit, and sympathetic support from her quiet but strong Welsh mother encouraged their only daughter to pursue a childhood dream of a career at Interpol.

Montjoy paused at a small bridge that passed over the waterway. "I've arranged for you to take a personal leave of absence." He handed Anderton an envelope. "A new passport."

"As I have had absolutely no personal life since joining MI6, no one will believe that as the reason."

Montjoy smiled. "You're a French tourist on vacation, until further notice."

Anderton pocketed the documents and joked, "Staying at a five-star hotel with a luxury spa?"

"Actually, yes, though not in the way you hope," Montjoy replied. "Before you see how the other half lives, however, I need you to collect something for me in Germany."

CHAPTER TWENTY-EIGHT

London, England

Tomas Karlson sat in a corner of the Grenadier, away from a raucous party of half-ripped revelers crowding one man's iPad and watching a Rugby derby between two London sides. A second set of tipplers lined a tap-laden bar, and the comfortable tavern remained relatively low-key, notwithstanding an intermittent crescendo of cheers from the corner.

The Belgravian pub, quintessentially English, was the type of place in which Karlson should have *huzzahed* a daring and successful operation three decades earlier. A feat of espionage that would still be fêted amongst what was left of the old guard. The walls and ceiling were covered with varying denominations of currency from around the world, an imaginary debt paid by customers for a young soldier reputedly beaten to death centuries earlier after having been caught cheating at cards. Karlson should have been able to tack his own bill up years ago, after hoisting a pint in honor of having beaten the Stasi and cheated death. He would have married a pleasant girl from the country and at that very moment be sitting across from his own son, himself a proud soldier at home on leave.

Instead, Karlson sat opposite the vacant reflection of an abandoned and broken man staring back at him from a lager advert bar mirror.

Karlson sipped a cask ale and pushed away the remnants of a lamb rump as he waffled on whether to start in on a sticky toffee pudding.

Though he had tentatively accepted the contract on Banastre Montjoy while in Sweden, Karlson discovered that his desire for retribution had only become more inflamed the closer he came to the people he held responsible. Once his new target had been reacquired by Karlson's handler, the failed spy-turned-assassin would continue his rampage through the SIS hierarchy that had cast him out.

Karlson finished his beer. He walked to a nearby wall and pinned a one-pound note atop several others. Amidst the droll platitudes and drunken names scribbled on everything from dollars to outdated Deutsche Marks, Karlson penned one word and two numbers.

Exodus 21:23

Karlson pushed through the crowd, all oblivious to the man who would soon see to it that an eye would indeed be taken for an eye.

CHAPTER TWENTY-NINE

Strasbourg, France

Banastre Montjoy refolded the note, penned from a text he had received on an abandoned phone an hour earlier, just after tea time. The message had been sent to a mobile left in his office, and from which Montjoy knew someone could tap into to theoretically track his movements.

Only a select group were privy to the number and it was no small measure of luck that he had been made aware of the missive at all. Abbot, having been charged with rooting out which Cold War cases involved Lindsay, Charlton, and Halliwell, happened to notice the blinking notification light on the phone in the drawer. He had taken liberties, considering that his boss was on the move and not planning to return to London anytime soon. The text was from a nurse at the *Rechts der Isar* hospital in Munich, who stated that in their care was an elderly patient rescued from a river five days earlier. The man had been unable to give his name or any other pertinent details, though before he lapsed into a mini-coma he had requested that the attached message be sent to the number provided.

The hospital had included its details and requested that if the recipient of the message were able, to please contact Dr. Martin Becker immediately. Montjoy skipped past the remainder of what amounted to a lengthy diagnosis the German doctor had included with the text, before he reached the single word that William Lindsay had begged them to transmit.

Spindle.

CHAPTER THIRTY

Zurich, Switzerland

*P**aradeplatz* buzzed with its typically frenetic mix of business and pleasure. Once a pig market in the seventeenth century, Zurich's main public square now boasted expensive shops and restaurants, in addition to serving as the de facto epicenter of Swiss banking. While its streets weren't literally paved with gold, what was massed in bunkered vaults beneath the asphalt amounted to arguably one of the largest concentrations of wealth in the known world.

Sean Garrett exited a tram at a nearby junction, where the volume of public transport in the popular square rivaled its collection of banks. Had it been any other location in Europe, the dynamic would have been reduced to organized chaos, with trams running late, cars laying on horns, and people bouncing off one another like pinballs in a machine lined only with pop bumpers.

But this was Switzerland, a country that invented in more ways than one the concept of "running like clockwork."

Garrett crossed the busy square and spied the main branch of Credit Suisse. The financial powerhouse, celebrated for its strict client confidentiality, was housed in a centuries-old structure that was an impressive fusion of sandstone, marble, and priceless art. He palmed a safety deposit key, one that had long been concealed by Madeleine Halliwell in her cottage in the Scottish Highlands. Montjoy had been made aware of its existence only after their grandmother had retired from MI6. Though Halliwell had not elaborated on the contents of what was kept in Switzerland, Montjoy was instructed that it wasn't to be touched while she was alive and to be extremely cautious should it be accessed after her death. When Garrett pressed his brother as to how exactly he would be allowed entry to the box, Montjoy answered that grandmother would have taken care of that contingent, and not to worry.

Not to worry, Garrett thought to himself, with Madeleine Halliwell, Geoffrey Charlton, and William Lindsay dead or missing, and Banastre fortunate enough to still be above ground.

The interior of the bank was ornate, spotless, and though busy, almost completely quiet. Garrett passed through the main lobby to a set of stairs that led to the vaults. Contrary to what Hollywood depicted, where state-of-the-art hand and retinal scans were overseen by suspicious employees flanked with hypervigilant security guards, Garrett encountered one polite and professional member of staff who asked only to verify a photo ID. After being shown to a small box in a sea of some thirty-five hundred others two stories below ground, dual locks were turned simultaneously using a sister key and Garrett was left alone.

The box was the size of A4 paper and little more than three

inches in height. It contained what Garrett guessed was close to thirty thousand British pounds in various denominations and currencies, a small-caliber pistol, and several passports, most of which were outdated and some from countries that technically no longer existed.

Garrett pushed the contents of the container to one side and saw, sitting beneath the cash and credentials, a leather-bound journal entwined with a single ribbon. The book was old and worn and its pages appeared to be filled with a collection of names, dates, and notes pertaining to past SIS operations. There were also random photos clipped to differing sections, organized by location and year.

Garrett emptied the contents into a backpack, closed and left the box on the counter of the privacy cubicle, and exited the bank.

CHAPTER THIRTY-ONE

Santee, South Carolina

The overflow lot at the put-in for the main boat landing at Santee State Park, in the span of twelve hours, had come to resemble a used car lot for black SUVs. Government-issued vehicles jammed every space, while a large grassy area adjacent to State Park Road had been commandeered as a landing area for no less than two helicopters.

What had set the circus in motion was a local scuba class using Lake Marion for an open water course. The man-made body of water, like many throughout the South, had long been a popular spot for divers of all skill levels. Some came to practice, while others explored the once-thriving mill and lumber "ghost towns" that littered the depths, swallowed up a half-century earlier with the coming of electric plants and the dams needed to power them.

A day earlier, a scuba shop from Leesville had brought a group of intermediates to snorkel the shallows of the lake. A few of the more experienced divers had ventured farther out and stumbled across a sunken speedboat with two bodies lashed to its transom. One man had nearly drowned when he panicked at the sight and, as he began to hyperventilate, instinctively tried to pull the mask from his face in order to breathe in more air.

It did not take long for local authorities to recognize they had something bigger than their limited manpower would be able to manage, and since the FBI would soon overrun their jurisdiction anyway, a call to the field office in Columbia had burgeoned into a sideshow of agents trying to determine what had happened.

Agent Brandon Wells, recently reassigned to South Carolina from Maryland, stood by himself along a bank and watched a team of Bureau divers work offshore. It had taken an hour to properly cable the jon boat to a barge towed in specifically to bring the sunken crime scene to the surface intact. It was clear the vessel had not been in the water long, considering the condition of the bodies. It took authorities less than ten minutes to identify one of the men as the missing DNR agent from Charleston, whose vehicle local authorities had discovered at a boat landing on the Stono River several days earlier.

The other man had been fingerprinted and his sets sent to headquarters to be run through IAFIS and NGI databases. Wells had wanted to expand the search from the outset, but had been overruled by his superiors, who did not want to turn the scene into a multi-jurisdictional pissing contest until it was absolutely necessary.

A more in-depth inspection of the DNR agent had turned up an all-weather notepad and an entry dated the morning Jeffrey Cox had disappeared. It contained the make and model of a vehicle, a GMC Denali, with a partial license plate. A BOLO alert had been issued for the SUV, and though nothing had yet turned up, the passport and driver's license for the second man, Kevin Greene, had come back as counterfeit.

What was of particular interest to the agents who crowded the body once it had been pulled from the depths, photographed, and gone over with the proverbial fine-tooth forensic comb, was the HK 9mm pistol in the man's waistband, five thousand American dollars in his pocket, and tattoos of stars below each knee, inscribed in Russian.

Wells recognized he was dealing with something far bigger than the Columbia office would be allowed to investigate. The call he received an hour later, from FBI headquarters in Washington, D.C., confirmed that his role in whatever was going on, was over.

CHAPTER THIRTY-TWO

St. Gallen, Switzerland

Sean Garrett downed a ham and pickle sandwich near a pretzel stand in the main station at *Bahnhofplatz*. His train from Zurich had taken just over an hour, and while he waited, a steady stream of travelers cycled between the platform and terminal exit. He checked the time again, and kept his eye on a My Post 24 kiosk near a set of escalators, which workers had cordoned off and were repairing.

Garrett had rented a temporary address at the anytime post collection point in St. Gallen for the forged identity papers from Sokolov, and had been notified via text that the package had arrived earlier in the day. He had spent the better part of an hour surveilling the depot, and decided to use the momentary chaos of the next train as cover to grab the package. As if on cue, an SBB from Zurich pulled to the platform, on time to the minute, and several crowded cars emptied out directly in front of Garrett's position.

A group of commuters, eyes on their mobiles, failed to recognize that the nearest escalator was closed until they merged en masse at the partition. A muted comment from the construction foreman at the group's expense elicited laughter from the rest of the work crew, and Garrett moved quickly through the disgruntled bunch, punched in his information, and removed the envelope from its assigned box. He momentarily mixed with the stragglers, some of whom were clearly weighing whether the need to find another way out should interfere with a selfie and social media post about the inconvenience. Garrett eased through the small crowd and exited near a supermarket.

A man standing near the entrance of an Italian café, dressed in casual attire and pretending to read a copy of *Blick*, folded the newspaper under his arm and followed Garrett from the station.

CHAPTER THIRTY-THREE

Calais, France

John Riker watched his reflection disappear from the interior window of a first-class seat on the Eurostar as it emerged from the darkness of the Chunnel on the coast of northern France. His high-speed train from London had departed just before lunch, and would take another hour to arrive at what would likely amount to a momentary stopover in Paris.

How long his sojourn in *la Ville Lumière* would last was up to the team assigned to monitor the unknown man who had made contact with one of Chénard's Cold War stooges in Amsterdam. The former counterintelligence officer with the Czech secret police had long moonlighted as an underground forger for whomever and from whichever side could pony up the exorbitant prices he charged for false credentials. Riker wondered how the eccentric agent had been allowed to operate with such impunity, until he learned that Chénard had discovered Sokolov's scheme in 1986 and allowed him to continue, with the caveat that he pass along the fake bona fides of his growing list of Eastern Bloc clients. The lucrative habit continued after the fall of communism.

A surrogate for Banastre Montjoy, dropping the deputy chief's Cold War code name *Zephyr*, had surfaced in Prague, calling in a back-owed tit-for-tat from the former StB operative in the form of a U.K. passport. Sokolov, ever the lackey looking to curry the smallest amount of favor, had reached out to his former KGB contact once rumors began to circulate three days earlier through old espionage back channels that Banastre Montjoy had taken a leave of absence from MI6. Moreover, a sizeable bounty had been offered for any information concerning his whereabouts.

Montjoy's proxy in Amsterdam had ordered delivery of the false credentials under the name Gareth Walker to a drop box in St. Gallen, Switzerland. Chénard hoped that the man would lead him to Montjoy and had immediately stationed his team of ex-Alpha Group operatives at the station. Upon receiving word from Sokolov, Chénard had also activated Riker in London, and sent him to Paris to await an update on his target's new location.

No matter how quickly that information was supplied, Riker gauged he would have at least enough time to patronize the red-light district in Paris, which straddled the city's 9th and 18th *arrondissements*.

He was tired, but not that tired.

CHAPTER THIRTY-FOUR

Lindau, Germany

The pair of killers had shadowed their target for two hours. After the man from Zurich retrieved his passport from a mailbox in the main station in St. Gallen, he had departed on an early afternoon train that took him, and them, to Rorschach, a small lake town in the north of Switzerland. He then boarded a ferry, a combination sightseeing vessel and car transport, which sailed across Lake Constance to the Bavarian town of Lindau, in Germany.

Mykhail Vann knew well the large body of water that conjoined the borders of Germany, Austria, and Switzerland, as his maternal grandmother had been born and raised in the small West Austrian alpine village of Höfen. His mother had married a Ukrainian soldier two years after World War II, and Vann had been born in Kiev twenty years later to the day. He was the last of eight and the only child to never know his mother, who died of sepsis during his birth. He and his father fought constantly, with both secretly blaming the younger Vann for her death. Their contentious relationship was one of the reasons the son joined the Red Army at eighteen, in defiance of his father's wishes, who wanted him to attend university and become an engineer.

The young soldier quickly distinguished himself, and within three years had joined the ranks of the Russian Special Forces. When the Ukrainian branch of Alpha Group was formed in 1990, the Spetsnaz sniper was one of the first to pass its rigorous selection program. It was during a routine training exercise that Vann met a colonel with the KGB, Alexei Arkipov, who secretly recruited him into a squad that would soon deploy to Chechnya.

After the death squad disbanded in 1996, Vann remained with *Alfa* until he retired to join the ranks of ex-soldiers paid handsomely in a new and swiftly growing private sector economy. His small company, setting up security for wealthy Muscovite businessmen, earned him a comfortable living by Russian standards.

It was at the moment Vann considered expanding his business that he received a call from his old commander, who had purportedly died in 1996. Arkipov, who now went by the name Emile Chénard, was someone for whom Vann would do almost anything, particularly when it paid one hundred thousand Euros. The opportunity to assassinate a retired MI6 spy in Munich, which would team Vann with one of his former Alpha Group comrades, Artem Ivanenko, had been too good to pass up.

Vann refocused his attention on the man he and Ivanenko had been instructed to follow from Switzerland.

Their target exited the ferry and strolled into the center of the small island located in the harbor just offshore. Vann and Ivanenko trailed the man in tandem from a safe distance, mixing with the crowd of tourists who had disembarked the ferry and spread out over the main shopping district. The men had just approached the bridge terminus that accessed the mainland and the main section of Lindau when their mark turned back along the road and entered a *biergarten* near a marina on the north side of the island. They watched him take a seat on the patio and order something to drink.

The pair split their surveillance, taking up discreet positions on either side of the small outdoor restaurant, and waited.

CHAPTER THIRTY-FIVE

S ean Garrett sipped a drink at a shared patio table at *Milchpilz Lindau Biergarten*. Several excursion ferries had disembarked one after another, and a mix of tour groups spilled out across the harbor town like water from an over-turned cup. He rotated his surveillance between a line of docks near a boat rental service in the marina and a walking bridge that connected the small island to the Lindau mainland.

Garrett spied a tall, attractive female in his periphery emerge from a nearby park. She turned a row of heads as she crossed the road and entered the outdoor seating area. When the woman paused and glanced around for an open seat, several men at a nearby table moved over to make room, though she ignored them and casually made her way to a seat opposite of Garrett. "*Ist dieser Platz besetzt?*"

"I'm sorry, I don't speak German," Garrett replied, lying.

"It's no problem," the woman answered in English, with a British accent, before asking, "do you mind if I sit down?"

"Better you than someone else."

The woman pushed a pair of Wayfarers to the top of her

head and tucked long, blonde hair behind her ears. "I hear this place serves the best hot dogs."

"Better than Coney Island."

The woman smiled. "I'm Sam."

"Sean," Garrett replied. "I hope the train in was uneventful."

"More so than yours, I suspect," Anderton said. "I see you have company, near the playground."

Garrett nodded. "His partner is across the street. They were waiting near the mail drop at the main station in St. Gallen."

"Then Mr. Montjoy's hunch about Amsterdam was correct."

"These two are likely the opening act. Whomever Sokolov alerted is waiting to see if I link up with Banastre."

"What's the play?"

"My brother told me you can handle yourself."

"That's kind of him, and yes, I can."

"Let's throw these two for a loop." Garrett reached into his backpack and pulled out the journal from the safety deposit box in Zurich. "What time does your train depart?"

"Twenty minutes."

"I want to see how these two react when you leave for the station, alone."

"Will they split up?"

"If so, it signals that whoever is running their operation has someone else waiting in the wings to finish the job."

"Mr. Montjoy suspects the same."

"Which means," Garrett replied, handing the book

Anderton, "that Banastre is foolishly looking to hang himself out as bait to draw in the assassin."

"He said you'd say that," Anderton replied. "What are you going to do?"

"See what I can get from whichever of the B-Team sticks around."

"I'll give you two to one odds it's the one in the park."

"You're on, for a drink after this is done."

"Good luck," Anderton said, pocketing the journal and pulling out her phone. She stood, but then said back over her shoulder as she began to make her way to the station, "You'll be buying, by the way."

Garrett smiled, and used the window of an adjacent delivery truck to observe the man across the street. Garrett watched him hesitate, before the operative dumped the newspaper he had pretended to read in a garbage bin and fell in step a block behind Anderton.

CHAPTER THIRTY-SIX

Strasbourg, France

B anastre Montjoy leaned against a window overlooking *Rue des Moulins*. He had checked into the Pavillon Régent Petite France a day earlier under the alias William Shaw, one of his covers that had not been used since the Cold War. The timber-framed inn was small but charming and situated directly on the Ill River. Montjoy had booked a room at the location not just because it offered good food and a comfortably relaxed atmosphere—it also provided a direct line of sight along the picturesque bridge from which the back entrance of the hotel could be accessed.

Montjoy suspected that he had little cause to worry, as the possibility that he could be found so quickly under an assumed name was remote. However, someone had been able to track down four MI6 operatives in as many countries, and had clearly been in possession of Montjoy's travel itinerary to Charleston. That he was still alive was simply the result of blind luck, in the form of a rescheduled meeting with his counterpart at the CIA. Accordingly, the deputy chief on leave and under operational cover in a small hotel on the French and German borders took no chances.

Montjoy had picked up his room phone to order afternoon tea, when his mobile rang. "This is William."

"Hello, sir," Abbot replied, knowing he was to keep the conversation as short and ambiguous as possible. "I've got the information you requested."

"Go on."

"I've narrowed the cases down to nine possible during the stipulated time frame. Seven in East Berlin and two in Moscow. There were three others, two in Hungary and one in Czechoslovakia, which I've dismissed as per the parameters of the search. Most of the operations focused on intelligence-gathering in East Berlin, with two of them coordinated to bring assets over. One was shut down after the informant got cold feet and disappeared. The other, in November of 1984, failed when our agent, coded *Castor*, was captured by the Stasi. The name of that operation was *Safeguard*, but there is no accompanying information in the file. It looks like someone has removed or scrubbed quite a bit of the details related to the mission."

"Keep looking. I want to know what happened to our agent."

"Yes, sir."

"What news of our man in Munich?" Montjoy asked, referring to William Lindsay.

"He's still not regained consciousness, but we've sent someone down to monitor the hospital and begin the paperwork to bring him home, assuming he wakes up."

"Keep me updated." Montjoy hung up, and called down to cancel an early dinner order he had placed with the kitchen. He did not know the details of *Operation Safeguard*, but did remember that a British agent had gone missing in the fall of 1984. The consensus was that the man had been arrested, tortured, and eventually executed. The alternative was that the operative had willingly defected, and had chosen, for whatever reason, to stay underground for the last three decades.

With Lindsay's warning, Montjoy realized that he was running out of options. It was time to come out of hiding and attempt to piece together what was taking the shape of a very troubling Cold War puzzle.

Considering who and what was potentially involved, Montjoy decided to gamble on reaching out to someone he hadn't matched wits against in three decades.

CHAPTER THIRTY-SEVEN

Lindau, Germany

Sean Garrett finished a plain hot dog and downed the remainder of a lemon-lime drink that had long since turned lukewarm. The man who shadowed him, the one from the park and who represented a losing bet to Anderton, had alternated his surveillance between various points around the restaurant for the last two hours. He was good, but not a professional, Garrett suspected, and so he had intentionally drawn out their silent standoff into the early evening in order to mentally wear his counterpart down.

The man's adrenal glands would quickly override any dulled senses the moment his mark stood to leave, but Garrett knew that his pursuer would nonetheless be tired and hungry and his tradecraft prone to slippage the longer this played out. Whatever the operative's ability to monitor a target lacked, Garrett had to assume he was no pushover. Professional or not, most people were able to call on seldom used reserves in a fight or flight situation. Trained killers even more so. Garrett needed to utilize the element of surprise, or the face off he would soon force could prove terminal for the wrong person.

Twilight approached, and the descending cloud cover intensified an evening fog that had formed and was beginning to drift across the harbor. Garrett stood and bid a *"guten Abend"* to an older gentleman with whom he had carried on a sporadic conversation over the last hour. He exited the patio and strolled to a walking bridge that connected the Lindau mainland. After crossing the causeway at the bridge terminus, Garrett turned back along a path that ran parallel to the shoreline. He did not need to fabricate some credible reason to turn and discreetly verify that the man was still following him, for Garrett could sense his trailer was not far behind.

Garrett continued through the park, over a main road, and into the outskirts of a large farming complex. He walked along the entrance driveway and passed several tractors that had been parked beside a newly plowed field. As there was no longer any kind of crowd to effectively disguise the pursuit, Garrett knew he needed to draw the man in closer before his shadow considered dropping back and out of any direct line of sight.

The trick, Garrett had learned from a childhood spent fishing the lochs of the Scottish Highlands, was to reel in the jig neither too fast nor slow.

Garrett approached two large parcels of land, clearly part of a rotating crop system. A line of newly planted trees separated the fields and grew into a thick copse as he moved along its perimeter. He resisted the urge to instinctively turn and check that his pursuer was still behind him, as Garrett neared what appeared to be the center point of the narrow wood. He decided it was time and quickly ducked through a gap in the grove, before doubling back along the opposite side of the hedgerow. Garrett knew the tense situation would play out in a very different manner then he envisioned if the man had decided to conceal his own pursuit by using the same field that Garrett had just entered.

A thin dirt path that had been worn along the timberline remained empty, so Garrett retraced his steps cautiously, all the while calculating how his trailer might adjust his own tract to intersect his target. Garrett continued to move quickly along the parallel path and then stopped behind a column of adolescent junipers that gave him the smallest window to observe the route from which he had just come. In less than a half a minute, the man appeared, slowly and with his right hand clearly gripping a pistol in his pocket.

Garrett crouched low until he was certain his pursuer had passed, and then quickly stepped from the bushes twenty feet behind the operative, who sensed the presence a moment too late. By the time he spun, Garrett's Glock was at high-ready, and Mykhail Vann knew that he would not be able to outdraw the man who had just outmaneuvered him.

Garrett stepped closer. "*Sprichst du Englisch?*"

Garrett picked up a muttered expletive in Russian, before Vann answered, "*Ja.*"

"Ditch it."

Vann tossed his pistol on the ground.

"Let's fast-forward past whatever bullshit story you've concocted," Garrett said. "Who is your target?"

Vann decided to play along, until he could exploit a lapse

of concentration long enough to get to his back-up pistol. "A man with British Intelligence."

"His name?"

"I don't know," Vann replied. "I have a photo."

"How did you know I would be in Switzerland?"

"My handler."

"Who is he?"

"I don't know."

"Bollocks you don't."

Vann equivocated, gauging how best to gain an advantage against someone who was well-trained, and worse, had clearly been expecting him. "My commanding officer from the war."

"Chechen?"

"*Da*," the man replied. "Yes."

"What's his name?"

"Anatoly Ivanov," Vann answered, lying.

"What a coincidence, that's mine as well," Garrett replied, seeing through the deception.

Vann didn't respond, his attention now focused on getting to his second gun as quickly as possible.

"How do you make contact?"

"Encrypted mobile communication."

"When was your last?"

"When I marked you at the station."

"What kind of code do you use?"

"What?"

"Deep-six the halfwit routine," Garrett warned, growing impatient. "Prearranged words to signal a compromised transmission."

Vann hesitated. "If I communicate in Russian, all is ok. In English, and it indicates a problem."

"Were you part of the Scotland operation?"

Vann did not immediately answer, and Garrett stepped closer with his pistol raised, causing Vann to quickly bring his hands closer to his face. "I wasn't in Scotland. We were sent to Munich."

"William Lindsay?"

"Yes," Vann nodded his head. "Lindsay."

"What happened to him?"

"We killed him."

"How?"

Again, Garrett picked up the slightest pause before the man responded. "We shot him and dumped his body in the Isar."

"You're lying, or you would have said 'I' shot him. There's no way your buddy back at the restaurant is the triggerman," Garrett replied. "What happened to Lindsay?"

"He suspected he was being followed and jumped into the river to escape."

"Did he?"

"I don't know."

"How often do you check in with your handler?"

"Every twelve hours."

"Take out your phone and transcribe this message."

Vann produced a mobile from his pocket and pulled up a screen. "What do I say?"

"'The target has been acquired,' in English."

"He'll know there's a problem."

"You were lying about that as well," Garrett replied. "Type it, but before you send it, place the phone on the ground and back away."

Vann did as he was ordered. Garrett picked up the mobile and when he verified that the message was in English, he hit send. "Where is your handler located?"

"I don't know."

The phone vibrated that it had received a reply. It was also in English, and queried Montjoy's location. Garrett answered back with the Baur au Lac hotel, in Zurich.

The reply was immediate.

Stay in place and monitor the objective. Someone will arrive within eight hours.

"Who will he send?"

"Someone who will not fail," Vann replied, and flashed Garrett a smile.

Garrett ignored the ominous warning. "Where is the photo of your target from MI6?"

Vann gestured at the phone.

Garrett tapped a JPEG image saved on the home screen. It was a smartphone snapshot taken of a picture, the one of Montjoy on the steps of 10 Downing.

The photo missing from their grandmother's mantel in North Ballachulish.

"Who sent you this?"

"A force that represents an operation bigger than you or your little team will be able to stop."

Garrett eyed the operative standing in front of him. There

was no rapid rise in his pulse, no rush of blood to the fringes, nor any flash of rage that Garrett needed to control.

He was beyond that now.

The man had just opened his mouth to say something when Garrett calmly leveled his .45 and put a suppressed hollow-point into the forehead of Mykhail Vann.

CHAPTER THIRTY-EIGHT

Prague, Czech Republic

"Smoking a churchwarden in a Barbour on the Charles," the man said as he passed behind Banastre Montjoy and came to a casual stop beside him. He leaned against a wall of the bridge and pulled a white and blue carton from his jacket, which he rhythmically tapped on top of the stone partition. "You should don a Gatsby and round out the cliché."

"It's bloody cold and dreary and I've always favored this view of the Vltava," Montjoy replied, as he watched the man pinch one end of a cigarette nearly flat before lighting the other.

"You and every Jap with a Kodak."

"One of those has gone bankrupt and the other is politically incorrect, mind you."

"You British and your sensitivities." The man took an extended drag. "This is why you lost the Cold War."

"*Pravda* is still writing your headlines, I see."

"We were ahead on points when the Curtain came down. Everyone knows this."

"I noticed no one stood and clapped for an encore." Montjoy extended his hand. "You haven't aged a day."

"Cheap cigarettes and women," the man quipped, returning the gesture. "Both cost more each year, thanks to your capitalism."

"But a drop in the Black Sea, considering all you've gained."

"I lost my dacha near Praskoveevka." The man then muttered to himself, "Goddamned *glasnost.*"

"It's just as well. We had it wired not long after you moved in."

"And all you recorded was me fucking for hours on end." The man gestured at a random brunette who walked by.

Montjoy smiled. He had liked Anatoly Laskin the moment they first met, thirty years earlier in a London pub. The Russian spy had introduced himself as a businessman from Austria, the nuances of his put-on *Vorarlberger* dialect nearly indistinguishable from that of a native of the picturesque Alpine region bordered by Germany, Switzerland, and Lichtenstein.

Moscow had sent Laskin to England in the summer of 1987 to winnow out potential recruits among MI6's up-and-comers. Montjoy had recently returned from assignment in West Germany and knew to be wary of KGB groomers trolling hot spots in search of the next George Blake. Under the cover of Jonas Bauer, a banker from Bregenz, Laskin had approached Montjoy one evening in an upscale tavern in Mayfair and presumed an Englishman's love of football as the pretense to strike up a conversation. Laskin was engaging and polished, and better yet, as far as Montjoy was concerned, a prolific drinker.

A few good laughs turned two lagers into an open tab, and though the lively back-and-forth allowed Montjoy to momentarily forget himself, it was the simplest of slip-ups that roused his suspicion. Laskin had jested in passing of England's failure to qualify for the 1978 World cup. Montjoy responded in German that he had been gobsmacked by "*Das Wunder von Córdoba*," an allusion to Austria's improbable victory over West Germany in Argentina. Even in his inebriated condition, the young operative could see that it took *Herr* Bauer the blink of eye to place the reference, something any true Austrian would have instinctively reacted to with immediate and unrestrained exuberance. Montjoy did not betray any misgivings at the time, and agreed to meet for pints two weeks later.

A fortnight on, in the wake of another epic bender, an SIS team shadowed Laskin back to his modest flat in Clapham. His ensuing behavior would have been credible enough for the agents to dismiss their mark as a waste of time and manpower, had it not been for Montjoy's initial hunch. The persistence paid off the following weekend, when Laskin was surveilled at a sit-down with a known KGB case officer operating out of the Soviet Embassy at Kensington Palace Gardens.

It was determined that Montjoy would continue to meet with Laskin and gradually assume the guise of a disaffected spy. Geoffrey Charlton tutored Montjoy on how to play an effective *dangle*—an agent feigning interest in becoming a double. Montjoy performed the role to perfection. Over the coming months, in between bouts of laughter and shouts of

Tsum Vohl, the Russian began to skillfully chip away at what he believed to be a legitimate crisis of conscience.

England offers much in the way of excess, but it doesn't provide for the collective. Why should such a small minority of wealthy and the well-off benefit off the backs of the worker?

As Montjoy simulated a growing concern as to what could be done to compensate for the imbalance, Laskin suggested a sharing of ideas, in order to bridge the gap between the two extremes. Through Montjoy, MI6 fed the Russian just enough viable intelligence, scattered amongst outdated and useless information, to entice Moscow to pressure their "mole" for greater access. And just when SIS pieced together the makings of an elaborate *dezinformatsiya* operation that had the potential to bear real fruit on the other end, Laskin was abruptly recalled home.

It wasn't until after the Wall came down and his transition to the newly formed Foreign Intelligence Service that the ex-KGB operative begrudgingly accepted he had been an unwitting pawn of the British. Nevertheless, Laskin and Montjoy kept an arm's-length respect for one another, and had remained in touch through back channels between SIS and SVR.

Laskin took one last pull on his cigarette and flicked it over the side of the bridge. "You were a very convincing *podstava.*"

Montjoy watched the meandering river break over a weir and spill around a loch chamber in the distance. "You were a worthy adversary, Anatoly, and up to the challenge."

"If only Moscow shared your view. It took two years to get out from behind that damned desk and back into the field."

Laskin's mobile began to ring, but he ignored it. "I should be angry with you."

"We enjoyed some good times, regardless of our mandated ideologies," Montjoy replied, an intimation that he believed Laskin had been more enamored with Western ways than he let on.

"Perhaps," Laskin replied, "but I suspect it wasn't the need to reminisce that motivated you to contact me, as you English say, out of the blue."

Montjoy began to walk, and Laskin followed. "I need any information you can divulge about a failed operation in the fall of 1984."

Laskin only shrugged his shoulders and produced another cigarette. "Your failure, or ours?"

"Both, perhaps."

"Where?"

"The Oberbaum. We lost an agent. You lost considerably more."

"I didn't realize you were attached to that MI6 fiasco," Laskin noted. "Not withstanding recently deceased SIS officers, where does this come from, after so many years?"

Montjoy took note of Laskin's reference to Lindsay, Charlton, and Halliwell, but effectively downplayed the man's subtle search of a reaction or response. "A ghost has reappeared."

The Russian smiled. "Which one?"

Montjoy took a long draw on his pipe, held it a moment, and let it out as slowly. "*Spindle.*"

Laskin stopped abruptly and shook his head, accentuating

the gesture by waving his finger back and forth. "This is no good for you, Monty. You should walk away and save us both the trouble."

Montjoy decided that in the wake of his uncertainty as to *Spindle's* identity, ambiguity and feigned presumption was the best way to flesh out more from Laskin. "Rumor had it the *Kontora* took care of that problem in the waning hours of the late unpleasantness." "We always took care of our problems," Laskin replied. "Only, *Spindle* wasn't our problem. He was yours."

"He was someone else's as well, if memory serves." Montjoy replied, still fishing.

"We dealt with Malinovsky."

Neither man spoke, Montjoy hoping that Laskin would continue to offer up clues, while his counterpart waited for the subject to be changed. After another moment, Laskin's curiosity got the better of him. "Something for something?"

Montjoy nodded. "That depends on your definition of something."

"Malinovsky was one of yours?"

Montjoy eyed Laskin, whose bearing had taken on a far more somber bent. He was referring to *Operation Failsafe*, MI6's penetration of the *rezidentura* in East Berlin in the early 1980s. The venture proved fairly successful, involving a number of lower-rank staff, until it was blown open by an informant. Though the Soviet station fell into temporary disarray, SIS never discovered who was responsible for *Failsafe's* exposure. "That operation never reached the upper ranks," Montjoy assured Laskin.

"But you would have known, *Da*?"

"I would have known," Montjoy lied again. He was too subordinate at the time to be allowed full access.

Laskin seemed to relax at the revelation, though he continued to probe. "Someone high-up had been turned, of this we were certain."

"Some around SIS believe you were the mole, and the intelligence I've seen makes a compelling case," Montjoy replied as the men neared the end of the overpass.

Laskin stopped to light another cigarette, but did not respond.

"Quid pro, Toly—"

"Markus Heinrich is not his real name."

"Not exactly a company secret." Montjoy kept up the pretense that he was already privy to what Laskin revealed.

"But you did not know that *Spindle* isn't German, did you? Heinrich was born Alexei Arkipov, a Russian. The best spymasters always are, and *Spindle* is one of the finest we ever produced. He disappeared in 1996, in the wake of the accusations against him because of Chechnya, lies created by the CIA as retaliation for his Cold War heroics against the West," Laskin said proudly, donning his hat. "If not for that, Arkipov would be running the FSB today."

Montjoy was about to respond, but Laskin cut him off, assuming that Montjoy was already aware of the circumstances of Heinrich's vanishing act, and his alternate identity. The Russian was clearly growing annoyed that everything he divulged seemed to be information Montjoy was already knowledgeable of. "There is something else." He reached into his jacket, and pulled out a weathered Polaroid photo. "This is Sergei Malinovsky talking with the British agent we captured in 1984. It was taken just before the Oberbaum incident. Proof of what you pretend to be unknowledgeable of."

Montjoy glanced at the photo. "There is nothing in our files that points to Malinovsky as the mole, Anatoly, nor am I certain what happened to our man."

"And you think I know?" Laskin returned the favor of playing dumb.

"Did the KGB glean anything during its interrogation?"

"Such things can slip the mind, so many years after."

Both men stood in momentary silence. "Some secrets can remain safe, Anatoly, as would your place with the SVR."

"It's easy to make such a claim, working in the West. The memories, and rivalries, run deep and remain bitter in other places," Laskin replied. "What you're asking, I have no answers to. But for anyone who is still curious, I would suggest they seek out a man named Egon Schultz, a guard stationed at the Oberbaum during the time your agent went missing. Who can say what some men know?"

Montjoy eyed Laskin for a moment, and then held up the photo. "Can I keep this?"

"*Da.*"

"Thank you."

"That's more than you gave me, and you're welcome."

"I owe you."

"Yes, you do." Laskin turned and disappeared into the crowd.

PART III

CHAPTER THIRTY-NINE

Helsinki, Finland
January 1985

*T*he fishing boat struggled to maintain its course in the rough waters of the Baltic Sea. In the constant pitch and roll, the battered agent splayed out on a wooden bench in the small vessel cycled between nausea and semiconsciousness. He labored to piece together the last fifteen hours, amid violent bouts of vomiting the small amount of food and water he had been allowed.

He could remember being jostled awake in the middle of the night. This time, there were no bright lights to prevent the return of much-needed sleep, no shouts or insults, nor shots to the back of his neck with a rubber baton. He would have barely noticed it anyway, as there was little left to bruise, break, or burn. His right arm hung useless at his side, having been fractured days earlier, while his left eye was swollen shut. The ache of the engorged socket was interrupted only by the flaring pain of cigarette burns on his eyelids.

He could recall the fresh air, and freezing cold. It was the first time he had left the sweltering confines of the basement cell and interrogation chamber in almost two weeks, by his best guess, and the sudden drop in temperature was a welcome shock to the system. He remembered the smell of nicotine and the fumes of a vehicle idling nearby, and guards speaking in low voices. Of being loaded into the back of a truck and driven a short distance before the vehicle slowed and he was shoved out.

The taste of dirt, and the glorious scent of wet grass.

Lying in a ditch for what seemed an eternity.

The approach of another vehicle, the scrape of shoes on the road, and the ties and blindfold removed.

Keep still and don't make a sound, the agent hardly needed to be warned as he was hustled into the boot of a black Volga. The drive from Riga to Tallinn, on the Estonian coast, had lasted almost seven miserable hours. The circuitous route, he had been informed in English when they arrived, was necessary to avoid main roads and roving patrols.

The agent stood on the bench to which he had clung for much of the passage across the Gulf of Finland and could see the faint lights of a coastline through the brackish mist frozen on the glassed-in cabin. The pilot had not spoken since they pushed off a rocky embankment in the pitch-dark three hours earlier, though the man now muttered to himself in Swedish as he searched the shoreline.

He throttled down as they approached a dock that jutted from an unpaved road, near two men standing alongside a car and another who guided the boat to a stop, before securing the bow cleat with a rope hitched to a wooden piling.

A man on the bank, dressed in a black suit and trilby, spun his finger in a rapid circle, the gesture to hurry.

The agent thanked the skipper, who only nodded. He stepped

shakily off the stern and onto the wooden slats of a ramshackle jetty in Helsinki.

Onto firm ground, and freedom.

CHAPTER FORTY

Strasbourg, France

Banastre Montjoy flipped through a newspaper inside an Illy Express coffee kiosk in the main station in Strasbourg. As he glossed over mind-numbingly vacuous articles, the deputy chief considered what he had learned from his conversation with Laskin. The SVR head of section in Prague had divulged far more than Montjoy expected, particularly where outstanding intelligence from a long-forgotten operation was concerned.

Time had a way of watering down old rivalries, and wounds, but what his former Cold War nemesis revealed went well beyond some newfound notion of Nixonian-era *détente*.

It was *glasnost* on steroids, and Laskin could be more than just called on the carpet should his superiors in Moscow become wise to the Charles Bridge conversation. The Russian had chosen to pass on what went well beyond office gossip for a reason, and Montjoy needed to determine what that motivation was.

Laskin had disclosed that *Spindle* was Alexei Arkipov, a KGB agent who had operated under the name Markus Heinrich while stationed in East Germany. Montjoy could vaguely recall a Stasi officer named Heinrich during his own posting in West Berlin, but he certainly remembered when the rumor began to circulate that a rising star in Russian Intelligence had drowned while on vacation at the Black Sea in 1996.

Montjoy had little knowledge of Sergei Malinovsky's disappearance and assumed murder in late 1984, though its significance had likely fallen by the wayside in the wake of successive intelligence failures in East Germany after the Oberbaum incident. What was still uncertain was the fate of MI6's agent in East Berlin, and what information a lowly border guard named Egon Schultz could possibly be privy to that would still be relevant.

Montjoy's meeting with Laskin had solved one small part of a puzzle at the same time it created more pieces. He would have to locate Schultz quickly and hope the man would be willing to meet, remember small details from something that happened three decades earlier, and be induced to disclose what he knew. Until then, the deputy chief needed reach out to someone else he had never met, but whom his grandmother had trusted more than any other colleague during her tenure at SIS. Verity Scott was a legend around MI6, and Madeleine Halliwell had once confided to her grandson that Scott would serve him well if he ever found himself in a spot he could not readily work his way out from.

Montjoy's flight to Brest Bretagne, where Scott resided, was due out in less than ninety minutes, and Samantha Anderton was running late. Montjoy had just considered hopping the fast shuttle to the airport when she casually approached the stand-up counter and set down an espresso and a scone.

"Just in the nick," Montjoy said in a low voice and without addressing her directly.

Anderton pulled out a Paperwhite and pretended to read. "Apologies, the train from Lindau was delayed."

"You've got the package?"

Anderton pulled the journal from her bag and placed it on the bar between them. "I've also got a trailer in tow."

"Do you see that person now?"

"No. He looks Eastern European, stands at just over six feet with black hair, and is wearing dark blue jeans and a light-colored jacket."

"He's only here to monitor and report my location, I'd wager," Montjoy replied.

"Where will you go?"

"I'm off to the coast, and while I'm away I need you to find someone, which might amount to a difficult task. A man who went by the name Jean René Bertrand when I knew him in West Berlin. The last I heard, he was a winemaker in the Moselle Valley in Luxembourg, using his vineyard as a front for black market truffles."

Anderton stifled a laugh. "There's a black market for truffles?"

"There is a black market for everything. If you don't believe me, visit the Camden Town markets on the weekend."

"Who is he?"

"That is a good question. Bertrand was reportedly born in Paris sometime around 1955 and raised across Europe until he joined French Intelligence in the late 1970s. He was stationed in West Germany during much of the 1980s, operating on both sides of the Wall, literally and figuratively. Rumor had it he was attached to the *Direction de la Surveillance*. However, as the DST was a small counterintelligence agency that was not supposed to operate outside France, no one was really certain."

"He liaised with MI6?"

"*Liaised* is one word for what he did," Montjoy replied. "Bertrand seemed to know everything about what was going on in Berlin, which could only mean he was flirting with the other side on occasion. Perhaps the French were dangling him out to see if Moscow would bite, and it's possible they did. I know Bertrand was the man to see to fill in gaps, and SIS used him as much as the French spy deigned to entertain an audience with us. Be forewarned that he is urbane and charming, and I'll leave it to you to decide if you trust him enough to ask for and accept his assistance, should he have anything to offer."

"How well did you know him?"

"I'm not sure anyone really knew René, but we got on well enough and shared a few stories over a drink now and again back in the day."

"Anything else?"

"He'll do everything he can to seduce you, so mind your back."

"Among other things," Anderton joked.

"Indeed," Montjoy gave her a sideways glance.

"I see the man who's been following me," Anderton said,

using the interior glass to monitor the exterior of the coffee shop behind them.

Montjoy glance up momentarily. "With luck, he's not seen through our clumsy attempt to chat surreptitiously. Stay here long enough to ensure your pursuer picks you back up. Head to the Régent Petite France and Spa, the five-star down the bridge from where I am lodged. Loiter in the lobby long enough for him to assume that you, and by extension I, are staying at the hotel. Once you're certain your shadow has taken the bait, shake him, and find Bertrand."

"Yes, sir."

"Sam, I don't need to warn you to look after yourself. It's me they're after, but it doesn't preclude an attempt to extract information from you."

"You as well, sir."

"We'll rendezvous when I return from Locronan."

CHAPTER FORTY-ONE

FBI Headquarters
Washington, D.C.

Fingerprints returned from the Europol database, the law enforcement agency of the European Union based in The Hague, listed the dead foreigner from Santee as Andrei Beslan. The forty-three-year-old Chechen was wanted foremost by Interpol for his links to organized criminal gangs operating throughout Eastern Europe. The former lieutenant in the Russian Army was also suspected of committing war atrocities during the Second Chechen War.

Beslan had dropped off the radar three years earlier. How and why he turned up in a lake in South Carolina shot twice in the chest and tethered to a sunken speedboat with a dead DNR agent, was the reason Special Agent Clair Donnelly had cleared her desk of all other cases for the foreseeable future.

Donnelly, in the highly efficient and ordered manner that had seen her promoted quickly through the FBI ranks from a field office in Nebraska to the Holy Grail of locations, Washington, D.C., had already organized the known and assumed facts of the case into a single dossier for the team assigned to her. Since assuming the investigation from a local field office in Columbia, Donnelly had moved quickly to determine what she was dealing with.

She knew that Beslan had arrived into Charlotte Douglas almost two weeks earlier as Kevin Greene, a Raleigh businessman supposedly returning from vacation in Hamburg. He had connected through Frankfurt, spoke passable German according to an attendant who remembered flirting with him in the first-class section of his Lufthansa flight, and the man's false passport showed that he had flown out of North Carolina two weeks before that, ostensibly on a business trip abroad. The stamps, it turned out, were fake, as was his driver's license.

Donnelly had a good idea of who the Chechen wasn't. What he *was* doing in the United States, traveling on false credentials and carrying an unlicensed Heckler & Koch, along with a large amount of cash, was proving difficult to determine. The tattoos on his knees, single stars on each, was a Russian sign of respect and warned that Beslan would bow before no man.

The other victim, Jeffrey Cox, had been with the Department of Natural Resources for eight years. Before that, he was a police officer in Richland County, South Carolina, and prior to joining the force, the Airborne Ranger had been highly decorated during three tours in Afghanistan. He had been happily married, by all accounts, for twelve years, and he and his wife were expecting their third child that December.

The last entry in Cox's waterproof logbook had been for a GMC Denali, with a partial North Carolina license plate consisting of three letters and two numbers. It was assumed that he had been knocked unconscious, based on the contusion at the base of his skull, while writing Beslan a ticket.

How the officer ended up next to Beslan, who Donnelly assumed was shot by the same man that strangled Cox, was the missing link her team were struggling to connect. Video footage from Charlotte Douglas showed that Beslan had not flown into the U.S. with anyone, at least no one who stood out. Those seated around the man on the flight did not remember him, and each of those passengers had been cleared, for the moment, as having no obvious or suspicious links to the Chechen. Passengers checked on either side of Beslan through passport control had also passed interviews and security checks.

Everyone else on the Lufthansa connection from Frankfurt had also been checked and dismissed, so if Beslan had a partner, he had not arrived on his flight. The passenger manifests of other planes that had landed the same day, and other inbound flights on either side of that Wednesday, were proving to be a time-consuming headache to track down and interview, and Donnelly feared it would amount to little more than a pointless endeavor.

Donnelly had also begun to suspect that Beslan was connected to the death of a New York businessman, gunned down nearby the same morning the DNR agent disappeared.

Donnelly's phone rang. A black Denali with North Carolina tags, faked and not registered with the DMV, had been located in Boston. Waterfront cameras had recorded a man exiting the vehicle and ostensibly linking up with a second person along the Harborwalk. Hats and sunglasses made facial recognition an impossibility, and the pair had split not long after entering the MBTA stop at the aquarium.

The second call came in an hour later. The FBI, Donnelly was informed, would continue to assist as needed, but the case was being commandeered by another agency.

The line went dead before Donnelly could inquire which one.

CHAPTER FORTY-TWO

Gorky Park
Moscow, Russia

Vasily Markov waited near a paddleboat rental at *Golitsynskiye Prudy*. It was a pleasantly crisp day, colder than average for late September, and the queue at the dock stretched back beyond the turnstile. He watched a teenage worker attempt to disentangle a pile of life jackets left in a twisted heap, finally cursing aloud when the young man realized he was making it worse.

The afternoon was overcast, with rain expected to begin at any moment and grow heavier through the early evening. Markov had stupidly left his umbrella in a café near Moscow's Red Square earlier that morning. He had realized the mistake after only one block and quickly returned to retrieve it, but someone else had decided they needed it more than he did. It had been a gift from his wife, an expensive James Smith & Sons purchased in London during her last trip to the U.K. She had settled on a bright red brolly because it was assumed her husband would not so carelessly misplace something that was seemingly impossible to miss, and which also cost five thousand rubles.

Markov's frantic search through old KGB records had so far turned up nothing out of the ordinary, at least any incriminating information that intimated he might have engaged in unapproved contact with the British during his final years in East Germany. He had collected perhaps half the files that involved Charlton, Halliwell, and Montjoy, but they too had failed to tell him anything he didn't already know.

What prompted his surreptitious trip to Gorky Park that morning had come in the form of a newly intercepted transcript of a bugged conversation between an SVR station chief in Prague and the man everyone seemed to be searching for, the deputy chief of MI6. In the conversation with Banastre Montjoy, Anatoly Laskin had revealed details of a top-secret KGB operation from the Oberbaum in 1984, further intimating that a guard from the bridge that day might be in possession of information beneficial to the British.

Why Laskin had now chosen to engage in such obviously treasonous behavior was something Moscow would certainly investigate as soon as the recording made its way through the proper channels. What troubled Markov more than Laskin's stupidity was that they both had served together in East Berlin, and had worked closely on more than one operation. The timing of Laskin's contact with the very man who was clearly investigating the coordinated attack against retired SIS operatives could not be coincidental. With each passing day, and new revelation, Markov was becoming worried that if he didn't act quickly to cordon off what appeared to be a growing conflagration, he would soon be caught up in some belated interagency cleaning of house linked to Cold War treachery.

Markov had just checked his watch for the fourth time in as many minutes when it began to drizzle. He turned his collar up and searched for a covered area within walking distance, but then caught sight of the woman with whom he had arranged to rendezvous. She was on the opposite side of the man-made lake and moving fluidly through the crowd that mingled outside the Ostrovok Restaurant. Markov decided to meet her en route and began to walk along the waterfront path. He increased his speed, hoping to get less wet by doing so, though the trick never seemed to work.

Markov had crossed paths with Elena Mullova several times over the course of her career in the *Glavnoye Razvedyvatel'noye Upravleniye*. The thirty-two-year-old Muscovite was born to influential parents who had at one time been part of the *nomenklatura*, which would have guaranteed their daughter a comfortable ascension up the Communist hierarchy. Because such positions had dried up as quickly as had Russia's GDP after 1990, the promising university student at Moscow State University abandoned her studies to join the GRU. Eventually rising to the rank of senior lieutenant in the Main Intelligence Directorate of the Russian Armed Forces, the athletic and highly intelligent officer worked primarily in the Second Directorate, which oversaw operations in the Western Hemisphere. Mullova was clever and capable and tasked with liaising with Department Three, in charge of operations that involved Spetsnaz operatives.

Two years earlier, Mullova herself had gutted out the rigors of Special Forces training, one of the first women to do so, and upon completion was reassigned to Directorate S, which oversaw the SVR's "illegals" program of infiltration agents operating under unofficial cover abroad.

But Markov suspected that Mullova possessed another skill, something her father had been particularly adept at during his time in the KGB's infamous Thirteenth Directorate, the department that specialized in "liquid affairs."

Markov intercepted Mullova at a bridge over a smaller pond. She did not greet him, nor smile, and when Markov turned in the direction of the Moskva River, Mullova followed without speaking. The rain had eased up, so Markov bypassed the protection of the underpass in favor of a circular overlook in the shadow of a large pedestrian bridge that spanned the river. The pair stood in silence and waited for several sightseers to pass by.

Markov lit a cigarette. "I assume you weren't followed."

"Only by several drunken sailors after I stepped off the metro at *Oktyabr'skaya.*"

"How is your father?"

"In the hospital. Stomach cancer."

"I'm sorry."

"So is he."

Markov offered her a cigarette, but Mullova shook her head. She watched a couple strolling along the promenade suddenly come to a stop, the second time they had done so. A child caught up to them and the family continued down the river walk.

Markov allowed his gaze to linger on Mullova a moment longer than would have been deemed acceptable had she been looking directly at him. He decided that while Mullova was not attractive in the classical Russian sense, her sharp, dark features, long black hair pulled perpetually back in a braid, and shapely figure made her as desirable as any woman Markov had seen in Moscow.

Markov shook off the growing desire to attempt to seduce the young officer, and refocused on the job at hand.

The last time he had worked with her father was thirty-five years earlier, when their respective intelligence departments were collaborating on *Operation Ryan*. While the KGB's ambitious attempt to monitor U.S. military bases, radar, and communication in an effort to determine whether their nuclear-capable nemesis was massing for a first strike had been bold, it ultimately failed.

There was something about Victor Mullova that Markov had not entirely trusted, though his reputation as a committed Party member was beyond dispute. What Markov knew of his daughter, other than her background, was that she could be as ruthlessly cold and efficient as her predecessor.

"I need you in Europe," Markov said, certain that Mullova had caught him staring in her periphery.

"The assignment?"

"One we cannot simply smash with the proverbial Russian hammer."

"Which means, I assume, it is unsanctioned."

Markov took another drag on his Marlboro, before dropping the half-smoked butt to the ground and grinding it out with his toe. "It means you'll report only to me, is that understood?"

"*Da*," Mullova replied.

"Eight days ago, two, possibly three, retired MI6 operatives, all high-ranking officers, were assassinated across
Europe. In the aftermath, the current deputy chief of SIS, a
man named Banastre Montjoy, took a leave of absence and left
England. Yesterday, he turned up in *Czechia* and met secretly
with the SVR's *rezidentura* in Prague, a man name Anatoly
Laskin. Laskin has long had the reputation of being a little
too forthcoming with our adversaries in the West, and there
are some who believe he is guilty of a much more grievous
offense. Accordingly, we have had him intermittently followed
and bugged over the last few years.

"In his conversation with Montjoy, Laskin referenced, in
the *present* tense, a former Stasi operative and KGB agent code-
named *Spindle*, a man named Alexei Arkipov, who supposedly
died in 1996. Laskin also gave Montjoy a photograph of a
British Cold War agent meeting with Sergei Malinovsky in
1984, a Russian officer who was subsequently executed for
suspicion of being a double agent."

It had begun to rain again, and the two climbed the stairs
to the Pushkinsky Bridge in order to cross the Moskva River.
Markov began to turn up his collar and pull it closed when
Mullova handed him her umbrella.

"Take mine," Mullova said.

"Are you certain?"

"I have another."

"*Spaseeba*," Markov said, popping it open. "In his conversation with Montjoy, Laskin also foolishly disclosed the name
of a border guard who had been stationed at the Oberbaum
Bridge where the MI6 operative was arrested after meeting

with Malinovsky. I need to know what information a man named Egon Schultz is privy to, and if and how it relates to the recently deceased British agents. Schultz still lives in Berlin, and now works as a mailman."

"All of this is tied together?"

"You'll let me know, I'm certain," Markov replied. "Find out what Laskin is hiding and what Schultz knows." He pulled a thumb drive from his jacket, along with a mobile. "All the files you'll need. Memorize them and then burn it."

CHAPTER FORTY-THREE

Montreal, Canada

Emile Chénard stood and surveyed the intelligence that was splayed across nearly every inch of an oak table in the dining room of his two-story flat in the oldest section of Montreal. With its cobblestone streets, centuries-old buildings, and quaint collection of cafés and boutiques, *Le Vieux-Port* possessed all the charming character and ambience of Old Europe, with a fraction of its logistical headaches and expense. Chénard's converted apartment, sizeable by the typical standard of Saint-Paul Street, was located along the Saint Lawrence River and afforded him an enviable vista of the harbor and St. Helen's Island.

On the other hand, Chénard's former bird's-eye view of the meticulously coordinated plan to eliminate four MI6 officers had since been narrowed to the size of a pigeonhole. Instead of overseeing the operation from the proverbial thirty-thousand feet, he was now standing at ground level, four thousand miles away and reliant on someone else's skill and surveillance capabilities to relocate the deputy chief of SIS.

Chénard cursed to himself, not for the first time since

Riker mishandled what should have been the clean and tidy sanction of Banastre Montjoy.

He again shuffled between maps and hand-scribbled memos in the hopeless endeavor of second-guessing where his remaining target might be. Chénard had received conflicting reports from his Alpha Group operatives concerning Montjoy's movements and whereabouts. Mykhail Vann had confirmed that the deputy chief was holed up in a luxury hotel in Switzerland. Artem Ivanenko had split from Vann in Germany and followed his mark to France. The operative had witnessed the woman from Lindau rendezvous with someone in the main Strasbourg train station whom he was certain was Montjoy. Ivanenko had been unable to follow the man, so he tailed the woman to a five-star accommodation in the *La Petite France* district of the city, and had been sitting on the hotel since.

It was a two-hour journey by rail between the two cities and entirely possible that Montjoy had in fact been seen in both places at what seemed to be the same time during his transition from one location to the other.

Chénard poured himself a vodka and wondered if he should risk flying to Europe to oversee the operation from ground level. He had decided against it at the last moment, and now realized that he had little choice but to rely on the skill of his operatives. Riker, who had been awaiting orders in Paris, was now en route to the Baur au Lac hotel in Zurich, while Tomas Karlson had been dispatched from London to Strasbourg to monitor the Régent Petite France and Spa.

He would pay whomever was first to the prize.

Chénard considered how the deaths of Charlton, Lindsay, and Halliwell might be playing out at MI6. That all had occurred in a twenty-four-hour period would have grabbed the attention of someone at SIS, though perhaps not enough to arouse sufficient suspicion to conduct an official inquiry.

At least, not yet.

Before that happened, the death of its deputy chief was paramount. It was intended to be a violent reprisal for what had been done to Chénard twenty-two years earlier.

Montjoy was the key.

CHAPTER FORTY-FOUR

Federal Security Service
Moscow, Russia

B oris Golitsyn finished dinner at his desk in a corner office at FSB headquarters on Lubyanka Square. It had been a fairly calm week in the Directorate of Counterintelligence Operations for Russia's Federal Security Service, other than the parade of rain clouds that seemed to descend and pass over, regroup, and then storm the square once again. Golitsyn peered across the street at the massive structure that once housed the FSB's famous predecessor agency, the KGB. He was certain he could make out the window near the top floor that had once been his, when he was with the First Main Directorate, responsible for foreign operations and intelligence.

When things used to be done the right way, the Soviet way,
Golitsyn thought to himself.

The nephew of a respected NKVD officer, Golitsyn had graduated from Moscow State Institute of International Relations before his posting to the Soviet Embassy in East Berlin in 1974. While stationed in East Germany, the young agent had been particularly adept at reading people and situations.

He was soon promoted and put in charge of a section tasked with infiltrating foreign businesses and embassies.

Golitsyn's MO for turning assets varied, depending on the individual and circumstance, though he found the most effective way to be through the use of honey traps. Employing female operatives and local whores, Golitsyn would target vulnerable men, disaffected with their jobs or dissatisfied with their wives. Once a mark had been singled out and seduced, a signal would be placed in the hotel window, and an agent playing the "husband" of the woman pretending to be the adulterous wife would burst in to interrupt the illicit carnal interlude. Faced with exposure and the reality of losing both a spouse and a cushy position abroad, a small number of American and British diplomats elected to spy for the USSR. Others refused, and suffered the consequences. A few, rather than be blackmailed in order to save their cover from being blown, chose instead to blow their own brains out.

By his eighth year in the GDR, Golitsyn had created more double agents willing to spy for the Soviet Union than anyone ese in the KGB office or the Stasi directorate with whom they liaised. The talented officer rose quickly through the ranks, and in the fall of 1983 was made head of station.

It was then that everything changed. In the span of just six months after being put in charge of the *rezidentura*, Golitsyn began to realize that formerly reliable assets were suddenly turning up empty-handed, or in possession of worthless intelligence. Moreover, some of the KGB's deepest-cover operatives and double agents were being exposed, arrested, and expelled from Western countries.

No matter what precautions Golitsyn took in an effort to ramp up its security protocol, the station continued to suffer a noticeable lag in its performance.

A deficit that Moscow would have soon noticed as well.

By the summer of 1984, Golitsyn recognized that he had a mole, either inside Stasi headquarters, or in his own office.

Golitsyn turned his attention back to a stack of files he had requisitioned, searching for anything that might relate to the arrest of a British agent in East Germany in 1984. His fruitless search was interrupted by a knock on his office door. Golitsyn saw Elena Mullova standing in his entryway and bid her to enter and shut the door. "What did Markov want?"

Mullova handed her chief the thumb drive and detailed everything that Markov had discussed.

"And the umbrella?" Golitsyn asked. "Did he take it?"

"*Da.*"

Once he got wind that Markov wanted to more closely monitor Anatoly Laskin, SVR's head of station in Prague, Golitsyn decided it was time to watch the watcher. Both Markov and Laskin had been posted to East Germany during his tenure, and Golitsyn had never fully trusted either man. It had been Laskin who had Sergei Malinovsky arrested on suspicion of spying for the British, and while the leaks originating from Golitsyn's office slowed in the aftermath of Malinovsky's execution, they never fully stopped. Moreover, Golitsyn suspected there had been other overtures from the British that both Markov and Laskin had failed to fully disclose during their tenures in East Berlin.

Markov himself clearly suspected that Laskin was hiding

something, and so, by keeping tabs on both men, Golitsyn could kill two birds with one stone. Because there seemed to be no small number in Russian Intelligence, even some hardened KGB holdovers, who wished for the past to remain buried, Golitsyn chose to keep his operation against Markov off the books. He bypassed the bureaucratic headache of requisitioning formal surveillance and instead resorted to old-school tactics. Golitsyn had several FSB agents follow Markov over the course of several weeks, knowing he would at some point put down or potentially leave behind the umbrella the man always seemed to carry. When Markov finally did, at a coffee shop near Red Square, one of Golitsyn's men snatched it. Mullova then offered hers in the park, which had been specially upfitted with a listening device and mini-transponder.

Golitsyn pocketed the thumb drive. "Report back to me once you've talked with Laskin and Schultz."

"Yes, sir."

"And if necessary, do what needs to be done."

CHAPTER FORTY-FIVE

Airspace over France

The flight from Strasbourg to Brest Bretagne, a three-hour nonstop, was smooth compared to everything else Banastre Montjoy had been attempting to sort out over the last week. En route to the northwest corner of France, the deputy chief began to worry that his gambit using Anderton as a lure in Lindau would fail if he couldn't coordinate his own end as bait for an unknown assassin who had surely been alerted to Montjoy's presence in Strasbourg.

Coasting at thirty thousand feet and momentarily safe from what was happening far below, Montjoy decided to enjoy a scotch and a small snack before taking a crack at the journal. He finished what was clearly an inferior whiskey and had just requested something better, when he finally opened the worn ledger and began to flip through its pages. The book itself looked ancient, and his grandmother had been diligent in recording the details, albeit limited, of operations between 1961 and the collapse of the Soviet Union. The existence of such a compilation would be considered a violation of espionage protocol, but Halliwell had only included dates, code names, and locations.

That she felt compelled to keep the journal at all, as well as hide it away from all others, spoke to some misgiving his grandmother must have had. What that concern was, Montjoy hoped he could uncover.

The deputy chief leafed through the earliest entries with only a passing interest, though it was obvious that his grandmother had been attached to some of the more famous operations in British Cold War intelligence. He would backtrack through the years at a later time, for at the moment Montjoy was interested in one date only. He flipped to 1984 and thumbed forward to November.

There, his grandmother had clipped two photographs and penned two lines.

Safeguard. Castor.
Turnkey. Pollux.

CHAPTER FORTY-SIX

Remich, Luxembourg

The rail ride through the countryside between Strasbourg and Remich had been pleasant, despite the last leg of the trip finishing on a crowded bus. It was Samantha Anderton's first visit to Luxembourg, a country Montjoy liked to muse was one whose residents clearly believed that their hands and pockets were inseparable. Known as the pearl of the southeastern winemaking region, the small town on the Moselle River that split the border with Germany was idyllic, and Anderton made up her mind to return on holiday.

Despite Montjoy's uncertainty, it had taken Anderton little effort to locate Jean René Bertrand. The man was listed in a directory of well-known vineyards in the Moselle Valley, which included an address and business number. He had been pleasant over the phone, and when Anderton asked if Bertrand was available to discuss a possible partnership with her new restaurant, he had agreed to host a get-together once he was able to free up time in his very busy schedule. Bertrand then suggested they conclude their conversation over FaceTime in order for him to get a better idea of who he would be working with. After seeing Anderton, the winemaker proposed they meet the next day.

Anderton quickly covered the short distance between the train station and the posh restaurant where Bertrand had arranged to meet for a late lunch. As she approached, a well-dressed man in a crème-colored suit smiled from the portico. He was tanned and handsome, and his lightly graying hair was stylishly coiffed back.

"You must be Samantha."

"Mr. Bertrand," Anderton replied, extending her hand. "Call me Sam."

"How wonderful to meet you, Sam," Bertrand replied, but instead of shaking her hand, he clasped her shoulders and leaned in to give Anderton a customary kiss on each cheek, allowing the second peck to linger a bit longer than ceremony dictated. "Call me René," he said after stepping back and giving her the once-over, for a second time.

"Certainly, René."

"You must be starving, after such a long journey."

"The trip was only two hours and I ate something on the train."

"Nonsense," Bertrand said, as he led her up the stairs of Domaine La Forêt, past the maître d', and to a nice table he had reserved near the window. "Here you will find a lovely French fare, in addition to specials that feature the best of the Luxembourgish cuisine." He pulled out her chair and Anderton sat down with a "Thank you." Bertrand touched the arm of a passing waiter, who paused and addressed him deferentially. "*Oui, Monsieur Bertrand*?"

"*Une bouteille de vin rouge, s'il vous plaît, Michel.*"

"*Bien sûr.*"

Anderton stopped the server before he left. "*Un thé Earl Grey, s'il vous plaît.*"

"*Avec plaisir, madame.*"

"Someone from the U.K. who speaks something other than English? Now, I am impressed. And here I thought you were merely a pretty face."

"You flatter me, *monsieur*," Anderton replied. "Something at which I'm certain you are quite practiced."

"And you insult me, *mademoiselle*." Bertrand gave her a mock frown and clasped his hands in feigned offense. "Do you suggest I act this way with all beautiful women? And, let me add, you are quite beautiful."

"No, I'm sure I'm the first," Anderton replied good-naturedly.

"Tell me about yourself. What can I do for you and your restaurant?"

Since time was of the essence, Anderton knew she was forced to broach the actual reason for her journey in a less nuanced way than ceremony would typically dictate. "I hear you're the man to see about truffles."

A subtle smile indicated that Bertrand recognized Anderton had not come to discuss wines, or anything else concerning the culinary business. "Indeed," he finally replied, "but, they can be quite expensive, depending on what kind of truffle you are looking for."

"Something small. Something that wouldn't cost you very much, and which might help a friend."

Bertrand shrugged his shoulders in an exaggerated manner. "I have many acquaintances. You must be more specific."

"Someone who, like you, would give the same response were the situation reversed. Call him an old friend."

"I had many of those too, my dear, provided the price was right." Bertrand raised a hand as Anderton was about to reply. "Let us see how well I do, discovering who this particular friend might be. You are English on one side, but something else on the other. Neither French nor Belgique, I think, and though your complexion suggests distant Spanish or Northern Italian, I would wager Welch."

"I'm impressed," Anderton replied.

"Not yet." The Frenchman held up a finger to signal he wasn't finished. "I still need to determine what kind of palate you have. You're far too interesting to be drawn into the ranks of those line cooks at Thames House. Such a boring appetite, always sniffing around their own house and feeding off the scraps," Bertrand said, making an unflattering reference to MI5, England's Security Service. "No, I think yours is a more refined taste, something exotic and better served a bit further down the river, at the Embankment. *Oui?*"

"*Oui*," Anderton answered. "*Très bon.*"

"Excellent! Then you'll indulge an older man and drink with me."

"Only if you'll indulge me with a few answers."

"That depends on the questions."

"The Cold War kind."

"By which you mean, the variety best kept in some dark place."

"Like a truffle, I imagine."

Bertrand smiled. "Someone so clever would have found their niche nicely back in that day. Nevertheless, the answers you seek are still the sort which can be damaging to some, so many years after." Bertrand refilled his wine glass. "What has our mutual friend told you about me?"

"That you were a man with his fingers in a lot of pies."

"True, in so many ways," Bertrand replied, and smiled as he took a sip of wine. "I am a man of varied taste, and I can say with certainly that trafficking in intelligence is no different than truffles. It all depends on what someone is willing to pay."

"What would a small bite cost me?"

"You have so much to offer, *ma chérie*." Bertrand embellished the gesture of looking Anderton up and down. "For a truffle, mind you, I can get one thousand to three thousand Euros for French blacks and Italian whites, respectively."

"What I'm after is seldom black and white."

"Information rarely is, and, were we back in West Berlin, that which you seek would be priced at more than what you might be willing to give up. Such was the cost in that time and place. But, for Monty, I'll make an exception."

"Bravo. *Monsieur* Bertrand," Anderton replied. "He said you were very shrewd."

"Please, I must insist you call me René, though I would beg you to wait until I can be of some assistance before you thank me. I hope Banastre is doing well."

"In a bit of trouble, I'm afraid."

"The kind that would have to do with Geoffrey, William, and Madeleine?"

"Possibly."

"You imagine I would know something about their deaths?"

"Perhaps, indirectly. Mr. Montjoy suggested you might be able to cast some light on an old operation."

"I prefer the shadows."

"He said that you seemed to know something about everything going on in East Berlin."

"Better than knowing everything about nothing, like so many British agents back then," Bertrand replied disdainfully.

"What do you know of one who disappeared in November, 1984?"

"The same as everyone else, that he went missing."

"Where were you?"

"The same place as everyone else, *there*." Bertrand took another sip of wine, and gestured at Anderton to follow suit. "Perhaps a better question would be, why did your agent just up and vanish?"

"He panicked and was apprehended."

"Panicked, or was he betrayed?"

"Both, perhaps."

"But they are quite different, *non*?"

"What do you know?"

"That depends on what you can tell me."

Anderton hesitated, remembering Montjoy's warning. "Very little, at this point. Someone has removed or destroyed much of the files related to the operation."

"Which would lead me to assume it was the latter."

"Our agent disappeared after he was arrested."

"As was the fate of most who ended up in the care of the KGB."

"Did you liaise with anyone from MI6?"

"It depends on how you define the term. I liaised quite frequently with some of your comelier female agents."

"Did anyone in particular stand out?"

"Someone always does," Bertrand replied, reminiscing. "I was smitten with a woman ten years my senior, an agent named Verity Scott. You might even call it love. In the end, I think she was only using me for information."

"You remember something, don't you?"

"I heard something, perhaps," Bertrand replied. "A name attached to the Oberbaum operation, and the disappearance of your agent."

"From what source?'

"Our wonderful friends at Langley," Bertrand answered sarcastically.

"What was the name?"

"*Gemini.*"

"*Gemini*? As in, twins?"

"Literally, Latin for twins, yes," Bertrand replied. "Two men on a bridge, *oui*?"

Anderton shook her head, not understanding what Bertrand meant.

"Picture its zodiac symbol."

Anderton did, and suddenly nodded in agreement. "It does resemble two men on a bridge. What does it mean?"

"Nothing to me."

Anderton frowned. "Do you recall anything else?"

"I'm afraid not, nor can I guarantee that *Gemini* has something to do with anything."

The two sat quietly for a moment as Anderton considered the implications of what Bertrand had disclosed.

Bertrand broke the silence. "What else did Banastre tell you about me?"

"That you would attempt to seduce me."

"I've always preferred it the other way."

Anderton smiled. "Can I ask you another question?"

"But, of course."

"Do you still use pigs to hunt truffles?"

Bertrand shook his head. "Dogs are preferred, for they tend not to devour the profits when they find them."

Anderton laughed, and then stood. "I hope you'll forgive me one drink only."

"But, of course."

She gave Bertrand a kiss on the cheek. "Thank you, René."

"*Avec plaisir*, my dear. Perhaps the next time we will share a truffle, which I can assure will be the best you've ever tasted."

CHAPTER FORTY-SEVEN

Locronan, France

Banastre Montjoy made his way up Rue St. Maurice, toward the city center of Locronan. Dating to the Dark Ages, the charming village had been well-preserved since the eighteen century and was long considered one of the most beautiful in France.

Within a stone's throw of where tourists now sipped expensive coffees and grumbled about wait times for dinner, he quietly paid homage to the Montjoys who had come ashore under heavy artillery fire on a dark Tuesday seventy-four years earlier, some of whom never made it off Sword and Gold Beaches at Normandy. Montjoy's late grandfather, Sir Nigel Aldrich, had been stationed at Bletchley Park during the war, and had been instrumental in overseeing the signals-intelligence operation that cracked *Enigma*, the German cipher machine deemed unbreakable. It had been Aldrich who first suggested conjuring up a master spy, later coded *Boniface*. The fictional agent and his phantom espionage ring in Germany would be credited, via deliberate leaks, as responsible for the intelligence gathered through *Ultra*, in order to mislead the Nazis concerning the real source of their intercepted communications.

Montjoy had little idea what to expect as he neared the crêperie where Verity Scott had agreed to meet. Her tenure at MI6 was the stuff of legend, though he suspected that some of the tales of her brazen exploits as a Cold War operative in the Eastern Bloc must have been only that. Regardless, the woman's brilliance was matched only by her stunning beauty, while the savage gusto with which she reputedly meted out wonton acts of violence against the enemies of SIS still resonated around Vauxhall Cross.

Fluent in four languages, Scott was preceded by the myth of her mother's own wartime derring-do. Code-named *Foxtrot*, Vera Scott had been dropped into Belgium in the summer of 1942, unescorted, thanks to an SOE cock-up. She combined charm with good looks under the guise of a bored homemaker from Hamburg to beguile her way into the beds of young Nazi officers, many who unwittingly betrayed military secrets as harmless tidbits dropped into chitchat over a post-coital cigarette. By the onset of *Operation Overlord,* the Abwehr considered the agent they coined *Aphrodite* as the Allies' most damaging spy, and the reward for her whereabouts topped all others most wanted by the Gestapo.

Though Vera Scott had been a contemporary of Madeleine Halliwell, it was only after the war that the former saboteurs met, when Scott's daughter was being recruited into SIS. Verity picked up where her mother left off, during a period when the Oxbridgian gatekeepers no longer took for granted that British Intelligence would eventually settle back into its cozy antebellum patriarchy. When she demonstrated little ambition to assume the role of a long-lashed, mini-skirted office liaison, the reaction was predictable. That the younger Scott was the sordid consequence of the slag mother shagging her way through the *Wehrmacht* ranks became the whispered scuttlebutt amongst the Old Boys, scattered between their own attempts to bed the up-and-coming agent.

Verity persevered, thanks in no small part to Halliwell, who recognized the potential of the Scott progeny. She was transferred from London to West Berlin to train under Halliwell's tutelage, and was one of the first operatives sent into the Soviet sector by the newly promoted case officer. Masterful at gleaning useful information from the most innocuous conversations, and at turning everyday East Germans into effective intelligence gatherers, Scott was also renowned for her hatred of, and single-handed retaliation against, the Stasi and KGB.

She was rumored to have skewered a Stasi colonel through the neck with the broken end of a spoon in the bathroom of a bar in Dresden, either because he attempted to seduce her or deduced her identity, depending on which side of the Wall the story originated. One KGB report, found in the Mitrokhin files that were smuggled out of Russia in 1992, detailed an incident in which an unnamed British agent, purportedly Scott, shot her own informant when he panicked and came close to compromising an exfiltration attempt at Bernauer Straße in 1972. Anecdotes of her conduct routinely turned up in the debriefings of absconding Soviet operatives, though it was usually determined that the defectors were simply passing on sensationalized hearsay.

In the end, Scott commented little on her own clandestine activities, or methods, which only bolstered her reputation, both good and bad.

Montjoy bypassed the charming farmhouse decor inside the restaurant for the café terrace. It was comfortably crowded and cool in the waning hours of the teatime sun. Verity Scott sat at a corner table, and either by design or coincidence was silhouetted in the converging shadows of a large planter and cantilevered parasol. She was subtly monitoring the patio, though her attention had been firmly affixed on Montjoy from the moment he stepped outside.

Montjoy had seen a photo of Scott from her early days with MI6 and didn't need to speculate whether he had the right person based on how she might have aged. The patron in the corner was by far the most beautiful woman on the patio. Scott also looked ten years younger than the seventy-two years she had weathered, and appeared to be in remarkable shape.

Montjoy stepped to her table, but before he could introduce himself, Scott spoke.

"Aren't you the handsome devil. The mirror image of your late grandfather."

"You're very kind, Ms. Scott."

"Verity," she replied, "and few have accused me of that over the years, I can assure you."

She gestured to a chair opposite, and Montjoy obliged as he pointed to her drink and nodded at a server who stopped by the table.

Montjoy settled in without saying anything, and when he glanced up, Scott smiled. "You measured me up with the same look many have when they first meet me, so feel free to ask whatever you're wondering." When Montjoy did not immediately respond, Scott said, "Yes, I killed a Stasi officer, but it wasn't with cutlery in a restaurant lavatory."

"And here I always assumed it was Professor Plum with a candlestick in the kitchen."

Scott laughed, in spite of herself. "Clever, to boot."

"I've never been terribly curious as to how fellow operatives went about their business, only that they did," Montjoy replied. "The ends often justify the methods in our line of work, in my experience."

"Spoken like someone long enough in the field before being plunked down behind a desk, and there never seemed to be an abundance of those running around," Scott replied. "The short of it was, I had become friends with his wife. She was disillusioned and he was an abusive drunk. I was certain I could convince her to spy for us and then defect. When he made his less than delicate pass at me, in a locked cloakroom, as it were, I stabbed him through the jugular with a screwdriver. Soon after, she killed herself. Not my best moment."

"We've all had our share."

Scott eyed Montjoy, but then smiled. "Most of the other bits are rubbish."

"Perhaps, though I would imagine you seldom sought to downplay any of it, knowing the reputation that preceded you as a result served a purpose."

"Something which can only be appreciated by someone

with a similar MO." Scott then lifted her wine glass. "To Maddie. I was so sorry to hear of her passing. She meant the world to me and I owe her much of my career. Your grandmother was such a good soul for our line of work. I don't know how she managed it sometimes."

Montjoy decided not to mince words. "She was murdered, you should know."

Scott did not respond as her eyes reddened, and Montjoy watched the woman struggle to fight back tears. In the midst of it, he also noticed something else—that behind the genuine anguish, Scott did not seem surprised by the revelation. She accepted the handkerchief Montjoy offered and composed herself. Scott then downed the last of her cabernet, and when the server asked if he should bring another, she shook her head. "Scotch. Double. Neat."

"Who, and how?" Scott finally asked, after the drink was delivered. She offered the lowball to Montjoy, who held up his hand. "It wasn't a suggestion," she said flatly. "I don't drink alone."

He acquiesced and took a sip, letting it roll over his tongue. "Dalmore?"

"Another overworked and underpaid company man, I see."

"Quite," Montjoy replied, offering back the glass.

Scott took it, and a drink. "Now I understand why you tracked me down."

"Grandmother told me that you were the one to see if I was ever in a pinch."

"Or a vice, as it would seem in this case."

"A toxic dose of potassium chloride was administered—"

"To mimic cardiac arrest," Scott interjected, before something gave her pause. "You couldn't have known that without an autopsy, which you wouldn't have ordered because of Maddie's age. Something else is going on. What is it?"

Montjoy gave the patio a second onceover, and then lowered his voice. "Geoffrey Charlton was murdered in Italy last week, hours before Grandmother, likely by the same individual. William Lindsay has gone missing in Munich, and someone tried to assassinate me in the States. All on the same day."

Scott remained silent, and it dawned on Montjoy that she was weighing whether she might be in danger.

"We're backtracking through the case file that involved all three, through 1990, and—"

"*Castor*," Scott said. "The Oberbaum."

Montjoy held up the empty tumbler.

Scott shook her head.

"What operation were we running on that bridge and what happened to our agent?"

"Not here," Scott replied. "100 Rue Lann. One hour."

CHAPTER FORTY-EIGHT

Strasbourg, France

Tomas Karlson sipped a digestif outside a French bistro and mulled whether he should order dessert so that he could extend his stay on the patio overlooking the Ill River. While the ambience of the evening and vista of the canal were pleasant enough, the assassin was more interested in the Régent Petite France and Spa, situated directly across the water.

Two days earlier, Karlson had been contacted in London by his handler, who notified him that Banastre Montjoy had been located in France. Though the call had come late in the evening, Karlson had been ready to move, and was able to catch the Eurostar to Paris before connecting on a French TGV bound directly for Strasbourg. He had been in the city only one other time, two years after barely escaping with his life from Latvia. Unlike most visitors who loved its beauty and atmosphere, Karlson did not, primarily because of Strasbourg's close proximity to Germany and its painful memories.

The sooner Karlson could find and kill the deputy chief of MI6 and leave the country, the better.

The hotel at which the blonde woman with Montjoy had been seen could be accessed by several points, and Karlson had spent the better part of eight hours rotating his position between three spots on opposite sides of the five-star accommodation. Foot traffic over the *Rue des Moulins* had been surprisingly light, making it easier to cycle between faces, in search of the one he wanted. En route to France, Karlson had been sent a photo of the woman, who had been followed from Germany. It had been taken while she was getting coffee at a station kiosk, ostensibly during a changeover between Lindau and Strasbourg. The snapshot came from a mobile phone and the quality was good, but its acquisition had clearly been a risky maneuver.

Karlson would agree that the agent was far better looking than most, and certainly more so than he, but that wasn't difficult. Though two surgeries had nearly repaired his drooping eyelid, little could be done for the atrophy of the optic nerve in his right eye, nor the recurring bouts of epiphora.

Karlson finished his drink and strained to concentrate on the busy terrace around him.

A glassed sightseeing boat packed with tourists wearing audio guides glided through a narrow lock in the channel below.

A man and woman seated at a neighboring table began to argue about something in Hungarian, and though the language was considered Europe's most complicated, the couple clearly had no trouble articulating their displeasure at one another.

A server at an eatery downriver retracted a patio awning as if it were the last thing on Earth he wanted to do.

Karlson's phone buzzed a weather update.

The assassin suddenly snapped from his momentary stupor and recognized that he needed to refocus. Karlson decided it was time to alternate his surveillance point once again, and so he settled his tab and left the restaurant.

CHAPTER FORTY-NINE

Zurich, Switzerland

It had been twenty-four hours since John Riker checked into a deluxe double room with a courtyard view at the Baur au Lac hotel. He knew better than to park himself at some nearby café and attempt to monitor the premises in the off-chance of catching his target coming or going. This kind of reconnoiter, rotated or not, worked only on someone unseasoned or unsuspecting. The deputy chief of MI6 would pick up on the surveillance and disappear like a puff of smoke in the wind.

In Riker's experience, he needed to integrate into his environment as much as possible, and an interior room overlooking a central outdoor service area was both inconspicuous and far more comfortable than a park bench. From his target's vantage point, the accommodation was smartly chosen for its all-inclusive services, as Banastre Montjoy could theoretically remain holed up within the confines of the hotel indefinitely. Whether the man was actually still there, or ever had been, was dependent on Mykhail Vann, an Alpha Group operator with whom Riker had served in Chechnya. It was Vann who had followed Montjoy's proxy from Germany and twice confirmed that Montjoy had been seen in the lobby. Two return texts to Vann had since gone unanswered, something Riker had notified Chénard of only hours earlier.

Riker had already taken several turns around the property, feigned interest in its architecture, eaten both breakfast and lunch in the Pavillon and Rive Gauche restaurants, and passed several intermittent hours in the lobby through the afternoon. Thus far, there had been no sign of his target, and Riker decided to give his surveillance one more full day before he would be forced to consider changing his strategy.

The assassin paid for the drink he had nursed at a table on the interior terrace and decided it was time to recanvass a four-block perimeter, working his way inward. If Montjoy had stepped out, he would not stray far, or long, from ground zero. Riker consulted a city map and reconfirmed his perimeter as the canal that bordered the Baur au Lac, the Limmat River, Lake Zurich, and *Paradeplatz*. He had already gone two turns around the demarcated area that day, both without luck, and was determined to repeat the loop, changing his pattern, until his stay was finished.

Riker exited the hotel and made his way toward a water-front park on the lake. He rounded the channel bridge near twin ferry terminals and had just turned back along the main road that skirted a marina at the mouth of the Limmat when he spotted a man he had seen earlier. There was nothing about him in particular that stood out, only that it was the third time Riker had seen the same individual over the last ten hours.

It was at that moment that Riker's phone vibrated an

incoming call. It could be only one of two people, and as he pulled the mobile from his pocket, Riker saw it was from the number that Chénard had given him to contact Vann once in Zurich. He tapped the green icon to answer, and greeted the caller in German, when the line went dead.

Riker glanced back in the direction of the park, but the man was gone.

CHAPTER FIFTY

Sean Garrett stepped behind a food truck, part of a row of mobile trailers that lined the boundary of Stadthausanlage Park. He had been eating the same sandwich for nearly an hour, as he waited for the man he had marked the night before to emerge from the Baur au Lac. Garrett had rotated his surveillance between the park, the hotel, and the rooftop of a mixed-use building he had gained access to across the street, and had just made up his mind to change positions, when his target appeared.

Garrett recognized that Montjoy's ruse had worked the moment he spied the two-man team waiting for him at the mail drop in St. Gallen. The pair at the train station had likely been dispatched by whoever was behind the initial assassination attempt on Montjoy, and Garrett's guess was that they were put in place to monitor the unknown proxy who had met with Sokolov in the hopes he would lead them to their ultimate target. Neither of the men who followed Garrett or Samantha Anderton from Lindau was the one who would ultimately complete the mission.

But Garrett had a good idea who that would be.

The bullet meant for Montjoy had come from a tree line seven hundred yards out. While authorities in Charleston continued to publicly speculate that it was an errant round from a hunter's gun, Garrett knew better. Someone had hired a seasoned sniper to take the shot. That the would-be assassin had then up and disappeared without so much as a spent cartridge or bootprint indicated they were dealing with a skilled killer who had, for whatever reason, found himself uncharacteristically off the mark. The type of professional whose nature it would be to come after Montjoy until the job was finished.

Garrett had first become suspicious of the man across the street when he noticed him earlier exit the Baur au Lac and begin what amounted to a systematic sweep of a fixed sector across the small peninsula. He was casual in his movements and broke up the pattern enough to appear random. However, the counterfeit tourist strolling along the river walk without a care in the world had clearly been canvassing an area between the canal and the Limmat, up through *Paradeplatz* and back to the lake. The man had appeared again, just after lunch, and this time Garrett followed him as he retraced his surveillance of the same area, though in reverse.

Once back at the hotel, Garrett marked the hour and predicted that if his suspicion was correct, the man would reappear just before dinner to retrace his well-disguised reconnoiter, beginning this time from the river park. Right on cue, he did, and Garrett pretended to peruse what amounted to a

Swiss flea market as the man casually began his stroll along the predicted path.

Garrett had waited until the man passed his position to make the call. He used the mobile he had taken off the now-dead operative from Lindau to ring the number that had twice texted it in Russian. The man from the hotel suddenly stopped and produced his own phone, answering it in German. Garrett hung up, and watched his target do the same.

The man had then glanced once back over his shoulder, neither appearing suspicious nor overly concerned, and began to make his way up the river walk.

CHAPTER FIFTY-ONE

Locronan, France

Banastre Montjoy turned the corner at Rue du Prieuré onto Rue Lann, a picturesque, single-lane alley paved with hand-laid cobbles. He strolled between rows of quaint stone cottages linked by ivy-laden walls, and was forced to double back when he missed Verity Scott's unmarked residence on the first pass.

Her flat was adjacent to a *boulangerie* and Montjoy caught the scent of something laced with chocolate as he rapped on a glass pane of the front entryway. Two workers in blue overalls flecked with drywall mud approached from the opposite direction. The first man carried a heavy-duty vacuum with its extension cord slung over a shoulder, while his partner kept one hand in a pocket and smoked a cigarette with the other. The men glanced up as Montjoy came level with the flat beside the bakery and briefly made eye contact with him. Montjoy was in the split-second process of weighing whether he should put a palm on the pistol in his own pocket, when Scott suddenly unlatched and opened the door.

Montjoy stepped inside and shut it behind him, keeping an eye on the pair as they continued past the cottage.

"Do you recognize those men?"

Scott peered through a side window. "They've been working on the shop next door for the better part of a week. Why?"

"Never you mind," Montjoy answered, then noticed two suitcases by the front entryway. "Where are you off to?"

"Somewhere else."

"I shouldn't think you've anything to worry about."

"Of course not," she replied, "what with you jumpy at random day laborers and considering that everyone else connected to *Safeguard* has turned up disappeared or dead."

"Touché," Montjoy replied.

"What do you know so far?"

"Very little. The files on *Safeguard* have been scrubbed," Montjoy replied. "How were you attached to the Oberbaum operation?"

"Facilitating *Castor's* exfiltration out of East Germany."

"What went wrong?"

"Your guess and mine. *Castor* had crossed earlier that week with two other agents, Czech dissidents working with MI6, and everyone was clear with the parameters of the operation. The next thing we knew, he was on the bridge, and then in the Spree. Two days later, *Castor* was whisked off to God knows where on the wrong side of the Wall."

"Who ran the operation?"

"William Lindsay, from London, with Maddie coordinating *Safeguard* on the ground in West Berlin. I got out after the entire business went belly up. It was unclear whether my cover was blown, but I was forced to bugger off to Norway nonetheless. Do you know how bloody cold Oslo is in December?"

"And Charlton?"

"Everything liaised through Geoffrey." Scott turned off the lamp on a nearby table and checked her watch. "Out of curiosity, when exactly did you come on board?"

"1984, summer," Montjoy replied. "Geoffrey was my section head."

"And that November?'

"In West Berlin, on short assignment, but it had nothing to do with *Safeguard*."

"That you were aware of," Scott replied. "It can't be a coincidence you were targeted alongside everyone who was involved."

"With one exception—"

"Which is why I've packed my bags," Scott replied. She checked the time again, clearly worried. "And I refuse to take a chance on whether I'm suddenly out in the open, after all these years." She opened the drawer of a china cabinet and pulled out a small-caliber handgun, which she pocketed after verifying it was chambered.

"What was *Castor* bringing over?"

"I've no idea. All I can tell you is that *Castor* wasn't supposed to be at the Oberbaum that night."

"Yet, he was."

Scott did not reply.

"Were we running a parallel operation, possibly coded *Turnkey* and involving an agent named *Pollux*?

"Neither name rings a bell."

"What do you remember about an agent code-named *Spindle*?"

"A sadistic bastard of a Stasi operative," Scott replied. "He always seemed to be one step ahead of us. *Spindle* single-handedly blew up at least a half-dozen operations, and was directly responsible for the deaths of more than a few of our agents and informants. He is the one man I would have personally, and gladly, put a bullet into, even today. He scurried off with the rest of the rats when the Wall came down and the lights were turned up on what they were doing during those years. I'm sure that smug prat is sitting safely in a dacha on the Baltic Sea and sipping a loose-leaf Ceylon from a glassed *podstakannik*."

"Do you remember Sergei Malinovsky?"

"Malinovsky?" Scott asked, surprised. "He was an officer in the KGB, middling at best. Arrested in November of 1984 and executed a month later."

"Why would he have been in contact with *Castor* before the Oberbaum operation?"

"He wouldn't have," Scott answered.

Montjoy produced the photo that Laskin had given him and passed it to Scott. "Is that *Castor*?"

Scott nodded. "His name was Stanford Collishaw," she said as she studied the photograph. "Where did you get this?"

"It was given to me by an ex-KGB operative who was stationed in East Germany at the time."

"If it's legitimate, I can't explain it."

"Was Malinovsky one of ours?"

"Possibly," Scott replied. "Though, my memory and ignorance on the matter aren't a reliable gauge."

Montjoy produced the photos from his grandmother's journal, of Collishaw and an unknown agent, and handed them both to Scott. "Do you recognize this man?"

She studied the second snapshot. "He looks like every other young operative sent to an early grave. But to answer your question, no." Scott was about to hand the photograph back when she stopped and took a closer look. "This might be a Stasi officer MI6 we attempted to recruit once, without success. *What was his name?*" Scott said to herself as she closed her eyes. "Brandt, perhaps, but I can't be certain."

"Was he attached to the Oberbaum operation in any way?"

"Not that I was aware."

Montjoy put the photographs back in his jacket. "Why don't you return to London and let SIS protect you?"

"Better than one of its ex-chiefs, deputy chiefs, and senior controllers?" Before Montjoy could respond, Scott apologized. "I'm sorry, that was insensitive."

Montjoy waved her off. "Water under the bridge, literally. But, I'm not going to ground, and I need everything you've got on *Safeguard*."

Scott pulled an envelope from the same drawer as the gun and handed it to Montjoy. "Collishaw was an Oxford Don before the war, and from a fairly prominent London family on one side. Partly German on the other. I've jotted down everything I can remember about him and the operation, which is not much, I'm afraid."

"If you need anything." Montjoy handed her his mobile number on a scrap of paper. "Godspeed, Verity."

"If he's fast enough to outrun this."

CHAPTER FIFTY-TWO

Zurich, Switzerland

John Riker made his way along the Limmat river walk. He had been unable to pick up in his periphery or by using discreet surveillance practices whether the man from the park was still following him. The assassin knew it was pointless to second-guess his gut instinct, and as he walked, Riker cursed his carelessness. He had allowed a momentary slip in concentration to cast the smallest spotlight on himself, but that was all most seasoned operatives needed to mark their target. How long the man could stay locked on to him depended on how effectively Riker could shed the bright-red bullseye that he had proverbially painted on his own back.

He should have ignored the phone's vibration long enough to steal away to a secure location to answer it. He should have practiced better situational and tactical awareness. That its originator hung up as soon as Riker answered the call meant it had been made to single out whether or not he was expecting to hear from Vann. Which indicated Vann was either dead or detained, and that the man eating a sandwich by the river was privy to a host of other deductions.

Likely, that Riker was part of a larger team, and possibly, that he was the assassin sent to finish the job on Banastre Montjoy.

Since his failure in Charleston, Riker had operated under the assumption that British Intelligence was at least suspicious enough about what had transpired to put more than a normal security detail on its deputy chief. If MI6 were certain there had been a botched attempt specifically on Montjoy, Riker's task had just evolved from difficult to nearly impossible. If that was the case, then the game was up and Riker needed to get himself cleanly out of Switzerland and back to Canada as quickly and quietly as possible. He would later decide if his flat, his life, in Toronto was blown.

However, it was possible that Riker was wrong about the man outside the Baur au Lac hotel. Before he justified the need to completely abandon the mission, Riker first had to determine whether his pursuer's presence signaled some kind of surveillance to protect Montjoy, or, whether the man was nobody, and that Riker had presumed someone who didn't exist.

Riker decided to make his way to the tram depot in order to find out.

CHAPTER FIFTY-THREE

S ean Garrett adjusted his pace as he moved along the *strasse* that ran parallel to the river. Whether the man he shadowed was a professional or just someone whose missed mobile call was merely a coincidence would be determined in the next few blocks. He could not risk following too closely if it was the former, for any surveillance, no matter how veiled, would eventually be spotted.

There were only so many coincidences someone in their profession would endure before recurring happenstance converted it into suspicion.

Garrett stopped at the entryway of a delivery road that bisected a complex of buildings and stood just behind a locked iron gate. Within a few seconds, he saw the man reappear and pause at the opposite end of the tunnel to allow a lorry access to the narrow lane, before he continued up the avenue toward the Münsterbrücke Bridge. At the next junction, Garrett allowed himself enough lag so that the man could cross the adjacent corner and carry on, before correcting his own pace to reconnect with his target's assumed route.

If Garrett was right, the man would soon come around the corner by the church and make his way toward *Paradeplatz*.

At the next intersection, Garrett mixed with a group of sightseers standing outside Fraumünster and feigned interest in the guided tour as he kept an eye on the Limmat. On cue, the man came into view, lingered at the river overpass, and then turned toward the main square. Garrett stepped back beneath a gated archway at the church as the man continued in the direction of Zurich's largest tram junction.

He expected the man to cross the busy square where Garrett had days earlier acquired his grandmother's journal from the Credit Suisse main branch, before turning on Bahnhofstrasse and heading back toward the Baur au Lac.

When Garrett reached *Paradeplatz*, he saw that his target had not continued in the direction of the hotel, but was instead standing at a ticket kiosk.

The man purchased a fare and stepped onto a nearby tram just as the door closed and it pulled away from the stop.

CHAPTER FIFTY-FOUR

Department of Homeland Security
Washington, D.C.

J ason Whitlock, Special Agent with Homeland Security
Investigations, swore under his breath as he spilled coffee
on a brand-new pair of Bruno Magli dress loafers. "Could they
possibly buy cheaper cups around this place?"

Bobby Hanlon tossed his partner a wad of napkins from
a McDonald's bag still on his desk from lunch. "If they did,
we wouldn't get the big bucks."

"Right," Whitlock answered sarcastically. "What *have*
we got?"

"A gunshotted Chechen and a strangled Department of
Natural Resources officer bound to a jon boat in a lake in South
Carolina," Hanlon replied, then added, "I've been fishing down
that way a few times. Pretty country and freshwater angling
about as good as it gets."

"I reeled in a nice brunette in the Holy City just last
month," Whitlock replied, referring to Charleston. "Want to
bet I had a better time than you?"

Hanlon watched Whitlock gingerly dab his expensive

Italian loafers. "Why don't you wear normal shoes to work like everyone else?"

"That question, my friend, is why you don't get laid when you travel, and end up fishing." Whitlock gave up trying to clean his shoe and gestured toward the file. "DNR, I'm not interested in. That's got *wrong time and place* written all over it. Kick it back down to the FBI so they can feel like they're doing something useful. What do we know about the other guy?"

"Andrei Beslan. From Grozny, ex-military linked to criminal activities in Eastern Europe and wanted for questioning for his role in atrocities committed during Chechnya vs Russia, redux."

"How novel, a Chechen in a gang and wanted for war crimes."

"You shouldn't stereotype, it clouds the judgment. To wit, my great-grandmother was from Moscow. I bet you didn't know that."

"Actually, I did, *comrade*. Why don't you grab me another coffee while I singlehandedly figure all of this out?"

"*Nyet*," Hanlon replied, "which is Russian for '*fuck off.*'"

Whitlock smiled, and turned his attention to the file he had been sent over from the Hoover building a day earlier. "What was our friend Andrei doing at the bottom of Lake Marion?"

"DNR's vehicle was found at a boat landing not far from where the banker was sniped that same day."

"Was our man a shooter?"

"It doesn't say in his military record," Hanlon noted. "We can assume that Beslan was stopped and ticketed for an infraction, probably at the put-in. Maybe he panicked and strangled the DNR agent, and was then killed as a result."

Whitlock shook his head. "My guess is, our mystery man killed both of them." He held up a finger, as if he'd figured everything out. "The Chechen's buddy was the shooter. A professional. He kills the banker for whatever reason, probably hundreds of thousands of them in an offshore account. The sniper then decides to cover his tracks and tie up loose ends, and offs his partner in crime. Beslan, with a professionally forged passport and N.C. driver's license, entered the U.S. through Charlotte Douglas a few weeks ago, right? Our other guy, however, didn't jet in. Killer number two is more local, and came in through a connected border. Canada? He'd already picked up the vehicle with fake plates, unlicensed and untraceable high-caliber weapons, and a bag full of cash. He's the lead operative and the perpetrator of the assassination, and is now in touch with the mastermind behind the whole operation."

"Twenty bucks we find out his contact isn't local, and was staying at a nearby hotel."

"You're on," Whitlock replied. "The big boss, visiting Boston by your bet, has come out of the shadows and is pissed because the job has gone south in the form of a hardworking DNR family man just out doing his job who pulls the short straw for the poor-bastard-of-the-week-award."

"They should have sent you to notify next of kin."

"So, who and where is our sniper, and who's his handler?"

"Someone who served with the dead guy back in Russia? More Chechens?" Hanlon asked. "Any idea why the big-shot banker was targeted? We could work our way backward."

"The hedge fund manager was a 'swell guy,' by everyone's reckoning. Maybe he was secretly laundering money and cheated the wrong client?"

Hanlon shrugged his shoulders, and both men went back to shuffling through the stack of evidence. At that moment, a colleague rounded the corner with a file and a message. "The good news is, Holmes and Watson, we might have partials off the Denali steering wheel, and, it looks like the second man from the park was staying at the Marriott Long Wharf."

Whitlock glanced over at Hanlon, who smiled and rubbed two fingers together in the pay-up gesture.

"In addition, cell phones pinged in the Harborwalk area at the time of the meeting show several texts exchanged between a pay-as-you-go phone purchased one week earlier in North Carolina, and a burner with a Canadian prefix."

"And the bad news?" Whitlock asked.

"Something you requisitioned triggered a big, fat, say-goodbye-to-your-case red flag. Make sure you boys wave *adiós* as it disappears upstairs."

"We are the upstairs," Hanlon protested, then asked, "where?"

The man only pointed toward the ceiling as he turned to leave, then stopped and said, "And if you're going to wear those shoes to work, Whitlock, you should consider pairing them with a tux."

CHAPTER FIFTY-FIVE

Frankfurt, Germany

Banastre Montjoy sipped a club soda in the Fifth Lounge and Bar, at the Hilton by the airport. Samantha Anderton had arrived by train from Frankfurt Central Station only minutes earlier, and ordered a Thai red curry and a glass of white wine before settling across from Montjoy.

"How was the flight?"

"A question which answers itself," Montjoy replied. "I'd rather not sit very long in anything five miles up that possesses no vertical thrust whatsoever."

"It's the safest way to travel, much more so than a car."

"Which, when they crash, isn't at the speed of sound. How was the train from Remich?"

"Slow."

Montjoy smiled. "And the visit with Bertrand?"

"Charming, and to a point, worth it."

"I won't ask what you mean by that," Montjoy replied, tongue in cheek.

"It was on his mind, believe me, but I was referring to information."

"Which was?"

"Only a name. *Gemini*, with no context."

"Which provides us with one more random jigsaw piece." Montjoy pulled a notepad from his jacket. "From the files, we know that one of our agents, Stan Collishaw, code-named *Castor*, was captured while crossing the Oberbaum Bridge under *Operation Safeguard* in November of 1984. My grandmother confirmed as much in her journal, which also includes the code names *Pollux* and *Turnkey*. There is no accompanying date or details, but we can deduce, for the time being, that they must represent some other agent and operation.

"Included with the code names are two photos. One is Collishaw. The other, of a man appearing to be in his late twenties, is someone we've yet to identify, though Verity Scott suggested that he may have been a Stasi officer named Brandt, who MI6 attempted to turn without luck. It's possible that Brandt might have been *Pollux*, but we have no context for what his, or *Turnkey's,* purpose was. William Lindsay's cryptic, pre-coma missive from Munich is all of one word, *Spindle*, who a former KGB operative confirmed was an East German Stasi colonel named Markus Heinrich. Heinrich, it turns out, was actually a Russian, born Alexei Arkipov. Now, Bertrand supplies us with a single word, *Gemini*, which for all we know could have been the name of someone's bloody pet parakeet."

"If not for the fact that in Greek mythology, Castor and Pollux were the Gemini," Anderton noted, "whose zodiac symbol resembles two figures on a bridge."

"And the last Rorschach I was shown turned out to be

something to do with my mother, not two bats shaking hands, as I guessed," Montjoy quipped.

"How does everyone tie into *Safeguard*?"

"William Lindsay oversaw the operation from London, Geoffrey Charlton was head of section in West Berlin, Madeleine Halliwell was senior case officer, Verity Scott was *Castor's* point of contact in East Berlin, and I had just been assigned to West Germany."

"Fast-forward thirty-four years, Mr. Collishaw is long dead—"

"Presumed," Montjoy interjected.

"Conceded," Anderton replied. "Mr. Charlton and Mrs. Halliwell have been murdered, you and Mr. Lindsay escaped assassination, while Ms. Scott is alive and well in France."

"In a nutshell."

"Who is behind the operation and who is pulling the trigger?"

"Inside that nutshell, which we're no closer to cracking."

"It's simply a matter of rearranging the pieces."

"With no discernible edges to begin from," Montjoy replied, tapping his notes. "When is your train back to Strasbourg?"

"One hour."

"You are clear on what to do?"

"Yes, sir," Anderton replied. "And you?"

"I'm heading back to the Oberbaum, where this all began."

CHAPTER FIFTY-SIX

Moscow, Russia

Vasily Markov emptied out another carton of case files. He had quietly fumed for months about not only having to sort through the intelligence himself, but that the pile of boxes made a room already limited in space seem even smaller. Considering that he had neglected to organize the documents as he plowed through them, Markov had created a bigger mess than when he started. Moreover, he had so far been unable to locate the KGB summary on the operation that captured the British agent at the Oberbaum in 1984.

On top of that, Markov had suffered through nearly one full year of colleagues joking that he needed to "*tear down this wall*," parroting Ronald Reagan's famous challenge to Gorbachev.

Now that Markov finally had, the removed box partition revealed patches of mold in the corner.

While he thumbed through the Cold War clutter, Markov considered what the bugged conversations in Prague had revealed. In his monitored exchange with Banastre Montjoy, Anatoly Laskin had referenced the deaths of Madeleine

Halliwell and Geoffrey Charlton when questioned about the Oberbaum operation. In addition, he had mentioned Markus Heinrich's name in the *present tense* when asked about *Spindle*. Perhaps it had been a slip-up, or something simply misunderstood. However, Markov had listened to the audio several times and it certainly sounded as if Laskin knew what everyone else did not concerning the "death" of Heinrich, by that time Alexei Arkipov, twenty-two years earlier while on vacation at the Black Sea.

Death by drowning, the official report had concluded. That Heinrich had also been intoxicated at the time he went swimming near midnight made for a poor mix, but since no body had been recovered, the coroner could only speculate without an autopsy.

Markov closed his eyes and struggled to map his way backward over three decades. He could recall the capture of the British agent in 1984, but not the details of the operation. Markov did remember the situation had been unique in that the KGB did not parade the spy before cameras, as it was prone to do. Instead, the operative had been whisked away in secret to Russia for interrogation. Considering the events that preceded the arrest, Moscow had seemed certain that the agent was privy to the identity of a long-rumored mole in East Berlin.

It had also been Laskin who first accused Sergei Malinovsky of treason, thanks to a photograph taken by Heinrich. Markov thoroughly disliked Malinovsky, and had no problem that the man was quickly executed, never mind that Malinovsky had persuasively argued that it was he who had approached the MI6 agent in the hopes of turning him to spy for the KGB.

Boris Golitsyn, head of station in East Berlin at the time, had moved to close the case quickly. That Malinovsky might have been innocent, and the actual mole allowed to continue to operate in East Germany unfettered, either never crossed anyone's mind, or somebody at the highest level was covering something up.

Who that someone, and what that something, might have been, was cast back into the spotlight in the years following the fall of communism. In early 1996, a rumor began to circulate that old intelligence existed, in the form of a book taken off the British operative, which pointed to the identity of the double agent in East Berlin. Markov remembered that the news had momentarily thrown no small number of leftover KGB officers into a panic. The destruction of their entire system had created a vacuum where anything was possible. Simply because the KGB no longer existed in name did not mean that the old ways of dealing business had simply evaporated, particularly during a period when much of the upper hierarchy believed that simply advocating for the new Russia was considered treasonous behavior.

The accusations had flown even before proof of such intelligence could be confirmed, and everyone seemed to be caught up in someone else's alleged Cold War misconduct. Bribery and double-dealing had been a way of life when everyone either seemed to be involved, or at least, turned a blind eye to it. Now that the wool had been pulled back, no one wanted to admit that they had been complicit in such conduct, either directly or otherwise, particularly when said behavior could be singled out as one of the main precursors for the implosion of communism.

Everyone had been quick to denounce that the emperor wasn't wearing any clothes without first checking the mirror to see if they were themselves dressed.

In the end, nothing concrete ever surfaced. The rampant threats of recrimination petered out into muted grousing, while much of the hearsay was eventually dismissed as only that.

And now, out of the blue, Laskin openly admitted that Heinrich was still alive. He also hinted to the sitting deputy chief of MI6 that a border guard stationed at the Oberbaum in November 1984 might have information that would interest the British. Moreover, when Montjoy insinuated that he had seen intelligence that pointed to Laskin as the mole, there had been no scoffs, clever tongue-in-cheek put-offs, nor protestations. Laskin had simply said nothing. The man who had been humiliated and reassigned to a desk for failing to recognize an obvious SIS dangle in London years after the Oberbaum incident had chosen to remain silent when the very operative who had fooled him floated the notion that Laskin *was* the double agent.

And what else had Banastre Montjoy cryptically suggested to the SVR head of station?

Some secrets remain safe.

Markov checked his phone again. He had heard nothing from Elena Mullova, though he was sure she would have at least interrogated Laskin by now.

There was only thing Markov could do, so he opted to skip lunch and scour the remaining files.

CHAPTER FIFTY-SEVEN

Strasbourg, France

Sean Garrett's train to Strasbourg was ahead of schedule. While the journey from Switzerland had been uneventful, the same could not be said for the short walk into the Grand Île, as the sheer volume of weekend tourists who had arrived at the same time all seemed to be heading to the exact same place as everyone else. The dynamic reminded Garrett of trying to navigate Notting Hill crowds during Carnival, but he was finally able to exit the mass after crossing the river bridge and turning off the main thoroughfare into the city center.

It had been twenty-four hours since he had lost track of his mark at *Paradeplatz*. The man had jumped a tram, though Garrett could not be certain whether it was an evasive maneuver or merely the actions of a tourist with OCD sightseeing habits. Garrett had returned to the Baur au Lac and maintained a vigilance on the hotel from the adjacent rooftop, but had not seen the man return through the rest of the day.

Either Garrett was mistaken and the man was inconsequential, or he was a professional who had picked up on the surveillance and disappeared. Regardless, Garrett had decided to abandon Zurich in favor of Strasbourg.

Garrett had deliberately avoided coordinating with his brother for the last forty-eight hours, since learning of Montjoy's plan to visit one of their grandmother's MI6 colleagues in France. Garrett had used the fake credentials from Sokolov to purchase his ticket at Zurich's main station in case the architect of the operation against SIS was wired in well enough to monitor whether the false name popped up on any travel manifests throughout Europe. The same moniker, Gareth Walker, had been used to reserve a hotel room not far from where Montjoy had booked his own.

At the moment, Garrett was more concerned with keeping Montjoy on the move and out of harm's way. He hoped that his brother's fact-finding jaunt would bear enough fruit to direct him elsewhere in search of answers, though their communication protocol limited any kind of consistent contact. Both men had arranged to cycle out their burner phones for a new one every twenty-four hours, which required Garrett to notify Montjoy of his updated mobile number, before being contacted in return. Montjoy had yet to respond to the text Garrett had sent upon arriving in France.

Garrett crossed a footbridge over the Ill River and entered the Pavillon Régent Petite France. He stopped at the front desk and picked up the envelope that had been left for Gareth Walker. In the plain brown package was a key to the room Montjoy had reserved as William Shaw, and Garrett quickly found the second-floor corner suite.

He needed to think, and sleep, so Garrett lay down for a

short nap with his head tucked into the crook of his arm, the Glock in his right hand, and a chair back jammed beneath the door handle.

CHAPTER FIFTY-EIGHT

Prague, Czech Republic

Anatoly Laskin had gladly picked up the pricey prix fixe tab for two at the Bellevue Restaurant. He casually followed behind the young woman and watched her shapely stride as she strolled along the riverfront. She was a Muscovite, at least twenty-five years his junior, and in Prague on business for some Russian conglomerate that Laskin had caught the name of over drinks, but had already forgotten. It didn't matter, for he could tell that she had been interested in him the moment they made eye contact from adjacent lunch tables a day earlier at Petřínské Terasy.

The businesswoman from Basmanny was smart and attractive, Laskin was clever and clearly a man of power, and neither harbored any illusions as to what their relationship would entail until she returned to Russia in two days' time. Never mind that his current girlfriend, a twice-divorced middle-aged French ex-socialite of sorts, was out of town visiting family on the Italian Riviera. She wasn't expected to return until the weekend, and besides, Laskin missed the company of a good Russian *zhenshchina*.

The young woman remained a step ahead of Laskin, and both enjoyed their roles in drawing out the foreplay. Russian women were especially good at it, and Laskin began to debate whether he would even need to pop one of the blue pills he kept discreetly by his bedside. *Not tonight,* the head of station thought to himself. That evening would witness the return of the legendary spy who had bedded half of Berlin's contingent of Western women back in better times. Cold War conquests that his subordinates certainly still gossiped about, wherever that sorry lot had dispersed to since the fall of communism.

The woman spun as they entered Laskin's flat and the two began the ritual lovers' tête-à-tête, walking backward in an impassioned embrace while clumsily shedding clothes en route to the bedroom. At the door, the woman stopped and pushed her hand to Laskin's lips as he attempted to protest. She held up a finger as the signal she needed a moment, before she turned and made her way to the bathroom.

Govno, Laskin thought to himself. He hated wearing a condom.

He moved to the bed and removed his watch and shoes. Laskin decided to bypass the chemical assistance he typically required, especially for someone less attractive or whom he was seducing for matters of manipulation. He heard the water running and the toilet flush.

It was then that Laskin froze, and struggled to recall whether "Anna" had taken her purse to the bathroom.

She should have dropped it by the entryway.

His question was answered when the woman suddenly opened the door, her clothes buttoned and zipped back up, holding a pistol with a suppressor attached at high ready in one hand.

Laskin shook his head, disgusted at his momentary lapse in judgment. He always suspected it would end this way. "Do it, quickly," was all he said.

"That depends," Mullova replied.

Laskin eyed the woman. "Who sent you? Fedorov? Borodin?"

Mullova did not answer.

"Whoever did is attempting to cover his own tracks."

"I'm here because of *Spindle*, and *Herr* Schultz, in Berlin."

"I can see that Moscow is monitoring me again," Laskin replied matter-of-factly.

"You met with the deputy chief of MI6 three days ago, and were quite loose with your tongue."

"Join me in bed and I'll show you loose with my tongue."

Mullova fired a 9mm round just beyond Laskin's shoulder, causing one of the pillows behind him to explode in a cloud of synthetic filaments.

Laskin raised his hands in a mock gesture of surrender. "You missed," he replied, blithely. "What do you want to know, other than what your superiors have already heard me discuss with Banastre?"

"Where is *Spindle*?"

"How should I know?"

"You referenced him in the present tense."

"Of course I did," Laskin replied, laughing out loud. "Who believes Alexei Arkipov is really dead? A Russian man who drowns after he's had a few vodkas? You must be joking."

Mullova fired another bullet past Laskin.

"Yes, go ahead and kill as many pillows as you want. Nobody thinks that Alexei is dead, at least, not anyone who should still be working in the FSB or SVR or whoever the hell sent you." Laskin refastened his belt and gestured toward his liquor cabinet. "If you're going to shoot me, may I?"

Mullova nodded her head. "The deputy chief of MI6 mentioned that Arkipov has resurfaced. What did he mean?"

"What he said." Laskin threw one hand up in an exasperated gesture and walked to his array of bourbon bottles as Mullova kept her pistol trained on him. "I don't suppose you want a drink?"

She ignored the question. "Why did you reference recently deceased British agents when Montjoy asked about *Spindle*?"

"To see if the deputy chief would show his hand. Banastre is clever, but Madeleine Halliwell was his grandmother and so now it's personal. That he didn't show any surprise at my query indicates the British believe the recent assassinations of their retired operatives are somehow connected to Arkipov, and possibly, to something that happened at the Oberbaum Bridge in 1984."

"What do you know of the missing MI6 agent?"

"What I told Banastre, nothing," Laskin replied.

"Was Malinovsky the mole?"

"We executed him, didn't we?"

"You were quick to denounce your KGB colleague back in East Berlin."

"Better him than me," Laskin replied, without thinking.

"By which you mean?"

Laskin did not respond.

"Why did you suggest that Egon Schultz may have something the British agent would be interested in? What information does he have?"

"Schultz was a border guard at the time the MI6 operative was arrested. He found something, or at least bragged to his son that he did. I don't know what it was, but I suspect that it is information that has to do with that nasty little rumor which circulated back when you were still learning to walk."

"Concerning what?"

"Was it Markov? Golitsyn?" Laskin asked, still fishing. When she didn't answer, he said, "Ask yourself, why are you here? If I was worried about what some stupid little book had in its pages, would I still be in *Czechia*? Whoever sent you is clearly concerned about secrets the dead might give up in regard to their own role in whatever is going on."

"I've been authorized to take whatever measures are necessary to find out what you know."

Laskin finished pouring a whiskey, before opening his shirt and tapping his chest. "Do me the favor, *dorogoy*."

Mullova centered her pistol on Laskin.

Neither Russian spoke as Mullova cocked the 1911.

Laskin took a drink, shook his head in disgust, and tossed the glass in the bar sink, causing it to shatter. "Alexei once told me that he always favored the French-speaking part of Canada. That's all I know."

Mullova lowered her gun. "If you contact Schultz or Montjoy and warn either about me, I'll come back here, and it won't be to fuck you."

CHAPTER FIFTY-NINE

Strasbourg, France

John Riker smoked a cigarette while he leaned against a tree on a wharf at the confluence of the Ill River and *Canal des Faux Remparts*. He had arrived in Strasbourg that morning, having abandoned his room at the Baur au Lac after assuming that he was being followed by the man with Vann's phone who had called him outside the Zurich hotel.

After he hopped the tram at *Paradeplatz*, Riker traveled several stops before alighting near the main train station. He had with him the backpack he always carried when on assignment, knowing that at any moment he might be forced to abandon his plan. As such, the rucksack contained everything that was essential to him. The only things remaining at the Baur au Lac were a set of clothes and a few toiletries, which joined the company of other non-valuable items left behind at other hotels throughout the world. Riker knew that the vast majority of his uncertain hunches about a person or situation had been unfounded, and that his decision to leave at the drop of a hat was almost always unwarranted.

Then again, the authorities could miss as many times as they liked. Riker could be wrong only once.

At the train station, Riker had contacted Chénard and explained what occurred in Zurich. When the assassin wondered aloud whether it was prudent to scrub the operation until they could regroup, his handler was adamant there would be no third chance, reminding Riker that they were in this situation because of his failure in Charleston.

Riker realized that he was left with two options. He could either vacate the mission altogether, retire with a semi-stained reputation and potentially risk having Chénard come after him at some point in the future; or, he could finish the job he had been paid to do and take a chance that he might get caught in the net British Intelligence had potentially cast around their deputy chief.

Chénard had then disclosed that he had been in contact with another operative in Strasbourg, Artem Ivanenko, a former Spetsnaz officer who had been teamed with Vann. Ivanenko had followed the female operative from Lindau and verified that he witnessed her meet with Montjoy in France, and that the pair were staying at the Régent Petite France and Spa.

Riker acquiesced, perhaps against his better judgment, and had immediately traveled to Strasbourg.

It was then that fate smiled on him for the first time since Charleston. Riker had just begun his surveillance of the hotel when he saw the very man who had followed him in Zurich enter an adjacent accommodation on *Rue des Moulins*. It had been from a distance, and by chance, and Riker was certain that the sighting had not been a reciprocal one.

It was at that moment he realized that MI6 was not running any kind of protection detail to safeguard its deputy chief, or a team would have been alerted to Riker's presence and he would already be sitting in the back of some windowless van making its way out of the city en route to a secure location.

The assassin couldn't be sure as to what exactly was in play, but he was certain it could be contained and the mission completed successfully. Riker first needed to figure out who the man and woman from Lindau were and what they were doing in Strasbourg. Once both of them had been eliminated, he could find Banastre Montjoy and complete the contract.

Riker stamped out his Belomorkanal and decided he would also crush two birds with one stone.

He did not have to wait long before the man from Zurich exited through the front of his hotel. His target covered the distance down the quay quickly and crossed the bridge that led back to the Grand Île. Riker fell into step a block behind the man and followed him until he entered the patio of a small bistro by the water, sat down, and ordered something to drink.

Riker knew that he would be unable to trail the man around Strasbourg for very long, as he was clearly a professional and would eventually spot the pursuit. But neither could the man monitor Riker's movements, for the same reason.

He and his adversary were now caught in a stalemate, and Riker could see only one way out.

The assassin walked to the entrance of the patio, within sight of the man, and dialed the number for Mykhail Vann.

CHAPTER SIXTY

The bistro was comfortably crowded, and like most good restaurants in Strasbourg, enjoyed a constantly inter-changing mix of tourists and residents. The wind had died down and the sun had come out from the clouds, inducing a momentary swap of jackets for sunglasses for the majority of patrons on the patio.

Riker bypassed the hostess and kept his eye on the lone operative sitting at a corner table, whose own attention remained firmly fixed on Riker as he approached. The man's mobile was still vibrating from the call Riker placed to Mykhail Vann's phone a moment earlier.

"You should answer it." Riker held up his own mobile. "It might be an important call."

Sean Garrett eyed the man from Zurich. "It's a number that won't be in operation much longer."

Riker flashed a wry smile as he pointed to a chair. "May I?"

The man said nothing, so Riker sat down and summoned

a nearby server. "Balmoral if you have it, Talisker if you don't. Glenlivet if you must."

"*Bien sûr,*" the waiter replied, and then glanced at Garrett, who shook his head.

"Drinking on the job?" Garrett asked.

"Only those that don't present a challenge." Riker placed his phone on the table. "So, it was you who attempted to set me up by sending messages from my colleague's mobile concerning the whereabouts of our mutual friend. How very clever."

Garrett ignored the comment. "You should have stayed in Switzerland."

"I couldn't agree more," Riker replied. "The chocolate is better." He then twisted a finger into his cheek, an Italian gesture for both delicious and beautiful. "On the other hand, the women in France, no?" Riker noticed the man had slipped his hand into one pocket. "Are we going to draw on one another like the Wild West in front of all these people and on such a pleasant afternoon?"

"I've got a way out," Garrett replied. "Do you?"

"Men like us only have temporary escape routes, never a way out."

"It would be a mistake to think that you and I are alike."

"We are made from the same mold, *mon ami.* Do not deceive yourself of this."

"*We are never deceived,*" Garrett replied. "*We deceive ourselves.*"

"And the man whose phone is in your front pocket?" Riker asked, accentuating his point. "Lying in deep freeze in a city morgue or some ditch on the outskirts of town?" The waiter returned with Riker's scotch. He tapped his glass on the table twice, in a silent requiem for Vann, and then raised it. "To a long life."

"Drink up. You wasted the only chance you had." Garrett then added, "In Charleston."

Riker lifted his glass again, and then downed the remaining whiskey. "The penny drops."

"I'm coming for your handler as well."

Riker laughed. "It might help if you knew his name and location."

"Soon."

The assassin's tone suddenly took on a more serious tenor. "Since you are fond of quoting Goethe, allow me. '*Who holds Satan, let him hold him well, he hardly will be caught a second time.*'"

"Then you were right about being cut from the same cloth," Garrett said as he stood and tossed a ten-Euro note on the table. "I *am* the devil."

CHAPTER SIXTY-ONE

Tomas Karlson finished packing his convertible duffle, and reverified his ticket to Stockholm. He had decided that he would monitor the hotel where Banastre Montjoy had supposedly been seen for only one day more. Karlson's conviction was beginning to waver, again, waffling between the extremes of wanting to exact vengeance on his tormentors, and pitifully retreating to the confines of his miserable existence in Sweden. He decided that if hadn't spotted the blonde woman from Lindau or the deputy chief of MI6 in the next twenty-four hours, he would abandon the hunt and return home.

For the last three days, Karlson had rotated his reconnaissance between several points around the Régent Petite France and Spa. He made up his mind that morning that if he was going to waste more of his time, it would be at the eatery he had patronized during his first round of surveillance.

If the mission was going to fail, it would be over the best tiramisu Karlson had ever tasted.

Karlson verified that he had in his possession the photo

of the woman from Lindau, though he had stared at it long enough to be able to recreate the likeness by memory. He exited the hotel and took his time meandering down *Quai de Paris*, opting for the longer route to the scenic patio on the Ill River across from the luxury accommodation he had grown weary of staring at.

Fortunately, the wait at *La Corde à Linge* was minimal. Karlson looked forward to practicing his French with waitstaff who were used to tourists speaking every other language but their own, all the while assuming that servers must certainly be fluent in whatever the guests' native tongue might be. He asked for a table further back from the water, and the hostess, accustomed to the exact opposite demand, gave a Karlson a quizzical look, but obliged his request. The afternoon was chilly and overcast and the sparse crowd reflected the weather. This would have normally been fine with Karlson, who disliked people, if not for the fact that he would have preferred a larger crowd in which to disguise his presence.

The assassin sat down and ordered roast duck, while he set his sights on the adjacent patio. It was a fool's errand, he acknowledged, for either of his targets could have already checked out and moved on, or be using an alternate point of entry to come and go. Karlson kept an intermittent eye on the hotel through his appetizer, main, and dessert, and had just finished an apéritif when the patio door of the in-house restaurant across the canal opened.

The blonde woman in the photo, carrying a drink from the interior bar, followed the maître d' to a table set for two, and sat down.

Karlson canceled his order for a second drink, opting instead for a water, and waited to see if Banastre Montjoy would show.

CHAPTER SIXTY-TWO

Oberbaum Bridge
Berlin, Germany

F oot traffic along the Oberbaum was surprisingly light considering the time and temperate nature of the afternoon, though over the last hour a parade of crowded sightseeing cruises had passed beneath the iconic bridge en route to the Landwehr Canal. Banastre Montjoy puffed on his churchwarden while he waited, and admired the architecture of the cloister vault that bedecked the pedestrian entrance of the formerly closed-off East German borough of Friedrichshain.

The closest he had come to this side of the border checkpoint during a time when it was unwise to, was from the friendly bank of the Spree during an abandoned exfiltration attempt of a mid-level Romanian mole in 1985. SIS had learned, at the last minute, that the double-agent whom they were planning to smuggle over had been turned back by the KGB, which meant the man would offer little more than disinformation and intelligence dead-ends. Rather than permit the spy to cross and persuade him once again to work against Moscow, MI6 burned the engineer from Bucharest, fooling the ever-suspicious Soviets into believing their operative had become what amounted to a quadruple agent. Montjoy had never bothered to follow up as to what happened to the father of four, but such was the nature of their very nasty business.

An unassuming man, in his fifties and wearing a rather ill-fitting gray pinstriped suit, leaned against a brick support near a bridge lamppost and glanced intermittently in Montjoy's direction. He lit another cigarette and turned back toward the river, but not before peering over his shoulder one more time.

Montjoy casually made his way to a section of railing nearby. "It looks quite different with the watchtowers gone."

The man nodded. "For some, they remain."

"Egon Schultz?"

"*Ja*," the man replied, pivoting in Montjoy's direction while taking a long drag. "Call me Stefan."

"If you prefer." Montjoy extended his hand.

"Do you know the Richard Scarry books, about farm animals?"

"Certainly."

"In our version, the inchworm is called Egon," Schultz noted. "In addition to being born and raised on the wrong side of history, I was saddled with a terribly outdated family name. A cartoon *wurm's* name, which every German schoolboy was, of course, well aware of."

"It sounds like you picked the wrong parents."

The German snorted a stilted laugh. "As with everything else in the Eastern Bloc, we were given few choices. Once that godforsaken barrier came down, I moved to Kreuzberg and left Egon, and a great many other things, on this side of the river."

"Not as easy as you make it sound, I should think."

Schultz shrugged his shoulders. "I was one of the luckier ones. At eighteen, they gave me a rifle and told me where to shoot."

"And you were there that night, I was led to believe."

"*Ja*," he said, flicking his half-smoked cigarette to the ground. "Right here."

Montjoy began to speak, but Schultz interrupted him. "How did you find me?"

"A friend of a friend."

Schultz nodded. "You are all friends now, I imagine."

"Some more than others. The game has changed—"

"*Nein*," Schultz replied, shaking his head. "Only the players."

"Granted."

"Men of power are all the same, walls or no. Always looking to push around the little pawns, never caring what happens to any of them."

"I'm looking for one that disappeared."

Schultz pulled a hip flask from his pocket. "The man in the water," he said, offering a drink to Montjoy, who shook his head. The German threw back his own as he turned up the silver bottle. "Better than yesterday, and God willing, worse than tomorrow." He finished the sentiment with an exaggerated exhalation. "The first time they drank good scotch, members of the Politburo must have known their system was doomed."

"There are some who use the same argument against capitalism."

"The weapon of tyrants," Schultz scoffed. "Only someone with the luxury to reject such things could be so arrogant."

A U-Bahn crossed overhead, briefly muzzling the conversation. The sun moved from behind a cloud bank, and suddenly the overpass seemed congested with tourists and twentysomethings getting a jump on their evening revelry.

"About that fish," Montjoy said, interrupting the silence.

"So far to swim," Schultz murmured to himself, thinking back on the moment. "He was nearly halfway out when they shot him. There—" he pointed to a spot in the water. "Your man went under, and I was certain he would not resurface, until he did. I was shocked he made it back to the bank. We tended to panic back then and fire at anything that moved when it wasn't supposed to. He was pulled ashore just below my position on the bridge. I was ordered to come down and help by a young officer excitedly barking orders at anyone within earshot."

"Can I buy you a drink?" Montjoy asked.

"Does Dolly Parton sleep on her back?"

Montjoy smiled. "After you."

The men walked to a nearby schnitzel restaurant and found a table on the patio. Schultz ordered two radlers and a plate of pommes.

"The bullet only grazed his leg, slowed by the water, I suppose. They pumped half of the Spree out of him so he could talk." Schultz then muttered to himself, "Saving a man's life just to kill him."

"How long was he here?"

"A few days only. If I had to guess, and that's the only

thing we had back then about what went on, they sent him to Lubyanka, or some other hellhole in the USSR."

"Do you remember who was in charge of his interrogation?"

"*Nein.*"

"Do you know if the Stasi found what they were looking for?"

Schultz took a sip of his beer and lemonade brew and dipped a handful of fries into a concoction of ketchup and mayonnaise. "They didn't find the sketchbook, if that's what you are asking."

Montjoy's reaction was one Schultz had clearly hoped the revelation would elicit. The German himself smiled, pleased that someone of importance and connected to the operation was finally privy to the clever secret he had carried for so many years. "I fooled them all, the bastards on both sides. It's always been the weakness of people in high places, to underestimate those they see as beneath them."

"Clearly," Montjoy replied. "I should hope you still have it."

"I do," Schultz replied. "The drawings are quite good. Enough at least to have allayed suspicion that your agent might not be who he pretended. Until he shit his pants and jumped into the Spree."

"He was young. He panicked."

"Yet, he had mind enough to hide his sketchbook."

"How did you find it, and not the others?"

"I wondered the same thing for many years. Certainly, the Stasi wished to hold up the prized catch as their own, without Moscow's fingers all over it. Little Man complex, I think you

English call it. I was in the cell for much of the second day, watching the interrogators at work. They were a little overenthusiastic, to say the least. The prisoner continued to insist he was a West German artist and that he spooked because the dogs began to bark. He was convincing. I believed him, at least, but then, near the end, when he was a battered, bloody mess, he broke. I think he knew he was doomed and that he would soon be in the terminal company of the KGB. Your agent looked his interrogator in the eye, laughed and spit, and told him in English that the Oberbaum would never give up its secret."

"Meaning?"

"I thought little of it at the time, until weeks later, sitting over a loose-leaf tea that had lost whatever flavor it might have had long before. I had been stationed along the bridge entryway the evening of his capture, and it dawned on me that the man was suddenly at the back of the line, as if he had appeared from nowhere. I should have seen his approach, from Friedrichshain. I dismissed it at the time, but later I realized he must have been waiting beneath the bridge. At the end of my next rotation, I searched the edges of the underpass. And there it was, jammed between a narrow gap in the brick where the mortar had cracked and come loose."

"Why keep it to yourself? Why not bring it to a superior and curry favor?"

"For what, a disingenuous pat on the back and a bottle of cheap vodka? I had come to hate my system more than what I was brainwashed to believe yours represented. In the end, it was my secret alone."

"But you didn't keep it to yourself, or I wouldn't be sitting here," Montjoy said. "You told someone."

Schultz nodded. "My son, several years after."

"When you thought all that you had was some harmless Cold War trinket. A conversation piece at family reunions."

"Peter works for the government and is the product of a unified Germany. He was born two months before the Wall came down and is all too happy to reject one entire half of where we came from. As he and I were never close, I thought the sketchbook might connect us in some way, that it could be something which linked our family's, our country's, past and present." Schultz's tone had taken on a hint of despondency. "He swore himself to silence."

"I'm afraid your son didn't attach the same sentiment to the secret you shared. The younger generation seldom does. At some point, he himself was looking to impress, or seeking a back-scratch up the line. I found you easily enough, and you must know there are others, these 'friends' you spoke of, who might also be privy to what you have in your possession, and come looking."

Schultz glanced up with a measure of concern over the disclosure, one that was likely the residue of the fear East Germans lived with on a daily basis.

"They won't buy you a beer and cross their fingers you'll cooperate."

Schultz did not answer as he watched a boat chug up the Spree. He suddenly downed the last of his *Radler* and stood. "If I'm here tomorrow at this time, you'll have my answer, and your little book."

Montjoy masked his skepticism with a polite tip of his cap.

Schultz turned to leave, then stopped and smiled. "How did communists light their homes before candles?"

"You have me," Montjoy conceded.

"Electricity."

CHAPTER SIXTY-THREE

Strasbourg, France

Tomas Karlson remained a block behind the blonde woman as she made her way from the station at the Museum of Modern and Contemporary Art. She had taken lunch and three drinks on the patio of the hotel where he had first spotted her, and at which one of Chénard's operatives had confirmed she and Banastre Montjoy were staying.

The deputy chief of MI6 had never shown, though several other random men approached the table to chat with its lone, attractive occupant, only to be politely rebuffed. The woman had remained at the Régent Petite France and Spa for several hours, taking selfies and tending to her makeup, before heading unsteadily to a tram near the canal. She rode two stops and alighted on the outskirts of the city, pausing several times to get her bearings. The inebriated woman then made her way to a nearby park, where she turned down a path that ran along the waterway.

Karlson remained a casual distance behind, as the woman continued past families playing by the river. She suddenly stopped to double over a trash can, though Karlson could not tell if she had vomited. Even in her state, the further they moved away from the public park, the fewer people there would be for Karlson to mask his pursuit. By the time the woman came to where the paved path turned into a dirt trail, the surrounding area was completely free of anyone else. Karlson was now forced to make a decision. He knew the canal would continue for several more kilometers until it rejoined the Ill River. However, since only the two of them remained on the path this far out, if Karlson stayed close behind his mark for much longer, the woman might become suspicious and possibly draw attention to herself, and him.

Scheisse, he thought to himself. He did not want to drop his surveillance and be forced to find her again at the hotel, knowing that she, and quite possibly his primary target, could leave Strasbourg at any moment. He had shamefully made up his mind to abandon the mission only hours earlier, but now with his opportunity for revenge was so close, the conviction that first brought Karlson out of hiding, and the bloodlust that accompanied it, had returned with a vengeance.

The woman paused and began to play with her phone. Karlson glanced along the trail to ensure they were still alone. She once again began to move down the path, but then abruptly stopped, seemingly confused as to her whereabouts. Karlson dropped behind a tree line that skirted the trail. He decided it was time to confront the woman and kill her whether or not she gave him the information he wanted. Karlson had just stepped onto the path when the woman abruptly turned into a heavily forested area adjacent to the river walk.

Karlson adjusted his own pace and came level to where

the woman's course had deviated from the path. There were a series of trails cut into the brush, where young lovers or illicit drug users likely sought out concealed spots to indulge their indiscretions. Having sensed movement to his immediate left, Karlson slowed to a casual walk, before stepping off the trail at the same point as had his mark.

He immediately came face to face with the woman, standing only five feet away and leveling a pistol on him with a suppressor at high ready.

Karlson stopped dead and raised his hands in a half-hearted gesture to show that he was harmless. He made certain that his expression of shock, which wasn't one he needed to completely fake, came across as genuine in order to mask his purpose for being on that section of the walk.

"*Ma chérie, je n'ai pas d'argent,*" Karlson said, as innocently as possible, hoping to convince the woman he had no money and that he assumed she planned to rob him.

"The pistol on your right hip, lose it."

Karlson did not immediately comply, pretending that he hadn't understood, all the while considering how to keep up the charade long enough to get to his gun.

"You can do it with or without a bullet in your kneecap."

Karlson realized that the woman was neither drunk, lost, nor unsure of herself. "I should have known that was an act back at the restaurant," Karlson said, in English, disgusted with himself as he slowly pulled his Glock from its holster and laid it on the ground at his feet. He stood, and stared down the MI6 agent who had gotten the drop on him.

"Do I really need to tell you to step back?"

Karlson complied, taking several, toward the river.

Anderton picked up Karlson's gun and ejected the magazine while simultaneously racking the chambered hollow-point round out and onto the ground. She tossed the empty mag into the bushes near the bank and the pistol into the canal.

Karlson was about to commend the woman in the hopes of disrupting her attention, when he caught sight of a car pulling up behind her. The driver hesitated, then spied the pair and pulled off the road to wait. Karlson could make out a young man behind the wheel, which clearly wasn't the deputy chief of SIS, and it was then that he saw the distinctive Uber logo magnet affixed near the front bumper.

"You must be joking," Karlson said.

Anderton ignored the comment while she pushed her pistol into the waistband of her jeans and pulled her sweater over the grip to hide it. "The man you're after is not in Strasbourg. If you want to meet Banastre Montjoy, he will be at the Restaurant Seehaase in Berlin, at 1 p.m., in two days' time."

Karlson did not respond, but nodded.

"And if I see you anywhere else near my chief before then, I will kill you," Anderton added, as she turned and made her way toward the car.

CHAPTER SIXTY-FOUR

Berlin, Germany

E lena Mullova listened to music and finished a coffee as she sat by a window in first class on a Deutsche Bahn train outbound from Berlin Hauptbahnhof, heading to Frankfurt. She looked forward to a proper meal and sleep that night, before boarding her Air Canada flight the next morning, nonstop to Montreal.

Mullova had been in Berlin only fifteen hours, long enough to locate and question Egon Schultz. He and his modest flat had been fairly easy to find, and though the man was in his mid-fifties, he looked and moved like someone much older. She had surveilled him from a park across the street from his block housing, but had been unable to get him alone because a friend and his family had come for dinner and stayed the night. As a result, Mullova was forced to wait and follow the mailman the next morning from his apartment building to his tram stop and finally, to a local post office, where he picked up his assigned batch of mail for that day's delivery. Schultz had taken his time, drinking coffee and chatting with colleagues before methodically loading his yellow Deutsche Post bicycle and setting out from the depot with a small trailer in tow.

The Russian operative had trailed her target for over an hour. She kept an eye open for an opportunity to isolate Schultz, but the pace was steady and his slow, circular route was strictly contained to a crowded urban district. It wasn't until an early lunch, after Schultz left his mail carrier leaned against a tree in a park, that Mullova was able to induce the man to move to a space where she could more easily question him. She did this by stealing his bicycle while he took his time over a sandwich by a pond and with his back to the road. She pedaled to a nearby wooded area and hid it in a hedgerow. When he returned to resume his route almost an hour later, Schultz did exactly what Mullova suspected he would with his bike and mail inexplicably gone—he went home.

While Schultz poured himself a whiskey, likely wondering what in the world he would tell his boss when he returned to work, Mullova quietly let herself in. When he saw a woman standing in his living room, dressed in all black and holding a large-caliber weapon with a suppressor, Schultz only stared for a moment before adding another shot of bourbon to his glass.

His answers were as simple as her questions.

Yes, he had been a guard at the Oberbaum Bridge in the fall of 1984.

Yes, he had recently met a man who claimed to be from MI6.

Concerning intelligence taken from the agent who had

been captured long ago, no, he had no idea what she was talking about.

The bullet Mullova put into Schultz's leg caused him to drop his drink and howl in pain.

Yes, there had been a book and he had found it.

Yes, he told Banastre Montjoy about it, the day before.

No, he no longer had it.

Mullova fired another bullet into Schultz's other leg, just above the knee, causing him to scream louder. He whimpered as blood poured from both wounds, pooling onto the floor at his feet near his favorite easy chair by a small black and white TV. He held his hand up while he labored to control his breathing, which had begun to come in shallow bursts.

He had planned to keep the sketchbook, but then changed his mind and mailed it to MI6 headquarters in London that very morning.

Convinced that Schultz was telling the truth and that she would get no other useful information from him, Mullova let him live. When she contacted Boris Golitsyn with the disappointing news, his only reply was to remain in place. Eight hours later, Mullova was informed that she was booked on a flight from Frankfurt to Montreal, departing the next morning.

She was to link up with local FSB operatives in Canada, who would provide her with the information she needed to find Alexei Arkipov.

CHAPTER SIXTY-FIVE

Montreal, Canada

Emile Chénard downed the first sips of what he swore would be his last lowball of the afternoon. The pricey single-barrel bourbon, which two hours earlier stood at a quarter full, now sat empty on his desk, and he realized that something was needed as a proxy to breaking the seal on a second bottle of ten year.

That particular something should have involved a focused analysis, and if need be, a reorganization of the two-pronged operation unfolding in France. Chénard had since dispersed separate assassins to the same target, though both had so far failed to finish off the deputy chief of SIS. Nor had he received any updates in almost twelve hours, which meant that Chénard was, to his chagrin, at wits end for the time being.

Playing catch-up was a game the Cold War spy was most unfamiliar with. His rise through Russian Intelligence had been meteoric for a reason, namely a refined skill at navigating the labyrinth of misinformation and misdirection on a three-dimensional board. At this, the man known as Heinrich, *Spindle*, and Arkipov had been a grandmaster, anticipating six moves ahead of not only the British and American spy networks, but his own overlords in Moscow.

Chénard's impressive maneuvering, from an expendable Stasi operative to the KGB *rezidentura* in East Berlin and finally to the upper echelon of the FSB after communism exploded in the faces of the Central Committee like a laced Cubano, had been the consequence of a remarkable gambit. It was the type of genius which would have eventually been the subject of assorted post-Wall tell-alls from both sides of the former Bloc.

Everything had been unfolding as Chénard had foreseen, until his former nemeses at MI6 sprung a trap from which he could not extricate himself. In less than one year, the operative who had been fast-tracked for the pinnacle found himself 'drowned' in the black Sea and ingloriously relocated to Montreal.

He should be overseeing a vast spy apparatus as the Federal Security Service's head of intelligence, not looking over his shoulder under an alias in a frozen corner of Canada.

Chénard pushed the papers he had been mindlessly shuffling to the back of his desk, and still in a fog of mashed corn and malted barley, reached for another fifth of Old Rip Van Winkle.

CHAPTER SIXTY-SIX

Moscow, Russia

B oris Golitsyn skipped through the last hour of digital audio files recorded by the bugged umbrella in Markov's office. There had been few visitors and scant conversation, as the man seemed to do little more than shuffle through papers and mumble to himself. It was possible the entire routine was an act and that Markov suspected he was being monitored, something some of them wondered most of the time, and most were certain of some of the time.

Golitsyn could not be sure what Markov or Laskin were hiding. What worried him more than either man's potential involvement with the British during the Cold War, was what either man could and would accuse Golitsyn himself of. There was also the matter of intelligence carried by the captured MI6 agent at the Oberbaum and what it might reveal concerning the supposed leak in the KGB station during the 1980s, when Golitsyn was head of station. Egon Schultz had apparently sent the book to SIS headquarters in London, who would soon be able to determine what their missing agent had been attempting to exfil out of East Germany.

The entire situation was a time bomb waiting to go off.

Golitsyn clicked out of the audio files and tried to recall the more relevant details of the officers who had served beneath his command in East Berlin thirty years earlier.

All four men, Golitsyn, Heinrich, Markov, and Laskin, had overlapped their postings in the GDR by three years. Markov and Laskin had been typical KGB officers stationed in East Germany, many of whom were underpaid and overworked, much of the time in relative isolation. The most valuable of them all had been Markus Heinrich. Golitsyn had been head of station only a year before Heinrich first popped up on his radar. At the time, he was a Stasi operative who had recently been transferred to Berlin from Bonn. Little was known about Heinrich, other than that he had been raised in an orphanage in East Berlin and adopted by an older couple with long-standing ties to the Party.

Golitsyn's KGB office directly liaised with the Stasi directorate that housed Heinrich and several of the department's more successful Romeos, operatives assigned to find and romantically exploit vulnerable Western women. And, as Golitsyn like to joke, the charming and attractive Heinrich became one of his best penetration agents.

It was Golitsyn who had given Heinrich the code name *Spindle*. Through the late 1970s and early 1980s, the young officer's stock continued to rise among the KGB hierarchy, who at times were prone to see their Stasi counterparts, though ruthless, as somewhat less effective than Moscow would have liked. By the summer of 1984, Heinrich had risen to the rank of colonel, and it was only a few months later that

Spindle approached Golitsyn with knowledge that the British would attempt to smuggle high-level intelligence through the Oberbaum checkpoint sometime in November. Golitsyn was impressed with Heinrich's initiative and his information-gathering capabilities, and allowed him to design an operation that Heinrich believed would also expose the mole operating inside East Berlin.

He had come by proof in the way of a photograph taken of Sergei Malinovsky meeting with an unknown British agent, whom Heinrich was certain Malinovsky had been supplying with sensitive intelligence. Heinrich's plan was to spring a trap that would capture the MI6 agent during his attempt to cross back into the West, force him to confess, and then use the admission to confront Malinovsky. *Operation Trapdoor* began without a hitch when the alleged MI6 operative attempted to pass through the checkpoint in early November.

The problem, however, was that the supposed agent was not carrying any kind of incriminating documents. Moreover, the man's claim that he was a West German artist who crossed intermittently to teach classes in the East came off as genuine. The entire examination descended into farce when his interrogators disagreed as to what should be done, nearly coming to blows in front of a roomful of bewildered border guards. When the prisoner was finally questioned as to the whereabouts of his sketchbook and teaching materials, he panicked, and that single moment of uncertainly exposed who he was, or at least, what he was not.

The British operative was taken back into the Soviet sector and tortured, not only for information about Malinovsky, but any other Russian or East German official who might be supplying SIS with information.

Malinovsky was quickly arrested. He too was convincing in his protestations against the charge of spying for the British, arguing that the MI6 agent had approached him, and that it was he, Malinovsky, who had rebuffed the young man. When asked why he hadn't immediately reported the overture to his superiors, the KGB officer couldn't offer a good reason.

A month later, Malinovsky was shot.

Moscow had found its mole, and Heinrich was duly rewarded for his operational success. It was in the months that followed that the KGB discovered that Markus Heinrich had actually been born Alexei Arkipov, in Moscow. Upon learning that he was Russian, the KGB invited Heinrich to join Golitsyn's East Berlin station. Heinrich accepted, at the same time he changed his name back to Arkipov.

Comrade Arkipov began to rise through the KGB ranks as fluidly as he had the Stasi's, and when Golitsyn was recalled to Moscow, Arkipov took his former chief's place as head of station in East Berlin.

From his new position in KGB headquarters, Golitsyn kept tabs on his most valuable agent. When the Wall came down and communism with it, Golitsyn transitioned to the newly formed FSK, and then its successor, the FSB. His request to bring Arkipov into his counterintelligence directorate was approved, and Arkipov continued his upward arc in the new order of Russian Intelligence.

In 1994, Arkipov was put in charge of a unit that was sent into Chechnya to wage a covert war against the separatist army and the treasonous Russian officials who had joined them. The squad was ruthless and effective, and while Arkipov's results were championed internally, his methods were quietly questioned by a small minority who feared possible sanctions from the international community once the conflict came to an end.

When the whispers of wide-ranging war crimes finally came to light in early 1996, Arkipov's name began to appear in horrific stories coming out of Chechnya. Though Arkipov would never be extradited from Russia, before Moscow could decide how to best handle the situation internally and the PR externally, Arkipov drowned while swimming in the Black Sea.

Golitsyn sipped a tea and began to read through several pages that had been sent to FSB by what amounted to a small army of analysts pouring over records recently obtained by the SVR. Anatoly Laskin's bugged revelation that Arkipov might be alive and living in either Quebec or Montreal had sparked a quietly aggressive digital search for the supposedly dead man, even before Mullova had contacted Golitsyn with the outcome of her interrogation.

Five years earlier, SVR agents had momentarily found a way into the immigration systems of both the U.S. and Canada. Though the breach was only partial, the FSB had been able to assemble a large database of passport holders in both countries. With rushed computer-generated imagery of what Arkipov might look like in the present day, Golitsyn had a team combing the hacked IDs issued by the Canadian or American governments.

Almost immediately, a retired businessman named Emile Chénard living in Canada, whose photo bore a striking resemblance to the aged likeness of Arkipov, had been singled out as a possible candidate.

Golitsyn had studied the intelligence and agreed, and had, only hours earlier, redirected Elena Mullova to Montreal.

CHAPTER SIXTY-SEVEN

Strasbourg, France

Sean Garrett zipped closed his luggage and stowed the black convertible backpack in the closet of the hotel room he had booked a few hours earlier as Gareth Walker. He would not be sleeping there, but needed to establish a base of operations for the day, as well as to keep his shadow away from the inn his brother had earlier booked himself into as William Shaw. It had been four hours since the assassin sent to kill Banastre Montjoy had approached Garrett on the patio of an eatery by the canal. Though the man's arrogance was the impetus for the Chechen to surface and expose himself, allowing Garrett to see that he did not see him as any kind of threat, the killer had also used the sit-down to serve a tactical advantage. Though Garrett had ensured that the conversation was short and to the point, he noticed that another operative was waiting to tail him when he left the restaurant. No doubt the same man was now nearby, ready to pick Garrett back up once he left the hotel.

In fact, Garrett was counting on it.

It was nearing nightfall and he had just heard from

Montjoy, who had traveled to Berlin. There, he hoped to find the answers concerning a missing Cold War agent, and solve a mystery that began thirty-four years earlier on the Oberbaum Bridge. Garrett was to remain in Strasbourg and keep the man who stalked Montjoy at bay.

It had never been Garrett's nature to stand passively to one side, nor to be intimidated. Everything was in place; the trap was set.

He just needed to spring it.

CHAPTER SIXTY-EIGHT

Artem Ivanenko stood in the shadow of a party supply truck parked across the street from a row of restaurants and cafés in the *Quartier de la Gare*. He lit a cigarette and tossed the still-burning match on the ground, twisting it out with his heel after watching it smolder for several seconds. The Ukrainian took a long drag and glanced back up at his target, who had not moved from the open-air table of a mixed-fare takeaway at which he had been situated for the better part of an hour.

It was nearing 9 p.m., and the former Alpha Group lieutenant could be as patient as he needed in order to retaliate against the man who had murdered his partner. In truth, Ivanenko acknowledged that Mykhail Vann shouldered at least some of that blame, for his surveillance had clearly been sloppy enough for the target he tailed from Lindau to have noticed. That the man was now in possession of Vann's mobile meant only one thing. If Vann had managed his own mark as professionally as had Ivanenko, he would still be alive.

Ivanenko knew that it could be difficult to maintain an

elite standard if not practiced on a regular basis. But Vann had been one of the best soldiers in their Spetsnaz unit, so whatever slip he recently suffered, fatally, as it turns out, was unchar-acteristic. As far as he was concerned, Ivanenko's own role in the operation, to follow and obtain a photo of the woman in Lindau, had been seamless. He had since passed it off, along with surveillance, to another operative whom their handler had dispatched to France.

Ivanenko had taken over pursuit of Vann's killer that after-noon, after coordinating with an assassin sent to Europe who was tasked with finding and finishing off the deputy chief of MI6. The man, a former Special Forces sniper with whom Ivanenko had briefly liaised during their direct-action covert war in Chechnya, now went by the name John Riker.

Ivanenko refocused on his target, now sitting across the street, and the plan he and Riker had devised to corner and eliminate him. Ivanenko had first suggested tracking the loca-tion transponder on Vann's mobile, but the device was either no longer transmitting a signal or had been destroyed and dumped. The pair had decided that Ivanenko would keep tabs from a safe distance and coordinate a parallel pursuit through intermittent mobile and text communication with Riker.

If they were lucky, the men could trap the man from Zurich that night, kill him quickly and quietly, and toss the body in the Ill River.

The man paid his bill and exited the restaurant.

Ivanenko messaged Riker, who replied in kind from one street block over, and the two killers began to follow their mark as he turned off the main *rue* that ran toward the river.

CHAPTER SIXTY-NINE

S ean Garrett walked slowly toward the river, having just finished his meal on the patio of a Middle-Eastern take-away. The chicken korma had been excellent, and though a pitch darkness had descended over the city, the moonless evening was calm and pleasant. Garrett had settled the bill while he kept his periphery on the lone figure across the street, someone who had been monitoring him since Garrett sat down an hour earlier.

The man tailing Garrett had masked his reconnaissance in the shadow of a delivery lorry parked directly opposite the restaurant. He might have been more difficult to spot, if not for a moment of misfortune. Garrett happened to glance in the direction of the van at the same moment the headlights of a passing car shone on that stretch of the road. For a brief second, the bright lights backlit the back side of the vehicle through the windows, illuminating someone standing and staring intently in Garrett's direction.

Garrett came to a row of cafés and shops and turned into an alley that accessed the rear of a two-story clothier. He paused and glanced back through the double-paned display, with the mirrored window acting to disguise his own observation. The man suddenly came into view, and Garrett recognized him as the same operative sent to St. Gallen, whose partner Garrett had killed and who had ultimately followed Anderton to Strasbourg. It was also the same operative who had been tracking Garrett since he left the eatery where he had been approached by the assassin sent after Banastre Montjoy.

It was at that moment Garrett recognized that with each of the players on the board, and now known to one another, it was time to accelerate the showdown to its end move. It was a risky gambit, and one at which he would only be given a single shot.

Garrett quickened his pace and made his way through the *Quartier de la Gare*, before crossing the Ill River over the Barrage Vauban, a stone-bridged dam that dated to the seventeenth century. He passed the main complex of the University of Strasbourg School of Medicine and spied a section that was being renovated. Garrett turned off the main avenue and onto an unpaved road that intersected two buildings. It was poorly lit, and he came to a cordoned-off area where building materials had been stacked and stored. The chain that secured the metal gate had been left unlocked and its opening ajar, and Garrett squeezed through. He continued deeper into the job site, where several shipping containers and two large construction dumpsters buttressed one another, forming a barrier with a row of roll-off trash bins set beside a medical supply building.

An adjacent walkway had been sealed off with a cyclone fence, creating a dead end.

Garrett heard the shuffle of footsteps, stopped, and turned to face the two men who had entered the makeshift quad behind him.

CHAPTER SEVENTY

Berlin, Germany

B anastre Montjoy stepped beneath a portico outside South *Hackescher Markt Station* in the vain hope the rain would subside long enough for him to make and conclude his meeting without getting soaked. He was set to pop open an umbrella and walk to the rendezvous point on the river bridge when he spied Gavin Abbot in his periphery.

"Good evening, sir."

"Quite," Montjoy replied, as Abbot came level with an exterior railing and peered out into what was quickly becoming a downpour.

"Bloody storm," Abbot muttered as he handed Montjoy one of the two coffees he carried. He turned up his collar and pinched it closed and was set to venture from the terminal for the bridge, when Montjoy stopped him.

"No need to prove it's pissing out, mate." Montjoy instead motioned toward the opposite end of the market.

Abbot followed Montjoy through the mob that crammed a covered walkway, and both men entered a Bavarian-themed tavern just as a packed bar erupted over a stoppage-time equalizer in a Bundesliga fixture. Montjoy exited the main restaurant in favor of an outdoor patio, which was empty.

"Good to finally be out of London and in the mix of it," Abbot said, grabbing his lapels and snapping the rain from his jacket.

"Just long enough to hear what you've got." Montjoy eyed a man holding a large beer stein who popped his head out momentarily to check the weather.

"Yes, sir," Abbot replied, disappointed. He had long hinted that he hoped to one day transition from an office analyst to field operative, something Montjoy had subtly signaled in return would not be forthcoming. Abbot pulled a file from his sling case and passed it to Montjoy.

A day earlier, the sketchbook had arrived by anonymous post from Berlin. Schultz had failed to show the day after his meeting with Montjoy at the Oberbaum Bridge, but the former border guard had ultimately decided to turn the intelligence over to MI6. Abbot had opened the package and worked nonstop to decode its pages.

"The pad is in remarkably good shape considering its age," Abbot noted, as he thumbed through the first section of the sketchbook. "The code itself consists of seventy-five lines in five-letter groupings. The key, of course, could have been anything, but our man was clever, and so, might I add, was the bloke who deciphered it."

"No doubt," Montjoy replied, knowing that Abbot was the only one with access to the sketchbook since it arrived at MI6.

"The drawings provide the decrypt, literally. Collishaw

encoded the intelligence using replications of famous paint-
ings, twenty-six in all. The first letter in the title of each repro-
duction corresponds to the alphabet, in sequence. *Nighthawks*
is the initial drawing, N for A. *Sunflowers*, the second, S for
B, *Whistler's Mother,* W for C, *Guernica* for D, and so on. It's
absurdly simple."

"Something the Soviets would have eventually figured out
if they had taken possession of the sketchbook."

"Agreed, but for naught." Abbot paused for effect.

"Edge of my seat, old boy."

"Within the cryptogram is another code."

"Not unusual, but how are you certain your decipher is
correct if the cryptogram is also encoded?"

"Because the first and last lines of the array come from
the opening stanza of *Jabberwocky*. The second cipher sits
between the prose."

"*'Twas brillig, and the slithy toves / Did gyre and gimble in
the wabe—*" Montjoy recited.

"Also nonsensical, albeit, pleasingly so."

"And clever. Unless someone in their immediate ranks
was versed in Lewis Carroll, the Russians would have assumed
they had the wrong key."

"Any ideas?"

"Not at the moment," Montjoy replied, remembering the
poem to be one of William Lindsay's favorites. "Any luck with
the second batch?"

Abbot shook his head. "The cipher could be somewhere
in the files, or the book, but I doubt it. I would suppose that

whoever was running the operation out of Six was privy to its key."

"What about the photographs?"

Abbot produced both of the photos he had been sent, one of Sergei Malinovsky meeting with Stanford Collishaw, and the other of the unknown operative from Madeleine Halliwell's journal. "The first one is definitely Collishaw. It matches his university ID and the official snapshot we have of him on file. The man he is meeting with is Sergei Malinovsky, if the photo from the dossier we kept on him is accurate."

Montjoy flipped open the folder and began to glance at its pages. "Go on."

"As for the other, we have only one 'Brandt' on file. A Stasi officer, first name Kristof. He was East German, but part of his family hailed from the U.K. For that reason, I assume, he was approached in early 1984 with the offer to spy for us. Apparently, he turned MI6 down, and there's nothing more in the file about him."

"Well done."

Abbot paused, confused by the abrupt response, and then it dawned on him. "You've figured something out, haven't you, sir?"

"Perhaps."

Abbot did not reply, and only stared at Montjoy like a schoolboy waiting for a scoop of ice cream.

Montjoy took note of his subordinate's anticipation, but remained mum. "You know the drill, Gavin."

"Of course," Abbot replied, long resigned to his need-to-know role.

"However," Montjoy said, "I need you to deliver something for me, to Prague. A message, and there is some danger involved."

"Absolutely, sir," Abbot replied, smiling broadly.

CHAPTER SEVENTY-ONE

Strasbourg, France

J ohn Riker and Artem Ivanenko had increased their pace after the man pushed his way through a chain-link fence that should have been locked. Riker correctly guessed that it led into a construction site, which would be closed off to prevent oblivious students from wandering through while mindlessly tapping away on their phones. Riker whispered an order in Russian, and Ivanenko nodded and slipped through the opening, pulling his pistol as he did.

Riker followed, and was ten paces behind when both men turned into the enclosed square, approximately sixty feet wide and at least that long. Lines painted in uniform rows on the asphalt indicated that the space typically served as a parking pad, but two waste bins and several multicolored metal shipping containers now lined the area, back to front. Riker could see the man they had followed, and whom he had confronted earlier, unsuccessfully attempt to find a way over and through.

The man had just turned to face the pair, when Ivanenko stepped forward and assumed a modified Weaver stance as he leveled his PSS silent pistol. He ignored a repeated command of "*Nyet,*" from Riker, who wanted to corner and question the man rather than kill him straightaway.

Time slowed as Riker heard the suppressed report of a bullet, but it was not Ivanenko who fired it. The shot had come from behind them, and Riker watched as Ivanenko's head snapped forward and then bounced back violently, causing his body to crumple directly down in an awkward motion that resembled a dead faint.

Riker spun as he reached for his own gun, but a blonde woman with her own pistol trained on him from no more than a dozen yards away gave him pause. Riker showed his palms as she quickly closed the distance between them.

Samantha Anderton kept her eyes on her new target as she put another bullet into the chest of the supine and unmoving man she had just shot. Ivanenko's body jumped as if it had been shocked, before settling back in the same position.

Riker did not take his eyes off the woman or move, but spit on the ground at her feet, a sign of disrespect.

"Quite the entrance, luv," Sean Garrett said as Anderton motioned for Riker to back further into the enclosed quad.

He did so, keeping his hands up and his gaze on her. Riker was certain that he could draw and drop the female agent in time, but not before her partner reacted in kind.

"Toss the Tokarev," Anderton said calmly.

Riker cocked his head in a show of mock commendation. "Is that just a lucky guess?" he asked, as he slowly pulled the gun from his waistband and flipped it to the ground.

"And the one on your ankle."

"Which answers the question," Riker replied, doing as she ordered. "I won't wait for you to order me to lose my knife as well."

"Both of them."

Riker discarded the remainder of his weaponry and then embellished a full turn, holding his jacked hem up to illustrate he had nothing else hidden. "I'll assume you're both with—"

"Shut up," Garrett said to Riker, before addressing Anderton. "Did you sort out the other team?"

"Yes, though he turned out to be only a single," Anderton replied. "These two are the last of them."

"Perhaps." Garrett turned to Riker and addressed him directly. "I came across a squad of Spetsnaz operatives once, in a bar in Marrakesh. They were tough blokes, the lot of the them."

"Still are," Riker replied, then added, "every one of us."

Garrett glanced at Anderton. "You can go."

Anderton furrowed her brow, not sure she had understood what Garrett was telling her. "By which you mean?"

"I'll see you after."

Anderton suddenly understood what Garrett intended to do. "This is a bad idea."

Garrett nodded. "I've had worse."

Anderton was about to protest, when Garrett said, "Go, now."

Riker understood what was happening, and smiled as he shed his coat.

Anderton shook her head in disapproval, but complied

with Garrett's request and pushed the pistol into her pocket as she turned to leave. "You still owe me a drink."

Garrett did not reply as Anderton disappeared down the alley. He squared up with his adversary, leaving about six feet between them. "It's here for the taking, *derevyashka*." Garrett taunted the Russian with an insult meant to imply a useless and ineffectual adversary.

"*Da*," Riker replied. "And my name is Kostya, *mudak*."

Both men began to circle one another, reversing direction several times. Garrett kept his hands up, while Riker bounced his arms by his side, loosening his shoulders. Several times he feigned a step toward Garrett, bringing his fists up, but then dropped back. Both fighters were content to let the other strike first, preferring to use a defensive position to set up a quick counter against an attack.

The faulty street lamp overhead continued to buzz and blink intermittent light, basking the enclosed quad in a disconcerting strobe of black and white.

Riker brought both hands near his face, keeping his elbows close to his body, to protect his midsection. He noticed his opponent kept his chin tucked and his right heel slightly elevated, with his weight on the balls of both feet and with his right leg slightly cocked. The man was clearly trained in Muay Thai, and likely several other disciplines.

Riker was about to throw a half-punch to see how he would react, when Garrett suddenly flashed a lightning-fast left-handed jab. Riker did not have time to pull his head back or pivot to let his elbow parry the shot. It hit him square on the bridge of his nose, causing his head to snap backward and his eyes to water. Riker back-pedaled instinctively as he attempted to shrug off the simple but effective assault. He would have expected some sort of follow-up strike, but the man held his ground, switching his stances and moving lightly on his feet.

Riker shook off the effects of the jab and regained his composure. He now knew what to expect, and walked forward, focusing on the Spetsnaz Systema of redirecting an attacker's use of force against them. He knew he also needed to employ some form of psychological warfare against his opponent in an effort to knock him mentally off-balance. "When I am done with you," Riker taunted, "I'll track down your boss and kill him, too."

"Heavy is the crown," Garrett replied. "Come and fucking take it."

Riker stepped and feigned a left jab-right hook. Garrett stepped back, bringing his hand to his ear and turning his head slightly in anticipation of the combo. Instead, Riker snapped a low hook kick to Garrett's right leg.

Garrett couldn't react fast enough to absorb the blow, and the force caused his lower body to momentarily buckle. He quickly regained his balance and moved to his right, forcing Riker to pull back from any follow-up assault.

Riker smiled, feeling that he now had the advantage, and again stepped in, this time faking another leg strike to disguise a left elbow strike.

Garrett anticipated the deception and pretended to lean into the expected kick, while watching Riker's hands. When the left elbow came forward, fast and accurate, Garrett dropped his shoulder and head and fired a liver punch below the man's defenses. It caught Riker square, knocking his breath partly out.

Riker backed off, again, irritated at himself for having given away his attack. Fortunately, he had compressed his midsection and absorbed the shot before it could do any significant damage. He grew angry, in spite of his better judgment, and rushed forward in a violent but controlled attack. Garrett met his charge by dropping down and launching forward. Both men collided and clinched one another, each seeking an advantageous position to attempt a full-body throw.

Both fighters sought to unbalance the other, with neither gaining any leverage. Garrett struggled to retake control with Riker's left arm wrapped around his head in a lock, while his own hands grasped tightly around his opponent's back.

Riker loosened his grip slightly, and Garrett sought to counter by shifting his weight.

Garrett recognized a second too late what had happened.

Riker realized that his opponent had taken the bait, and as soon as he felt him pivot on his front foot, Riker switched his own stance and hip-threw his opponent. Garrett hit hard, and before he could roll and readjust to a defensive position, Riker swiveled on top, pinning him in a half mount while slamming several punches down through his guard. One connected, though several were parried when Garrett twisted his lower body to gain some traction from his ground position. Riker allowed enough movement to break the man's guard, while keeping him flat on his back.

Garrett struggled to keep Riker in his guard, but as soon as his opponent pivoted to one knee and pulled back while attempting to stand, Garrett felt his foot lock break. Riker rained down several more shots, but Garrett was able to hook both of the man's ankles with his hands, causing Riker to lose his balance and fall backward. Garrett kipped-up into a standing position as Riker rolled up over his right shoulder and to his feet.

The men were back where they started, and both were now breathing in short, heavier bursts. Garrett did not wait, and came forward with a flurry of kicks and elbow strikes. Riker blocked several and deflected another, but a well-placed palm strike caught him just below the chin.

When Riker attempted to step back and regain an advantageous position, Garrett suddenly slammed a hammer fist down onto his clavicle. It was a strike that most fighters did not anticipate, typically choosing to protect their neck and face. But the small bone only required nine pounds of pressure to break, and it shattered with a sickening sound.

Riker tried to back off, clearly in pain and cursing loudly. Garrett quickly followed with a fist to his throat, crushing the hyoid bone and causing Riker's larynx to spasm and collapse.

Riker's left arm was useless, his collarbone shattered. He couldn't control the dry, heaving reflux from the blow to his throat, and so he attempted to wildly punch at Garrett, who had taken a half-step back. An attempted right hook missed, causing Riker to lurch slightly off-balance. The pain along his entire left side prevented him from lifting his arm to protect himself.

Garrett leaned back and out of the path of the awkwardly thrown haymaker, before stepping forward again and connecting with an elbow to Riker's right cheek, breaking his nose and fracturing the lower jawbone. Riker was now leaking blood from his nose and mouth, and when he reached out in a vain effort to defend himself, Garrett took hold of his arm and pulled him forward as he flipped his own legs up around Riker's neck and shoulder, using their combined momentum to sling him violently down to the pavement. Garrett rolled to his back, and with his legs he locked Riker in a triangle choke hold.

Riker pushed himself to his knees and attempted to force himself out of the lock by thrusting his lower body upward. Garrett was too heavy to lift off the ground, though Riker tried several times. He could feel the blood draining from his head and a bleary unconsciousness beginning to take hold.

Garrett kept his legs locked tight, pushing his torso off the ground, while gripping Riker's right arm, which was pinned against Garrett's chest. The assassin continued to thrash back and forth, so Garrett took hold of his wrist and wrenched Riker's arm backward, using his own hip as a fulcrum. He could hear the radial bone snap, while the elbow dislocated. Riker again howled in pain. Garrett then rocked to his right side, releasing Riker from his hold.

Riker lay crumpled on the concrete pad, near the trash bins they had rolled beside. Garrett stood over him, and then took hold of Riker's forehead from behind, yanking back as he pushed his knee into the center of his back.

Riker's neck snapped, and he gurgled several final breaths before Garrett finally released him, allowing the assassin's body to slump forward into an unmoving mass.

CHAPTER SEVENTY-TWO

Moscow, Russia

I t was nearing nightfall when Vasily Markov located the files, and it should have come as no surprise that the case notes were misplaced in a collection of other operations catalogued with the wrong geographic region and year. As he began to sift through the documents, some mislabeled and with pages clearly missing, his memory began to slowly return.

There had been *two* operations run in November of 1984. One had been orchestrated by the Stasi, to stop an MI6 agent who was purportedly bringing across intelligence concerning citizens in West Berlin who were informing for the GDR. The other had been run by the KGB, based on information from an unnamed informant concerning a Stasi officer stationed in the South who planned to smuggle out of East Germany a list of Russian "illegals," sleeper agents working under non-official cover in France and the U.K.

Where the anonymous tip-off originated was anyone's guess, though Boris Golitsyn, the KGB head of station in East Berlin, speculated at the time that something so significant could not have come from a typical street informer, who often supplied what amounted to peanuts in the grand scheme of the battle between the Blocs. Markus Heinrich, it turned out, had been the mastermind behind uncovering both operations. It was he who had single-handedly gathered the intelligence as to the existence of two agents and their separate plans to exfil to West Berlin, and Markov could remember how quickly the once unknown Stasi operative began to climb the ranks in East Germany in the aftermath of the impressive intelligence coups.

Operation Trapdoor, run by the Stasi directorate in East Berlin, ensnared a British operative who had attempted to cross the Oberbaum Bridge under the guise of a West German artist teaching in the East. The captured agent was in fact not carrying anything, but under questioning, the young man eventually broke and blew his cover. He was taken to Lubyanka, further interrogated under torture, and then executed when it was obvious they would get nothing from him.

The second agent, captured at Checkpoint Bravo during *Operation Obelisk*, turned out to be a Stasi major named Kristof Brandt. Brandt, attempting to permanently exfil himself, along with a batch of high-level intelligence, almost made it through the gate, even though the guards had been warned to be on the alert for him. His handlers had done an excellent job with the double agent's papers, and of integrating the microfiche he carried into a nondescript math book.

Brandt had been taken in secret to Latvia, to keep his fate and final location hidden from the British and the Americans. He was tortured for weeks, though he never broke. It was on the day that Brandt was scheduled to be shot that Latvian agents working for MI6 and disguised as prison guards brazenly walked him out of The Corner House with fake orders that he be transferred to Lubyanka Prison.

And just like that, Brandt disappeared.

Markov finished reading the files and considered the implications, particularly in light of Anatoly Laskin's recent suggestion that a soldier on duty at the Oberbaum the night the British spy was arrested claimed to have knowledge about a key piece of information the MI6 operative was supposedly carrying.

Markov could recall when word first began to circulate about the rumored existence of damning intelligence related to the *Trapdoor* operation. It had been just after Christmas, 1995, and the possibility that proof in the form of photos or documented evidence might be floating around about the mole in East Berlin had all the Cold War rats scurrying. At the time, it had only been six years since their system imploded. And though that long-feared acronym, KGB, technically no longer exited, the agency was still alive and well.

As everyone cautiously joked, meet the new boss; he's the same as the old one.

Markov now wondered the same thing that many officers had been worried about over the years. How many overtures had been made by the CIA or SIS to Russians of all ranks stationed in Germany throughout the Cold War? How many KGB officers had accepted a sit-down, if for no other reason than a free meal and drink, and perhaps even to sniff out whether they could fool their potential Western handlers by only pretending to spy?

Everyone knew that it was far easier to cross the proverbial border between a dangle and a double-cross than the real one separating East and West.

One man's casual talk was another man's treason.

Markov continued to thumb through the volume of documents. Despite the incomplete file, there were tens of pages dedicated to the details of both operations, no matter how small or seemingly insignificant. No wonder the KGB had employed an army of analysts.

And then Markov saw it.

It would have gone unnoticed, if someone had not placed a single question mark in the margin alongside an encircled paragraph. It was a surveillance report, from the team assigned to tail Boris Golitsyn when he traveled into West Berlin. It stated that the KGB head of station's movements in August of 1984 had been unusual, frenetic, akin to someone attempting to lose a tail. Golitsyn had boarded and alighted a series of trams and trains over the course of two hours, before venturing to a restaurant in Kreuzberg. There, he had met with a man who was later identified as Geoffrey Charlton, MI6's head of section in West Berlin. There was no other information, no closure file or follow-up investigation, as to Golitsyn's explanation for his behavior.

Markov closed the file and considered the implications. He was certain that Mullova would have interrogated Laskin and Schultz by now, though he had heard nothing from her. It meant that she was answering to someone else.

Someone who was closing ranks and covering their tracks.

If the rumors were true, then anyone who had been posted

in East Berlin during that period would be thrust back into a very real career-killing zone. Or worse. Old allegations, like habits, died hard in Mother Russia, especially for agents who had not reported overtures made by the West.

Markov considered his own behavior during that period, even the appearance of impropriety, before pouring himself a black tea and contemplating how quickly he could disappear.

CHAPTER SEVENTY-THREE

Camaret-sur-Mer, France

Boats moored in the natural ocean harbor bobbed in the mild breeze, their owners seemingly unaware of the coming storm. The coastline was dotted with a scattered mix of tourists clinging to the last spell of enjoyable weather, and locals counting the days until they could momentarily reclaim their space.

Samantha Anderton strolled along a white sandy stretch that turned into a leeward inlet on a small peninsula that jutted into the Atlantic in the northwest of France. As she skirted a band of rocks that bordered the beach and high ground, her mind momentarily wandered back to Strasbourg, and the split-second decision she had been forced to make. The second operative at the construction site had been an easy, and satisfying, kill, but Anderton should not have allowed Garrett to convince her to leave him with the lone assassin. She could only hope Garrett was the better man, for now she had more pressing concerns.

Since speaking with Jean René Bertrand in Luxembourg, where the French operative had referenced Verity Scott,

Anderton requested permission from Montjoy to track her back down. Though Montjoy felt Scott had little more to add, he acquiesced, while predicting that the search would be fruitless, as the canny Cold War agent was certainly in the wind, as he put it, and not likely to be found anytime soon. Anderton had immediately visited Scott's abandoned flat in Locronan, and after thirty minutes of looking, believed she knew where to find the absconded MI6 operative.

Anderton eyed a row of houses set back on a grassy burn that rose off the beach, and spied the one she sought. The charming cottage, with painted white brick and a covered porch that wrapped around three sides, stood on a gentle slope overlooking a cluster of towering rock islands just offshore.

Anderton made her way up the embankment, before crossing a road that ran parallel to the coastline. She had the look and demeanor of a sightseer, the large .45-caliber Glock hidden in her backpack notwithstanding. As she pulled a long mass of hair back into a ponytail and removed her sunglasses, Anderton scanned the area around neighboring homes and a nearby restaurant. She stepped onto the shaded veranda and reached out to knock, but the door had already begun to open. An attractive older woman stood behind a closed screen door, and Anderton smiled.

Verity Scott responded in kind. "Yes?"

Anderton noticed that Scott's right hand remained behind her back, holding something. "I'm a friend."

"By which you mean," Scott replied, "with the Service."

"Yes, ma'am."

"In my experience, one thing doesn't always guarantee the other."

"Mr. Montjoy sent me. My name is Samantha Anderton, but please call me Sam."

Scott eyed Anderton for another moment before stepping back and inviting her in. "Banastre keeps on surprising," she said, and gave a quick look down the empty road. "How, exactly, did he find me?"

"He didn't," Anderton admitted.

"It's good to know they're still recruiting the best and the brightest," Scott observed. "And pretty." She walked to a small cabinet and set down her pistol, before holding up a bottle of whiskey.

"Sure," Anderton said. "Neat."

"I wouldn't serve it any other way, my dear." Scott handed a glass to Anderton and gestured to two chairs beside a large window, overlooking the sea.

Both women sat down and Anderton took a sip. "Straight Kentucky."

Scott laughed. "I'm not sure it's a good thing you already know that."

"My Welsh mother's father was American, and refused to drink anything else."

"To grandfathers with good taste." Scott raised her glass. She took a second sip, and set her drink down. "I'm not sure what to make of you, Ms. Anderton. It was easy back when there was a war and a wall to weed out the weak and the stupid. Hitler and Stalin at least guaranteed that. Times are different now."

"Ask me anything."

"Why SIS?"

"To cover up someone's dirty little secret."

"MI6's unofficial motto," Scott replied. "Have you killed anyone?"

"If you're asking whether I've blown someone's brain through the back of their head, the answer is yes, though I've facilitated more death than I've been the direct cause of. You'll let me know if there's a difference, other than ruining a blouse."

A faint smile flashed across Scott's face. "Good girl."

"And you?" Anderton asked.

"In my day, it was for Queen and Country."

"And now?"

Scott stared through the large front window and out over the ocean, before replying, more to herself, "To weather the storm."

"For someone who thought they might be in danger, you didn't stray very far from home."

"The proverbial last place someone would look, clever female MI6 operatives notwithstanding."

Anderton finished her whiskey and shook her head when Scott gestured toward the bottle. "To answer your other question, you have a photograph of a cottage on your mantel with a crêperie in the foreground. A hunch and a search at street level on Google satellite brought me here."

"Google," Scott said. "Something we could have used back in the day."

"From what I've heard, you didn't need it."

"You flatter me, but there's no need. Allow me to reward your cleverness by answering your questions, for that's no doubt why Banastre sent you."

Anderton smiled. "It was a genuine compliment, Ms. Scott. You're a legend around SIS, and not for the reasons that men whisper about like silly schoolboys. The female operatives know who you are and what you did. You and Mrs. Halliwell are an inspiration."

"Thank you," Scott replied, giving Anderton a thoughtful glance. "My generation is dead and gone, or close enough to it, so ask me what you came to, so that I might perhaps be of some use one last time."

"How long had you been Collishaw's point of contact in East Berlin?"

"Two months."

"Why was he on the Oberbaum that night, against orders?"

"Some run-of-the-mill cock-up along the chain of command, or, *Castor* panicked and didn't properly follow protocol."

"*Castor*," Anderton reiterated. "As in, one of the two Gemini twins."

"I suppose."

"I met with a French agent in Luxembourg named Jean René Bertrand, who referenced working with you in West Berlin."

"René." Scott smiled as she repeated his name. "A good agent and an even better lover."

"He lamented that you were just using him for information."

"It's true, but I still enjoyed myself."

"It was *Monsieur* Bertrand who mentioned hearing of an operative, or an operation, code-named *Gemini,* that was possibly being run by the CIA at the same time as *Safeguard*."

"I don't recognize the name, but that's not unusual. No small number of operational monikers were tossed about and then tossed out for one reason or the other."

Anderton was about to follow up with another query when Scott suddenly reached out and touched her arm.

"There is something." Scott's gaze narrowed as she attempted to single out a memory that had been stirred by Anderton. "*Gemini*, was it? I *have* heard a reference to that name before, in a passing comment I haven't thought about in thirty years. Geoffrey and I were in West Germany, on a weekend, perhaps a month after the Oberbaum setback. We were out for a drink. He'd downed one too many and was particularly cross about a directive that had come down from London. I remember he mentioned something about the twins being bollocksed. I dismissed it as the chatter of an inebriated and overworked agent. Then I distinctively recall Geoffrey, still annoyed, mutter to himself, 'It's always about protecting that bloody *Felix*.'"

"Protecting *Felix*?"

"That's all I can recall, I'm afraid. I didn't ask what he meant at the time and I never heard anything about it afterward. I'm sorry."

"Thank you so much, Ms. Scott, and I apologize for the trouble." Anderton stood to leave.

"The pleasure is mine, my dear. I'm just sorry I couldn't be of more assistance."

"One more question?" Anderton asked. "Any advice?"

Scott nodded. "Years from now, when you're alone in that dark place you'll sometimes find yourself and wondering whether everything you've sacrificed was worth it, just remember, you did your best, and it was."

"I've got the dark place down pat, though I've been unable to sort out the justification, or guilt, as of yet."

"Give it time," Scott replied, "and bash on."

"Thank you, Ms. Scott."

"Call me Verity," Scott said, as she hugged Anderton.

"I have something for you." Anderton fished through her backpack and pulled out the photo from Scott's flat. "Mind your back."

"And yours, my dear."

CHAPTER SEVENTY-FOUR

Berlin, Germany

Banastre Montjoy responded to the knock on his suite door at the Regent Berlin with a Beretta in one hand and a short pour of Scapa single malt in the other. He expected Samantha Anderton at any moment, but, as he had arranged to meet with the assassin who had been hunting him for a week, there was no guarantee the man wouldn't turn up with ideas other than a sit-down and friendly chat.

An oft-spun story had long circulated the halls of MI6 about an agent in Madrid who had been shot through the eye via a hotel peephole by a KGB operative who was able to gauge the man's position at the door from his approaching silhouette. Though he did not believe the anecdote for a minute, Montjoy nonetheless often found himself standing aside entryways while he queried who was on his stoop.

Speak friend, and enter, came the reply.

Montjoy smiled at the Tolkien reference, and when he opened the door, Anderton greeted him with a box containing several slices of *Bienenstich*.

"If that's Bee Sting Cake," Montjoy said, referring to the almond and honey treat, "then you may come in."

She entered and set the dessert down on a table near the door, before shedding her backpack and pulling a water bottle from a side pocket.

"You've been busy yourself, I hear," Montjoy said as Anderton sat down and unwound her hair from its double bun.

"Yes, sir."

"You met with the man tracking me in Strasbourg?"

"I did."

"And he got the message?"

"I should think so."

Montjoy removed the cake from its package and took a small bite. "I'll find out either way in one day's time."

Anderton stood and walked to the stack of handwritten notes and files that covered a small conference table. "What else do we know?"

Montjoy approached the jumble of intelligence and pulled from the pile the sketchbook and a single page. "Have a peek."

Anderton began to read through the summary, and then stopped. "Simultaneous operations?"

"Aye, but ones never intended to collide on November 9, 1984."

"Ms. Scott reiterated that Collishaw should not have been anywhere near the Oberbaum that night."

"Or any other checkpoint. *Safeguard* was a feint, a ghost operation."

Anderton considered what Montjoy had said, and then

nodded to herself as she began to put the pieces together. "To protect *Turnkey*."

"Clever girl," Montjoy replied. "It *was* to protect *Turnkey*, but not for *Turnkey's* sake, nor the agent assigned to it, *Pollux*."

The revelation confirmed what Anderton had uncovered earlier. "*Gemini*."

"Not twin agents on a bridge," Montjoy replied. "Twin operations."

"*Safeguard* and *Turnkey* were run independent of one another, and from separate sides of the pond?"

"MI6 sent in *Castor* and put together the Oberbaum ruse as cover for an operation at Checkpoint Bravo, and *Pollux*, who was being run by the CIA."

"What happened to Collishaw?"

"More than likely buried in some unmarked grave on the outskirts of Moscow for the last three decades."

"And *Pollux* was an officer in the Stasi who had recently been turned?"

"A major, to be precise, named Kristof Brandt. He was East German, but part of his family on his father's side hailed from Kent County. *Pollux's* East German end was coordinated by Madeleine Halliwell and run from West Berlin by Geoffrey Charlton. Ultimately, the entire operation was controlled out of Langley, who were interested in something far more important than intelligence that may or may not have been genuine."

Anderton remained silent while she continued reading the file, and then something dawned on her. "*Felix*."

"Aye," Montjoy replied. "*Gemini*, devised to cast suspicion on Sergei Malinovsky, was the umbrella operation created by the CIA to protect its most prized asset in East Germany."

"Enough to sacrifice an MI6 operative and blow the cover of an East German double agent who may have had viable intel?"

"*Castor* shouldn't have been in play, while what *Pollux* offered was likely a one-time intelligence grab, at best. However, no one foresaw that Collishaw had pieced together where the real deception lay, nor that the sacrificed pawn, *Pollux*, would survive Latvia, courtesy of MI6, and escape to safety in Sweden with information that could inadvertently expose the entire operation."

"Then why did *Pollux* come after MI6? After you?"

"You asked the question," Montjoy said as he gestured to the file Anderton was holding. "And you've already answered it. *Felix*."

Anderton wasn't certain she understood, and again thumbed back through the pages of Collishaw's pad. "I assume the answer lies in the deciphered code of the sketchbook?"

"Collishaw's sketchbook *was* the coded message, you see, one that contained a warning, hidden in plain sight, concerning the CIA's man in East Berlin, their mole."

Anderton eyed Montjoy for a moment. She considered what Bertrand had cryptically disclosed, as well as the backstory and seemingly inconsequential bits of intelligence that Verity Scott had confirmed. Anderton flipped the brief over and again reread the names.

Then it struck her—something that stood out amongst the

jumble of code names and ciphers, and the buried operations and dead agents.

The key that connected everything.

"Good God," she said, looking up. "Are you certain?"

"We'll know soon enough."

CHAPTER SEVENTY-FIVE

Langley, Virginia

Robert Riley, head of Europe Division for the Directorate of Operations at the CIA, sat quietly at his desk with both hands kneading his brow. He was several days behind on a stack of work because of a head cold, and laboring to make headway through a raging migraine. Riley downed several more Motrin and had already begun to count down to the end of the day when he became aware of someone in his office.

Gerald Fitton, head of Central Eurasia Division, was standing directly in front of Riley's desk and smiling. "That good of a day, eh?" He was the youngest division head ever appointed in the DO, and Riley liked Fitton not only because he was even-keeled and quick-witted, but exceptionally capable.

"I'd rather be waterboarded."

"Which can still be arranged, so long as you don't tell anyone in the media pool or on a congressional oversight committee," Fitton joked. "Not to add to your headache, but we've got a small situation, something you might want to take a look at."

"No doubt," Riley replied. "If I didn't hear those words at least once a week, I would know we were really in trouble."

Fitton dropped a file on Riley's desk.

"What is it this time?"

"A case which has made its way up the chain."

"Concerning?"

"A banker shot in Charleston, who might be linked with a DNR agent and a Chechen both found dead at the bottom of a lake in South Carolina, who might be associated with a Russian we're attempting to locate, who, you guessed it, might be involved."

"Those are a lot of 'mights' to get worked up about."

"That's what I told them," Fitton replied. "The inquiry should have been red-flagged miles back and fast-tracked straight through to us, but you know the Catch-22. Either we put old-school officers in charge of the computers, and good luck with that, or rely on some Gen Y half-wits to oversee the intelligence. Regardless, half the time we end up stuck on the double-yellow line and flattened from both directions. As it is, someone on high thinks this is important enough to clog up our trays with more crap." He gestured to a side table.

"My tray, I think you meant," Riley noted. "Why not let DHS, the FBI, or whatever other acronym is investigating this to sort out the maybes before we start stepping on toes?"

"It's been tagged as a matter of national security."

"Like everything else," Riley muttered to himself. "I miss the good old days, when so-called threats were actually ones that might have started a thermonuclear war."

"I wouldn't know. I was in grade school when you and your commie buddies had that little dustup."

"I won," Riley said, as he opened the file Fitton had delivered. "That's all you need to know."

"Speaking of way back when, weren't you knee-deep in those happy fun times in West Berlin?"

"Me and everybody else around here over sixty, including the coattail riders who like to pretend they were in the fight because they showed up for all of five minutes."

"They still do love to spin those stories."

"What triggered this? I don't see anything here that is particularly sensitive."

"What do you remember about any operations in East Berlin in November of 1984?"

"I know information like that would still be classified and not lying around near the copier," Riley replied, holding up the file he was reading. "Unless it came through the FBI or DHS, then it might as well be."

Fitton laughed. "My dad was a *Fibbie*. He would have taken exception to that comment."

"Your father did it the right way."

"Agreed," Fitton replied. "Actually, this comes from our BFFs over at Six, Banastre Montjoy, specifically. Some millennial newbie clearly doesn't know the difference between Europe and Eurasia and delivered the message to my office by mistake."

"You can't make fun of millennials if you're using terms like 'BFF.'"

"I'm impressed you know what it means. Maybe you're not so much the dinosaur as everyone whispers," Fitton joked.

Riley eyed his counterpart, but then smiled. "What's Banastre up to?"

"He's after anything we might have lying around about an old operative code-named *Felix*. Ring any bells?"

"*Felix*?" Riley asked, sitting up in his chair.

"Clearly so, judging from your reaction. Who was he?"

Riley read the message once again and then glanced up at Fitton. "Our most important Cold War asset in East Germany."

PART IV

CHAPTER SEVENTY-SIX

Copenhagen, Denmark
One year earlier

*T*he plain brown envelope was propped against Tomas Karlson's front stoop. It had been delivered during his daily stroll along the Københavns Havn, and did not provide a return address. He routinely ignored the scant mail he received, often for weeks at a time, but that morning curiosity got the better of him. The longtime East German expat prepared herbal tea, and split the seam with a kitchen knife.

Inside was a letter that claimed what the Cold War spy had long suspected, that his exposure wasn't by chance. He had been set up, sold out before he even stepped to that checkpoint thirty-four years earlier. That the Stasi had been tipped about the intelligence the German double agent carried for the Americans, and were waiting for him to attempt his exfiltration to the West. That Operation Turnkey was never intended to be successful, but only serve as a feint to protect the mole inside Stasi Headquarters.

That the young Stasi officer himself had been betrayed by the very people for whom he worked.

Karlson was taken back to the moment at that damned

border crossing when he knew he was doomed. To his arrest, detention, and weeks-long torture at the hands of the KGB. He could recall the night he was pulled from his cell, surely for the last time. Suddenly, dropped in a ditch on the outskirts of Riga, then standing on a deserted dock in Helsinki. Of being warned not to return home, of abandoning the name Kristof Brandt, and hiding in Norway on false credentials until the Berlin Wall came down.

He still carried the visible scars. His vision was blurred in an eye that never fully healed, its lid partially drooped. The agent's left arm ached whenever the weather turned cold, and he had difficulty raising it above his shoulder. Two smashed toes on his right foot had never regained feeling, and the pockmarked remnants of cigarette burns dotted his torso.

The psychological damage was considerably worse.

And suddenly, out of nowhere, the names, locations, and recent photographs of the retired, but very much still alive, British Intelligence officers who were behind the betrayal that ruined his life. Included were documents, in the form of decrypted correspondences between London and West Berlin, detailing the off-the-books operation that sealed his fate just four months before Mikhail Gorbachev came to power and declared glasnost and perestroika.

The missive also offered something the broken and disillusioned agent had obsessed over on an almost daily basis, forsaken to a small flat in what had once been a Viking fishing village.

An opportunity he was certain never to get, until Markus Heinrich reached out two weeks after the package had arrived

*with the details of a complex operation he had pieced together
and for which he needed Karlson. A mission that would also
give both men something each he had desperately longed for.*

    Revenge.

CHAPTER SEVENTY-SEVEN

Berlin, Germany

anastre Montjoy stood with his back to the wall in a corner at Berlin Hauptbahnhof, one hand firmly on the grip of an HK P30 pistol in his front pocket. Though he had extended an offer of a sit-down to Kristof Brandt, it was entirely possible the man would arrive in Berlin early and attempt to locate his target beforehand. Brandt would likely not risk confronting the deputy chief in plain sight, but the man was driven by rage and Montjoy couldn't be certain, so he kept the safety off and his attention on the only entrance from which he could be directly approached.

It was nearly a half-hour after the prearranged time Robert Riley had agreed to meet. Montjoy had reached out through Gavin Abbot, and Riley notified him that he was coming to Europe that very week and could spare time for a quick sit-down. Montjoy had resigned himself to wait ten minutes more, when Riley appeared around the corner, flanked by several serious-looking men in black suits wearing discreet, two-way earpieces.

Riley smiled and extended his hand. "Banastre."

Fallout

"Robert."

Riley jerked his head and his small entourage moved to a position nearby.

"I see you got my message."

"Several actually, sounding rather urgent."

"Abbot prepped you with the operations on which I need information?"

"Yes," Riley replied, "though I'm not sure what I can tell you that your own intelligence doesn't."

"Walk with me."

Riley followed Montjoy from the station and toward the Spree River. "I haven't had the opportunity to tell you how sorry I am about your grandmother. Madeleine was a wonderful woman and a pioneer at MI6."

Montjoy did not have time to be anything but direct. "She was murdered."

Riley stopped and faced Montjoy, clearly alarmed. "By whom?"

"The same man who assassinated Geoffrey Charlton in Italy, and made it look like a murder-suicide."

Riley donned his sunglasses. "Charlton's death, coupled with Lindsay's disappearance, certainly appeared to be more than coincidence."

"The hedge fund manager gunned down in Charleston that same day was intended to be me."

Riley eyed his British counterpart. "What's going on, Banastre?"

"The reason I reached out, Robert. All of this is connected with East Berlin, 1984."

"What do you need to know?"

"We ran an operation through the Oberbaum in November of that year, coded *Safeguard*. The CIA, in collaboration with MI6, was bringing something over at Checkpoint Bravo at the same time, correct?"

Riley nodded. "*Operation Turnkey*. We ran an agent code-named *Pollux*."

"You were also running an umbrella operation, *Gemini*, whereby *Safeguard* was piggybacked off *Turnkey* as a bluff. Our operative, *Castor*, was used as cover to bring *Pollux* over with key intelligence supplied by your mole, and, in the end, to protect your source."

"Langley feared that our man inside Stasi headquarters was on the verge of exposure, so Lindsay created a ruse to shift attention away from our end. Your agent was never supposed to cross over. His only purpose was to give the appearance that a significant intelligence operation was being run through Freidrichshain, information we purposely leaked to the Stasi and KGB. Lindsay hoped that if Soviet suspicion was sufficiently diverted, they would focus on the Oberbaum rather than the handoff at Bravo, where we were getting the proverbial keys to a small part of the kingdom."

"Which was?

"Moscow's list of sleeper agents in England and France."

"But there was no list, was there?"

"Our man was detained at the checkpoint, so we never found out. The feint didn't work."

"It worked alright, just not in the way anyone from our side intended it to."

"By which you mean?"

"As you know, our agent did attempt to cross that night, and he disappeared from the Oberbaum at the same time your informant was arrested at Bravo," Montjoy replied. "Did anyone ever attempt to piece together how that happened? Why there was a mix-up with *Safeguard*, and how *Turnkey* failed?"

"Miscommunication and bad luck. You remember how it was back then. Most of the time we were flying upside down and partially blind. You always do when relying on dead drops, coded messages, and informants."

"Did anyone ever suspect that your attempt at misdirection was actually hijacked and redirected back at MI6 and the CIA? That there was a problem with your mole?"

"Langley took pains to ensure that he was protected. *Gemini* was created to cast suspicion onto Sergei Malinovsky, and Moscow took the bait. Malinovsky dropped off the radar soon after, and our man, *Felix*, continued to operate for another five years."

"Who was your mole?"

"Markus Heinrich."

Montjoy pulled out his churchwarden and a packet of leaf. "And you are aware of his current whereabouts?"

"He's been living in Montreal for the better part of two decades. We helped him get out and disappear."

"You helped him do more than that. Heinrich is the mastermind behind the murders of Charlton and my grandmother, the disappearance of Lindsay, and the botched assassination in South Carolina."

Riley considered the implication of what Montjoy had revealed. "Why? To what end?"

"Because Heinrich wasn't just your mole, he was a triple agent."

"Bullshit," Riley quickly countered. "That's not possible."

"It was Heinrich who blew up *Safeguard* and *Turnkey*."

"Impossible," Riley countered. "It was Markus who compiled and gave the sleeper list to *Pollux* to bring to us."

"Let me ask you something. How effective was Heinrich as an informant?"

"Better when he was with the Stasi, but less so after he moved to the KGB as Alexei Arkipov. As you are well aware, it's not unusual for an informant's effectiveness to wane over time."

"It's not when someone is truly a mole and worried about exposure. In Heinrich's case, he initially betrayed the Stasi to curry favor with the CIA, but then feverishly worked against Western interests to bolster his own position in the KGB thereafter."

"Where is this coming from, Banastre?"

"We found and decrypted the intelligence our agent intended to bring over in 1984, the significance of which prompted his attempt to cross the Oberbaum when he knew his life would be in danger. Stanford Collishaw was aware that time was of the essence, but what he did not realize was that London had inadvertently sold him out. Collishaw's fate was sealed the moment he set foot on that bridge. On the surface, his sketchbook amounts to gibberish, which I initially assumed was the point of the operation, of our feint. In reality,

Collishaw, the shiny object dangled in front of the Soviets to protect the 'keys to the kingdom,' as you put it, was actually the one in possession of information vital to our shared interests in East Berlin. His coded message, using *Jabberwocky* as the key, *was* the intelligence. Collishaw had been tipped off by Malinovsky that everyone's prized spy inside Stasi HQ was not what he seemed. Knowing he couldn't get it back any other way in time, *Castor* ciphered his revelation in a way that would set off alarm bells in London, that what we were being fed by Heinrich sounded good, like Carroll's poem, but was essentially nonsense. A hidden-in-plain-sight confirmation that everyone was being played."

"If Markus was a triple, why expose *Turnkey*? Why not allow a bogus list to cross over? The KGB could have sprinkled enough viable intel amongst the chickenfeed to lead us astray for years. It would have allowed Moscow to protect its Western assets and cast suspicion on anyone who might have actually been inclined to turn and work for MI6 or the CIA."

"Because Moscow had no idea what Heinrich had been up to. He convinced you early on that he was a genuine double by betraying the Stasi to gain your trust. He then sold out *Safeguard* and *Turnkey*, operations *he* set up, in order to curry favor with the KGB. In what was likely his intention from the very beginning, Heinrich turned himself into a triple agent without Moscow ever knowing he had betrayed actual secrets, something which would have guaranteed his arrest and execution had anyone found out."

Riley remained silent as he cycled through years of operations and intelligence-gathering that involved Heinrich, while trying to process the implications of what Montjoy was telling him. The sudden recognition that everything one believes might only not be patently untrue, but the diametric opposite, began to splay across Riley's face. Like a man who realized he hadn't been wearing any pants at a large gathering where he had been the proverbial life of the party and from which he left thinking that everyone had been laughing *with* him. For a brief second, Riley was able to shake off his growing sense of panic and regain a faint glimmer of hope that Montjoy had erred. "The Kremlin wasn't stupid. They would have been suspicious of Markus."

"Perhaps, if Langley hadn't so effectively cast suspicion on Sergei Malinovsky. Call it a case of exceptionally bad timing and luck, but in the end, we sold out the one man who could have helped us in East Berlin to protect someone who ended up actively working against the CIA and MI6. As a result, Moscow wasn't looking anywhere else," Montjoy replied, "and neither were we. Let me ask you something. Whose idea was it to front Malinovsky as the patsy?"

"Markus'," Riley answered, and then paused, as if something had suddenly dawned on him.

"Heinrich used a photograph he took of Malinovsky with Collishaw to convince Moscow that Malinovsky was the mole." Montjoy pulled the Polaroid of the two men from his jacket and handed it to Riley.

"Where did you get this?"

"Anatoly Laskin."

"Laskin?" Riley replied. "Why would he do that?"

"Because Anatoly suspected that Heinrich wasn't dead,

and had come out of hiding to eliminate the former British officers connected to an operation that contained intelligence which was rumored to have resurfaced concerning the identity of the mole in East Germany. Information that could also cast suspicion on any number of officers from the KGB's station in East Berlin, many of whom are now high-up and comfortably nearing retirement. Anatoly was aware as to how easy it would be for someone in the SVR or FSB to manipulate whatever implications the sketchbook contained. However, he knew that if *we* got the intelligence, it wouldn't be buried. The opposite, in fact."

Riley stared at the photo, but said nothing.

"It was at the clandestine meeting with Collishaw that Malinovsky offered to pass on his suspicion of Heinrich if MI6 agreed to get Malinovsky out. Heinrich distrusted Malinovsky and shadowed him to the rendezvous with Collishaw, then presented the photo to the KGB to save his own skin while simultaneously ridding himself of his main rival in East Berlin. Fast-forward a decade. The border guard who found the hidden sketchbook told his son, who was working in the unified German government, of the discovery. Heinrich, at that time moving upward in the newly formed FSB as Alexei Arkipov, got wind that intelligence from a compromised Cold War operation involving a captured MI6 agent at the Oberbaum in November 1984 had surfaced. The very one he had exposed and used as his ticket to the upper echelon of Russian intelligence. A butterfly flapping its wings at one end because of Heinrich's behavior could have created dire consequences for him, as Arkipov, on the other. He feared the intelligence might contain information that confirmed what Malinovsky had suspected, that Heinrich had been a traitor to both sides. Even with the fall of communism, Heinrich had good reason to fear that remnants of the KGB could and would come after him. In the end, Heinrich used *Turnkey* as the means to apprehend Kristof Brandt at Bravo, expose Stanford Collishaw with *Safeguard,* and further KGB suspicions the CIA had already stoked about a middling KGB officer. Moscow believed it had found its mole in Malinovsky, and a champion in Heinrich. The CIA thought it was protecting a valuable informant while removing another piece from the Cold War board. In one fell swoop, Heinrich was able to dupe us, you, and Moscow."

Riley furrowed his brow, a sign that he was attempting, and failing, to convince himself that any of what Montjoy had divulged couldn't possibly be the case. "What did Lindsay know?"

"Nothing concrete, but sometime in the wake of the fiasco at Bravo and the Oberbaum it began to dawn on William that Heinrich was the architect of not just it, but a string of ensuing intelligence failures. When rumor of the sketchbook first surfaced, William began to float through Eastern European channels that SIS had a high-ranking informant inside Stasi headquarters in the mid-1980s, which was true, but thereafter in the KGB and FSB, which was not. If MI6 could push suspicion high enough in Moscow, coupled with intelligence that might surface at any moment and corroborate the ruse, someone might eventually recognize that Malinovsky could not have been the mole, or at least not the only one, having been exposed and then disposed of in 1984. William believed that if Heinrich had in fact been playing both sides, he would react accordingly."

"I've got a bad feeling that you're about to disclose that this occurred right before we faked Markus' death and brought him to Canada."

Montjoy lit his pipe and took several short puffs, illuminating the tobacco in an orange glow. "By early 1996, Heinrich had become aware that the damning rumor was gaining traction in his own intelligence ranks. He feared that it was only a matter of time before enough layers were pulled back to cast suspicion on him. Heinrich knew he needed to get out, so he reached out to the CIA. You thought you were providing cover to a reliable and trusted informant. In the end, not only did Langley give asylum to someone who was ultimately loyal to the KGB, it ended up protecting a man who would later be wanted for war crimes for his actions in Chechnya. Without directly subverting Langley's role in the operation, and compromising the relationship between Washington and London, William's move was probably made in the hope that he could affect Heinrich's capture before you were able to afford him safe haven."

"Why didn't Lindsay let us in on what he suspected, and was up to?"

"Certainly because of the Ames fiasco." Montjoy referred to Aldrich Ames, the counterintelligence officer in the CIA's Soviet division who had been spying for Russia for nearly a decade before he was arrested in 1994. "Ames had been reassigned to the Soviet/East European desk at Langley by early 1985, correct?"

Riley nodded.

"That was just five months after the Bravo and Oberbaum failures. Any chance Ames knew what Heinrich was up to, or was coordinating with him?"

"Rick didn't mention anything about Heinrich when he was debriefed following his arrest. But, as Ames was responsible for betraying to the Soviets over a hundred of our operations, that we are aware of, along with at least ten deep-cover operatives, there is no way of knowing."

"It's plausible Heinrich feared that Ames's exposure might lead to his own, which, coupled with the possibility of the emergence of long-hidden intelligence, and William's gambit, forced him to reach out when he did."

"It's possible we turned a blind eye to Heinrich *because* of Ames," Riley noted. "It would have been easy, and convenient, to attribute intelligence failures through 1994 to Rick, rather than Markus." Something then dawned on Riley. "Why did Heinrich come after you? You played no part in either *Turnkey* or *Safeguard*."

"It took me a while to put that piece together. It all comes back to Heinrich's betrayal. He couldn't be certain who from MI6's West Berlin station was behind the effort to expose him in 1996. When William tasked me with planting the seed of a longtime informant in Berlin and Moscow, he intimated that it was a ploy to sow discord and distrust in the ranks of the fledgling FSB. I was unaware that I was actually helping to flush out the traitor that William suspected had gotten the better of him, and MI6, back in East Berlin. Do you remember Nestor Petrov?"

"A Russian officer who liaised with the FSB," Riley answered. "We tried to turn him once, unsuccessfully, in 1988."

"That's because we had already turned Petrov. It was through him that I spread the information from William. If you recall, Petrov disappeared in the spring of 1996, not two months after he and I met for the last time. I can only assume now that Heinrich, who had by that time become wise to the snowballing rumor of a Cold War traitor still amongst their ranks, learned of what William was up to, through me, from Petrov, before killing him. Ultimately, Heinrich blamed each of us for the effort to destroy his future in Russian Intelligence. You brought him to Canada not long after, and that grudge has only grown over the last two decades."

"Son of a bitch," Riley muttered to himself as he shook his head and rubbed his brow. "Who killed Charlton and your grandmother?"

"Kristof Brandt."

"Brandt?" Riley replied, surprised. "He was arrested by the KGB and carted off to Russia. If the KGB suspected *Pollux* was ours, how is he alive and well?"

"When William found out where Brandt had been taken, he mounted a risky operation to get him out of the Soviet Union, to safety in Sweden. Brandt disappeared, became Tomas Karlson, and at some point afterward, Heinrich found him and convinced the bitter ex-Stasi officer that it was the British who betrayed him. For Heinrich, it was the ultimate act of irony and revenge. As you know, my grandmother was Brandt's point of contact in East Germany, and Charlton ran the British end of the operation from Berlin, so it was an easy sell. Heinrich offered Brandt the opportunity to exact retribution on those he was made to believe were responsible for his arrest, and at the same time Heinrich satisfied his own need for retaliation against those he assumed, rightly, had orchestrated his exposure."

"What happened to Collishaw?"

"Sent to Lubyanka, where he was tortured and shot by the KGB."

"And the assassin sent after you in Charleston?"

"Eliminated."

"Brandt?"

"Still in play, and possibly still after me."

"What do you need from me?"

"Only one thing," Montjoy replied. "Heinrich's current location."

CHAPTER SEVENTY-EIGHT

Moscow, Russia

Boris Golitsyn replayed the digital feed, focusing on anything he might have missed the first three times he listened to the bugged conversation. The nuanced exchange, between Anatoly Laskin and an unidentified man, had been recorded a day earlier by an FSB team in Prague that had been monitoring the SVR head of station for the last two months.

Golitsyn also studied several snapshots taken by the operatives assigned to Laskin. The proxy with whom the Russian had rendezvoused was nondescript, spoke with an English accent, and looked more like an analyst than an agent. He was heretofore unknown to the SVR and FSB stations in Prague, while the hat, scarf, and sunglasses he wore had rendered attempts at running him through a facial recognition program fruitless. That he was in Czechia and intimating knowledge of a Cold War operation that had suddenly popped up on everyone's radar pointed in the direction of Banastre Montjoy.

The man had in fact stated he was in Prague in place of "a friend," and, concerning a package that had recently been received from a mutual acquaintance. There could be no doubt in Golitsyn's mind that this was in reference to Egon Schultz and his foolish decision to turn over vital intelligence to the British instead of his own East German government, and by extension, the Soviet Union, when he had the chance three decades earlier.

Had Shultz behaved with the fealty demanded and deserved by the State at the time, none of its participants would be in this predicament now.

The enigmatic go-between told the story of a man, whom he called Mr. Jones, who had worked as a field hand on a large plantation. Golitsyn immediately assumed the name and reference to be an allusion to Orson Welles's allegorical tale of Stalinist Russia in *Animal Farm*.

Mr. Jones was in charge managing one small pasture of a large plantation. Unbeknownst to the owners of the estate, he was selling off a few animals from each litter to a rival, who in turn helped the field hand improve his own farm's husbandry in order to gain favor over the other laborers. His superiors were so impressed with the results that they rewarded him with a bigger field and more responsibility in the running of day-to-day operations. Meanwhile, his underhanded behavior continued until someone from a neighboring field discovered that Jones had been poisoning the well, which was the root of the constant outbreak of death and disease amongst the flock. Jones, however, was able to convince the owners that it was his colleague who was to blame. While the accuser was fired, Jones continued to prosper. He was duly promoted through the ranks until the day he mysteriously drowned in a watering pond, near the same time a rumor began to circulate that proof of who really owned the toxin had surfaced. The evidence also confirmed that other field hands had aided in the spread of the poison, and that those workers were still employed at the farm.

Golitsyn listened to the exchange several times before finally turning off the audio. He considered the implications of the coded message. That it was Markus Heinrich, someone Golitsyn had trusted with his life, who turned out to be the mole, would come as a shock to everyone who had worked with the man. What was more troubling was the existence of evidence that suggested additional officers from the KGB station in East Berlin had shared in the complicity and worked in concert with Heinrich, wittingly or not, to spy for the West.

Golitsyn realized he was caught in a Catch-22.

If the charge against Heinrich was sound, it would benefit Golitsyn to pass the information on to his superiors, who would then wonder how and why Golitsyn suspected the exchange between Laskin and the British agent concerned a long-dead and much respected KGB officer.

If he kept it to himself, and if Laskin or Markov reported their own misgivings, then suspicion could fall on Golitsyn, should anyone discover that he had also seen and heard the intelligence.

There was no telling what else the missing MI6 operative had uncovered in 1984, and whether it was the truth, speculation, or misinformation sowed by London during the Cold War. Considering that it might soon be widely whispered amongst the upper ranks of Russian Intelligence that Heinrich was still alive and a traitor to boot, anyone even remotely implicated in the sketchbook would be caught up in the frenzy.

It would matter little whether Golitsyn was actually guilty or not, if his name was listed in that book.

SIS might choose to keep the information in their back pocket for a later gambit, though Golitsyn suspected they would not pass up the chance to disrupt FSB operations at the first drop of a hat. If the British sat on the intelligence, however, the only thing anyone might discover was that Markus Heinrich was alive and well and living in Canada, and it would then come down to Heinrich's word against any others.

Golitsyn realized that he had but one hand to play, and very little time left to lay it down.

CHAPTER SEVENTY-NINE

Montreal, Canada

E lena Mullova stood beneath a pavilion near the old port and kept an eye on the front entrance of a multiuse building that housed several restaurants and a café. The top floor, she knew, was also home to a former Stasi and KGB operative, who for the last twenty years had gone by the name Emile Chénard.

Mullova had flown into Montréal-Trudeau International two days day earlier, cleared customs with no issues, and had taken a taxi into the city center. There, she met with two FSB officers stationed in Ottawa who had located Chénard's flat in Old Montreal and had been sitting on it for two days. One of the operatives was certain he had seen someone who he thought was their target leave and return only a few hours earlier. Mullova had since ordered the men to monitor the building from opposite ends of St. Paul Street, assuming that Chénard would likely alternate his entry and exit points of the premises.

Her mission had taken Mullova from Moscow to Prague to Berlin and now Montreal. The parameters of the original operation had been to question Laskin and Shultz to determine what information either man might be in possession of concerning the capture of a British agent at the Oberbaum Bridge in 1984. Intelligence that might also shed light on MI6's mole in East Germany in the 1980s.

When she found the man formerly known as *Spindle*, Markus Heinrich, and Alexei Arkipov, Mullova had been instructed to assure him that things had settled down, times had changed, and to ask him to consider coming out of the shadows and returning to Russia.

That morning, Mullova had received another message from Boris Golitsyn, one that notified her the assignment had a new objective.

She was to hunt down and kill the Russian hiding in Montreal.

CHAPTER EIGHTY

Berlin, Germany

Tomas Karlson stood in the shadow of Checkpoint Bravo near the bustling interchange of two *Bundesautobahns* and watched tourists snap photos. The sound of irate motorists laying on horns served as a stark reminder of what the region used to represent, when it was *sectored*. When people were desperate to make it to freedom, not to a business meeting or a casual lunch with friends.

He was a stone's throw from the *Großer Wannsee*, a recess in the Havel River that was arguably the most popular spot for sunbathing in Berlin. Despite the month and turn in weather, the meandering shoreline was still packed with sightseers drinking up the last bit of sunshine before a very German winter set in.

It took little effort for Karlson to summon the memory of that exact moment, when deliverance was only a few meters away. If he closed his eyes, he could recall the order to exit his vehicle and accompany border guards to an interrogation room in the overpass above. The young Stasi officer had been stationed far enough to the South that no one should have recognized his face or become suspicious over the fake papers he carried showing him to be a mathematics teacher. Karlson had been assured by his handler, Madeleine Halliwell, that his cover, and the operation to get him across, was foolproof.

What resonated more than any other detail that long night was the sudden, sinking feeling when he realized the commotion was because of him. Karlson could remember the surreal sensation that he was physically standing beside himself and watching the scene unfold. Of thinking that all he had to do was shake the shackled man until they both woke from their shared nightmare, dreamt from a safe house in London.

It was the same out-of-body experience he encountered through much of his torture over the following weeks.

From Berlin, Karlson had been transported a long distance, nearly fifteen hours by his reckoning. The blindfolded discomfort of the military truck was a precursor to the sweltering basement he was dragged to and locked in.

At first, the pain was searing and palpable, and the anticipation of the coming cuts, burns, and kicks was almost as bad as the abuse itself. He screamed and cursed, and lashed out against his restraints, which only drew rebukes in the form of more punishment. Karlson then recognized, through a heightened sensory haze, that this was what his interrogators wanted, a visceral reaction to their sadism. If they couldn't extract any useful information, his tormentors were at least determined to enjoy the spectacle. At some point the pain began to subside, even as the all-day assaults increased in their intensity, and Karlson began to feel like a bystander sitting in the room and watching his own torture.

There had been no point in denying that he wasn't involved in an operation of subterfuge, something his interrogators could deduce for themselves from the documents Karlson was carrying. An enciphered list of Soviet spies had been concealed in the math book, and it wouldn't be long before KGB code-breakers uncovered his secret. They had him dead to rights, and Karlson would have laughed at the irony of being caught *red-handed*, if it hadn't hurt so much.

At some point, the questions and the violence that accompanied them began to subside in frequency and ferocity. Karlson had felt a wave of relief, until he realized it meant they no longer needed him and that he would soon be taken to a concrete room and shot in the back of the head.

What happened next was a blur. A backseat of a truck, the boot of a car, a rough boat ride, and the sensation of near-frozen saltwater.

Then Finland, and freedom.

At least, the kind a man who had been beaten and broken and left with damaged vision, shattered bones, and torn ligaments might take comfort in.

Karlson turned his attention back to the present, and the familiar spot at which he now stood. The first time he had returned since that night.

Five meters.

It had been exactly one year since Markus Heinrich had contacted Karlson out of the blue. He professed to know a secret Karlson did not—the specific circumstances of his arrest in 1984. The man had asserted that declassified documents detailed an operation that had taken place at Checkpoint Bravo in November of that year, a smashing KGB success that allowed the Soviets to roll up an entire British network of spies in East Berlin, save one agent, a mole inside Stasi headquarters that the CIA controlled and who MI6 was protecting when it sold Karlson out that November night.

It was Madeleine Halliwell's idea to betray you. Her head of section, Geoffrey Charlton, was only too happy to give it the green light. The mole got away, you were taken to that hellhole in Riga, and the British agents involved all retired amongst huzzahs and service medals. No one involved deserved what they got, good or bad, but now you have a chance to remedy the injustice.

Karlson took a taxi to a restaurant overlooking the Wannsee. He was early, and decided to order dinner and down a few drinks while he waited. Karlson was shown a table on the back patio, where he ordered a schnitzel and a German stout, and sat where he could watch the patio entrance and still enjoy the sights of the small marina. He was served the beer just as Banastre Montjoy arrived.

The deputy chief walked to his table and gestured to the chair opposite Karlson. "May I?"

"Don't think I won't kill you here and now," Karlson replied in a tone that amounted to a whispered growl.

Montjoy ordered a scotch from a nearby waiter and then sat down, laying his hat on the chair beside him. "Not before we finish our drinks like civilized gentlemen, I should hope."

Karlson did not take his eyes off of the man he had hunted for the better part of a week. "You knew I was in Strasbourg and had me followed."

"Aye, and I see you got my message."

"You can pay my regards to your agent," Karlson said. "Now, what do you want?"

Montjoy was served his drink, and raised his glass. "To set right what was put wrong."

"I'm in the process of doing that."

"What you did was allow yourself to be duped into targeting the wrong people, and in so doing, slake another man's thirst for revenge."

"Which would be whom, exactly?"

"The same man who sold you out to the KGB thirty-four years earlier, at that former border crossing over there." Montjoy pointed back in the direction of Checkpoint Bravo. "Markus Heinrich."

"You would claim such a thing to save your own life."

"I might claim anything," Montjoy smiled, "for a good scotch." He took another sip. "And, to forego the need for both of us to draw our pistols on such a pleasant day."

"I don't plan to sit here longer than it takes to finish this pint and my meal."

Montjoy pulled a photo from his pocket and laid it on the table in front of Karlson. "That is Sergei Malinovsky, a KGB officer stationed in East Berlin, meeting with an MI6 agent in November of 1984. Malinovsky was in fact offering to give up Markus Heinrich in return for our protection. The other man is Stan Collishaw, part of a separate operation created expressly to protect you at Checkpoint Bravo. It was Heinrich who sold you and our agent out to the Russians in return for a seat at the big table, which Moscow granted."

Karlson kept his gaze on Montjoy, but did not respond. He folded his napkin into a triangle and pushed one end into the 'V' of his shirt as his schnitzel was served. Karlson took a bite, but then put down his fork. "You must think some doctored photo and contrived backstory will suffice to persuade me what happened that night is the exact opposite of what I was led to believe by Heinrich."

"Let me ask you, Kristof, who got you out of the Soviet Union?"

"My name is Tomas."

"It was not the Americans, that I can assure you, and certainly not Markus Heinrich," Montjoy replied. "Have you ever asked yourself this question?"

"Many times."

"And?"

Karlson did not respond.

"My head of section in West Germany, Geoffrey Charlton, ran *Operation Safeguard,* the feint MI6 created to get you out of Germany. Madeleine Halliwell, my grandmother and your point of contact, always considered its failure her fault. It was her biggest regret, you should know. She had taken a special liking to you, as well as Collishaw, who was on his first mission behind the Wall. '*Two brave fellows facing danger alone at those godforsaken checkpoints,*' she always said."

Karlson had stopped eating and sat unmoving with his attention now fully on Montjoy.

"Collishaw was captured at the Oberbaum at the same time you were arrested at Bravo. Our man wasn't supposed to cross over at all, mind you, but only give the appearance that we were running an operation of considerable importance through Friedrichshain. Collishaw, having been tipped by Malinovsky about Heinrich, risked his own life to save yours."

"How did you get his photo?"

It was given to me by a former KGB operative, the same man who ordered the arrest of Malinovsky after Heinrich convinced him that Malinovsky was the mole in East Berlin. In a single moment of espionage brilliance, Heinrich was able to betray you, Collishaw, Malinovsky, Moscow, and two joint operations run by the CIA and MI6, all for the simple reason of protecting himself and furthering his career."

"Then why come after MI6 after so many years?"

"Because we ruined Heinrich a decade later by pushing a rumor through the ranks of Russian Intelligence that they had a Cold War mole who was still operating in the FSB. Heinrich's downfall needed only a little shove, and we helped it along."

"And what about me?" Karlson asked. "Where was help when I needed it?"

"Once my deputy chief in London, William Lindsay, discovered where you had been taken, he pieced together a risky operation to get you out of the USSR. Your exfiltration cost two Latvian agents their lives, and was undertaken at a potentially great personal and political cost to Lindsay."

Karlson leaned back in his chair and reflected on what Montjoy had disclosed.

Montjoy reached into his pocket and pulled out a piece of paper with two names. "Aleksis Kode and Mārcis Lanka were the agents posing as guards in Latvia, in case you're interested. Kode had three children and Lanka was the only surviving son of a family who lost everything fighting the Russians. You're welcome to research the men yourself. The names were harder to bury than the bodies, you see. You suffered at The Corner House, and those scars never healed. But the level of torture you experienced was commensurate with the fact that your interrogators needed to keep you alive to elicit information. Your subsequent escape was a major embarrassment to the KGB station in Riga, a price Kode and Lanka were made to pay. It's rumored both men were given multiple blood transfusions and adrenaline shots so they wouldn't pass out from the pain. What they suffered was unimaginable."

Karlson picked up the paper and looked at the names, but did not say anything.

"You should also know that Heinrich sent a team to kill the very man who was behind your escape from Latvia at the same time he convinced you to assassinate Charlton and Halliwell."

Karlson listened in silence, then said, somberly, "If what you say is true, then you have more cause to kill me, than I you."

"Your manic and misguided crusade to retaliate led you to take the lives of not just Charlton and my grandmother, but an innocent young woman in Italy. You'll have to answer for that." Montjoy finished the last of his whiskey and stood, donning his hat and jacket. "Each of the other assassins recruited by Heinrich have been eliminated. If I wanted you dead, I can assure you that it would have already happened."

It was evident from Karlson's muted reaction that he

had begun to believe Montjoy, as well as consider the consequence of his actions. He glanced up. "And what happens to Heinrich?"

"Time will tell."

Karlson eyed Montjoy, but did not speak.

Montjoy began to leave, but then turned. "Heinrich's in Canada, you should know, hiding under the alias Emile Chénard."

CHAPTER EIGHTY-ONE

Quebec City, Canada

Emile Chénard finished packing the last of his bags. He again glanced out of the front window of the hotel he had checked himself into several days earlier and watched tourists mingle near a weekend market by the river. It was too crowded to tell if anyone stood out in particular, and the Russian knew that a professional would disguise their presence well enough to avoid detection anyway, so his vigilance was not only pointless; it was wasting valuable time.

Each of his operatives had gone dark.

Every single one, from Riker to Karlson to his Alpha Group team. Chénard had already discarded the three mobiles he had used to coordinate the operation against his MI6 nemeses from Berlin. Two had been killed, but the others had gotten away. Whether to eventually chalk the mission up as a success would be something Chénard would determine later. As a precaution, he had left Montreal, at least for the foreseeable future, and likely for good.

Chénard suspected that eventually he would need to put

his entire Canadian front behind him and create an entirely new cover for himself, potentially in Europe.

He checked the street view once more, and made sure his Beretta was chambered, before grabbing his backpack and suitcase and heading out the door.

CHAPTER EIGHTY-TWO

London, England

The traffic along Westminster Bridge was heavy, owing to a late-morning deluge, maintenance that was being undertaken on both ends of the span, and the fact that it was London.

Banastre Montjoy, Sean Garrett, and Samantha Anderton sat alone in an upstairs room of St. Stephen's Tavern, at the corner of Parliament and Great George Streets. The overflow space for special events was typically cordoned off during the weekday, but the proprietor, an ex-Royal Marine, turned a blind eye when Montjoy used the bar either for company business, or to get away from it.

Montjoy stared out from a corner window at Big Ben, enwrapped in construction scaffolding while major restoration works were undertaken. The famous bell, which had tolled every day for a century and a half, was scheduled to remain dormant for another three years. Montjoy acknowledged that while he had paid little notice to the recurrent ringing for much of his life, he now found the deafening silence eerily disconcerting.

Behind him, Garrett tapped his whiskey on the table. Montjoy turned as he lifted his tumbler in a toast. "To Grandmom."

"And to Geoffrey," Montjoy added, as he took a sip of his lager.

Anderton raised her glass of merlot, purchased by Garrett to honor their bet from Lindau.

Garrett walked to the window beside Montjoy, as the bustle of Central London sounded from the street below. "What's the fallout look like?"

"Contained, as usual," Montjoy replied. "The Italian police have officially ruled Geoffrey's death as part of a murder-suicide, something that will, unfortunately, forever tarnish his reputation. Grandmother officially died of a heart attack, an already eminent legacy only bolstered by her passing. She'll be honored at a ceremony at Vauxhall Cross next week, along with Grandfather."

"And Lindsay?" Anderton asked.

"Still in a coma, and the hospital won't agree to move him until he awakens. The official story is that an aging man, wandering alone in Munich, fell into the Isar River and nearly drowned."

Garrett finished his bourbon and poured another two fingers. "Brandt?"

"He will disappear back into the wilds of northern Sweden, I should think. In the end, the fate of Kristof Brandt, and Stan Collishaw, was the byproduct of bad historical timing. Each was born of English and German extraction, which only accelerated a destiny that would not have existed without the Cold

War. Both were used by their respective intelligence services, Collishaw because of his Oxford pedigree and that he spoke German, and Brandt because of some lingering familial loyalty to the West. MI6 employed God and Country, and of course, glory, to incent the agent who would become *Castor*, while the CIA promised defection and a new life to *Pollux*. Some might argue that Collishaw ended up better off than his East German counterpart. I doubt anyone will see Kristof Brandt again, and that's probably the way he wants it. As for you two, I can't thank you enough, as I wouldn't be here without your help."

"I had no choice," Garrett joked, "you being family and all. It's Sam I need to thank. She handled her end of the Strasbourg operation like a seasoned professional."

"You know the old saying, Sean," Anderton replied. "Flattery will get you everywhere."

"Case in point," Garrett answered, pointing to his brother. "Banastre's rise to deputy chief."

"Easy mate," Montjoy replied. "She still thinks I know what I'm doing."

The three shared a laugh, and decided on another drink, which Montjoy happily paid for.

"Abbot handled himself well in Prague," Garrett noted.

"Indeed," Montjoy replied, "but keep *schtum*, or he'll only pester me for more field time. In the end, Gavin simply verified what Laskin already knew."

"Will he pass it on to his superiors?"

"Laskin won't need to, as Moscow must certainly have him under surveillance, considering his history. Abbot's cameo served to intimate that other agents from their

East Berlin station were complicit in Heinrich's traitorous behavior—officers, I might add, who are still employed with Russian Intelligence."

"Who else *was* involved?" Anderton asked.

"No one, as far as I know. At least, there is nothing in Collishaw's sketchbook or our files that suggests it. To put it bluntly, I bluffed."

"How will everything play out in Moscow?"

"Notwithstanding the internal blowback, no one outside the center circle will be the wiser."

"And the CIA?"

"They'll also find a hole and bury their role in the whole affair as deep as possible. If the information ever got into the public sphere, it would be an embarrassment to both sides."

"Where is Heinrich?" Anderton asked.

"He'd be long gone by now, disappeared into the Canadian backcountry, or perhaps somewhere in Europe."

"And you?" Anderton asked, turning to Garrett.

"Back to the mountains myself, until Banastre conjures up some new drama."

"Don't hold your breath, brov."

"Something I've never heard before," Garrett joked, but then raised his glass. "Until then, cheers."

Montjoy and Anderton returned the salutation in silence, certain it would not be the last time that each of them would do so.

CHAPTER EIGHTY-THREE

Jacques-Cartier National Park, Canada
Two months later

The secondary road had been scraped of the most recent snowfall, but only far enough to the point where disoriented tourists in search of the ski resort would have realized they were off route and doubled back. Emile Chénard did not mind the difficult drive, for the remote cottage on the fringe of the provincial park would be the last place anyone would look for him. His new Jeep Rubicon, a recent present to himself, cut its way through the fresh powder, and he looked forward to a momentary sojourn in the wilderness north of Quebec City before he would decide where to permanently relocate.

The last leg of the winding approach shadowed the Jacques-Cartier River. The same rapids that provided some of the region's best white-water rafting during the warmer months were now frozen over and carved a brilliant white runway through the glacial valley. Chénard rounded the final turn that fed a steep grade to the property and elected to park at the base of the hill and walk the driveway.

He trudged up the icy incline and punched a four-digit code into the key lockbox. The house was cold, and it was clear it had not been used in some time. Chénard decided he would load and light the wood-burning stove and scout out several possible hikes while the cabin heated. Though the weather was forecast to worsen over the coming days with considerable snow accumulation, Chénard welcomed the challenge of climbing in such conditions.

He exited the mudroom door, which abutted a conical border of sugar maples and black spruces along the backside of the property. Several paths led up the mountain, and Chénard took notice of the clouds gathering across the ridgeline as he lit a cigarette. He stood quietly for several moments and savored it, there in the one place he felt completely safe.

The Russian reflected on the turn of events since September. The operation to eliminate the MI6 officers responsible for ruining his career twenty years earlier had resulted in the deaths of Geoffrey Charlton and Madeleine Halliwell, but had failed to kill William Lindsay, as well as the primary objective of the mission, Banastre Montjoy. Moreover, several of his assassins had gone missing, and he did not expect to hear from any of them anytime soon, if ever again. One was still due half of his payment, so Chénard admitted he would not be losing too much sleep.

The Russian had opted to leave Montreal, and knew he would never be back in the city again. Chénard had destroyed as many files as he dared before he worried he was fast approaching, and exceeding, the time at which it might be dangerous to remain in his flat. If anyone back home had determined that he was still alive, it was feasible they could, and would, eventually find and come after him. Chénard had since switched to an alternate identity, one of several he had created for himself since arriving in Canada two decades earlier. For the foreseeable future, Henri Cappelle was a French business-man touring North America on holiday. Chénard particularly looked forward to traveling across the American West, which he had never seen.

Chénard ground the burned-out butt into a black crater in the drift near the stairs and opted for the trail nearest the cabin. It appeared to be a demanding hike and Chénard resolved to see how far he could climb in thirty minutes.

No matter how difficult the going got, nothing could rival what the master spy had endured when the superpowers were balanced on a razor-thin edge, and he was one of the few people controlling its pivot. His father had long been a loyal Party member, but that provided him little currency in the power vacuum created by Stalin's death. It was an unchecked black hole into which the masses disappeared, and Chénard had grown up leery of those in power. He had learned to trust only his own instincts, which allowed him to see all sides and maneuver into a position where he had been able to manipulate his handlers in both the East and West.

He continued to grind up the slope, ignoring the burn in his legs, and had already cleared the first plateau by the time his watch sounded. Chénard turned and marveled at the view from the vast range, at the sheer openness and quietude of it all. He took in a deep breath, and the sight of wood smoke rising from the cabin below signaled all was right in his world at that moment in time.

Chénard sidestepped the downslope nimbly, and quickly,

and cleared the tree line in less than ten minutes. He considered another cigarette, but instead decided to prepare something to eat. The cottage had heated up nicely, and he estimated that a rick of cedar left on the back porch by a previous occupant would last for the duration of his stay. Chénard stripped his Gore-Tex jacket and stomped the snow from his boots, and poured himself a whiskey before moving to the den.

Chénard entered the room, but froze as he approached the comfortably warm wood stove.

The operative sitting in the recliner in the corner said nothing. Chénard had spied the person in his periphery a second too late, and only after reaching the fire to adjust its air flow. It was at that moment he realized the bed of coals was too large for the short stack of hardwood he had packed and lit before his hike.

Someone else had fed the flames.

Chénard should have noticed. The strong column of smoke pouring from the chimney should have been a warning. All his training and honed situational awareness, the lessons gleaned from a lifetime of subterfuge, should have been sufficient to avoid this situation.

Should have. The requiem of dead and missing operatives that echoed throughout history could be reduced to two words.

The agent in the chair did not speak, or move. The cocked hammer on the M1911 that rested on his knee, and a gaze ruthless and cold, were both zeroed on Chénard.

The Russian had never seen the man before, at least in person. Chénard gauged how fast he could get to the Colt clipped on his waistband before his adversary could pull his own trigger.

It would be close.

Chénard broke the silence. "Bravo, *monsieur.*"

Banastre Montjoy did not answer, and only gestured to a chair beside the stove.

"I'm speechless," Chénard admitted, sitting down.

"Soon enough."

"How did you do it? You're not good enough to find me on your own."

"You're someone a lot of people suddenly want to see go away, this time for good," Montjoy replied. "In the end, it was Laskin who sold you out."

"*Kuhynya,*" Chénard laughed. *Bullshit.*

"If it's any consolation, he didn't despise you as much as did Malinovsky."

"Sergei got what he deserved."

"He'll get his revenge from the grave. It was the photo of Malinovsky and our agent which you used to doom both men back in East Berlin that ironically sealed your own fate."

"You'll meet yours soon enough."

"If you mean the assassin sent after me in Charleston and Switzerland, he is dead, as is the Ukrainian team from Munich. If you are referring to Kristof Brandt, he and I recently shared a gentlemen's sit-down in Berlin. He returned to the void in which you cast him, though it was all I could do to keep him from sitting in this chair." Montjoy smiled. "You should have stayed put in your little corner of Canada."

Chénard muttered the expletive again, this time to himself,

as he reflected on the likelihood of what Montjoy claimed. Both men eyed one another, and Chénard grew angrier that he had allowed himself to be put in this position. He had outwitted the Stasi and KGB, outplayed MI6, and fooled the CIA. That it should end here and in this manner because of a singular moment of incaution was something he could not abide. "I assure you, I'm not going back to disappear into one of your prisons."

"No, you're not, *Felix*."

"How clever," Chénard scoffed. "You know my name."

"I know much more than that, old boy. As you deliberate whether you can outdraw me, you should know that at this very moment, a team is searching your flat in Montreal."

"They will find nothing."

"I would expect not, though what they leave behind will pique the interest of more than a few people who thought they knew you, whether it be as Markus Heinrich, Alexei Arkipov, or Emile Chénard. Long-forgotten Cold War intelligence, along with newly fabricated documents fingering you as a rat and traitor to the USSR, will be found in your crawlspace. The CIA has been made aware, as have key players in the SVR and FSB. At this moment, there are any number of ex-colleagues in a race to determine how best to cover themselves while exposing you in the process. Concerning your life in Montreal, that the quiet, older bloke in 5D was, by all appearances, a trafficker in child pornography and a serial pederast will no doubt shock your neighbors and anyone else whose path you crossed since fleeing Russia. And, I can assure you, the evidence we've manufactured will be widely shared."

Chénard struggled to mask the rising rage. He realized that anger would only hamper his ability to react when the time came, so he calmed his fury. "*Mon ami*, you're no killer."

"Not for a long time."

"It's a bluff. You haven't the stones for it. You're a button pusher who sends others in his stead."

"Indeed."

Chénard readied himself to spring from the chair and draw his pistol in one movement. He knew he would need something to create a split-second distraction, so he shifted his weight slightly and opened his mouth to speak. "It will—"

The flash of the muzzle caught the Russian by surprise, as did the speed at which Montjoy leveled his pistol and fired it. The bullet entered just below the right eye, snapping Chénard's entire upper body backward with explosive force. The spatter of brain fluid and gray matter splashed the bookcase, before Chénard's head finally bobbed forward, an expression of shock frozen on his face in morbid repose.

Montjoy did not move. The only sound was the squeak of the swivel rocker, still in motion from the violent energy of the fatal shot. The deputy chief of MI6 glanced through the front window and watched a massive shadow cover the front woods. The coming storm would slow his return hike, but the new snow would also mask his sets of tracks to and from the cottage. Montjoy finally stood and approached the lifeless figure slumped in the chair beside the fire. He calmly swapped his pistol for the 9mm in Chénard's lap, and closed the vent on the stove.

He considered the dead man in front of him, whose attempt

to erase his own tracks had been meticulous. Montjoy would ensure that the job was completed. The spy with innumerable identities would die faceless, literally, and ultimately, nameless. Time would bury down the memory hole the legacy of a former Russian spy whom everyone would eventually know was a longtime mole, while authorities and neighbors in Montreal would assume the feigned persona stemmed from the need to conceal a lengthy trail of degenerate behavior.

The former Stasi and KGB officer would end up little more than a miserable wretch who shot himself in a lonely cabin in the middle of nowhere, and that would be the only thing anyone would remember of the *Montréalais* who called himself Emile Chénard.

SIS would finally be able to close the books on a forgotten Cold War operation that had taken, and destroyed, so many lives.

Montjoy deliberated warming himself with a quick whiskey before donning his snowshoes and rucksack and backtracking eleven miles through biting wind and bitter cold. If he was lucky, he could summit the ridge and bypass the twin lakes on its windward slope in less than two hours in order to make his hired car before dusk. From there, a forty-five-minute drive would take him to Neuville Airport outside Quebec City, followed by a flight to LaGuardia, and then back to London.

He poured two fingers of Scotch from the newly opened bottle of Johnnie Walker Blue Label Limited Edition into a hip flask. Montjoy paused on the front porch of the cabin and raised it to the mountains, to the memory of Geoffrey Charlton, Stanford Collishaw, and Madeleine Halliwell.

He knew the way back would be difficult, but in the end, it was the only thing that ever made the journey worthwhile.

ABOUT THE AUTHOR

William Hunter's debut novel, *Sanction*, is an Amazon #1 International Bestseller and winner of 3 book awards. He has a PhD in history from the University of Cambridge, and specializes in the American Revolutionary War. Hunter has lived and worked in Switzerland, Germany, Scotland, and England, and now resides in the mountains of North Carolina.

Website: www.williambhunter.com

Made in the USA
Middletown, DE
09 October 2023

40493296R00236